SICILIAN UNCLES

Leonardo Sciascia

Translated from the Italian by

N. S. THOMPSON

Granta Books
London

Granta Publications, 2/3 Hanover Yard, London N1 8BE

First published in Great Britain by Granta Books 2001

Translated from *Gli Zii di Sicilia*, copyright © Giulio Einaudi editori s.p.a.,
Torino 1958. English translation copyright © N.S. Thompson 1986

Copyright © Leonardo Sciascia Estate, published in Italy by Adelphi Edizioni,
Milan

A CIP catalogue record for this book is available from the British Library.

3 5 7 9 10 8 6 4

Printed and bound in Great Britain by Mackays of Chatham plc

CONTENTS

1   The American Aunt   7
2   The Death of Stalin   53
3   'Forty-Eight'   85
4   Antimony   147

The American Aunt

I

It was three o'clock. Filippo whistled from the street, and I came to the window.

'They're coming!' he shouted.

I ran down stairs, my mother shouting something after me.

In the street, dazzling with sunlight, there wasn't a soul to be seen. Filippo remained half-hidden in the doorway of the house opposite. He told me that the mayor, the rural dean and the carabinieri marshal were in the piazza, waiting for the Americans. A peasant had brought them news they were coming, they were at the Canalotto bridge.

But, there were two Germans in the piazza. They had unfolded a map on the ground and one of them was indicating a road with a pencil. He pronounced a name and raised his eyes towards the marshal, who said, 'Yes, that's right.' Then they folded up the map and went towards the church, where their car was parked below the portico, shaded by branches of almond. They brought out a loaf of bread, some ham, and asked for wine. The marshal sent a carabiniere to get a flask from the dean's house. They were on edge, with the two Germans there eating peacefully; they felt fearful and impatient, so much so that the dean decided to let the whole flask go. The Germans ate, finished off the flask, lit cigars and left without a word. The marshal then noticed the two of us and shouted to us to go away, threatening us with a kick.

So, no Americans, only Germans. Who could say when the Americans would arrive? To console ourselves, we went to the cemetery. It was a high point, where you could see the twin-tailed aeroplanes hurl themselves down on the Montedoro road, then rise up again in the sky as black clouds sprouted along the road. Then we heard a sound as if barrels were exploding. Blackened lorries remained on the road in the expanding silence, then the twin-tailed aeroplanes returned and pierced it with more explosions. It was wonderful to watch them plummet down on the road, then suddenly they were up, high into the sky. Sometimes they used to wheel low above us and we used to wave our hands to salute the American we thought was watching us. But that very evening they brought a carter into town with his stomach torn open, and a boy of our age wounded in the thigh: they had waved their hands and down had come the man in the twin-tail waving his machine-gun. They played at target practice, those twin-tails; they even used to shoot at corn stooks or the oxen grazing in the stubble. The following day Filippo and I went out into the countryside, where the carter had been hit. There were cartridges lying about, as big as those for my father's twelve-bore, and we filled our pockets with them.

The whole countryside was ours, shining and resplendent. The peasants could not come out of town because the militia had set up roadblocks. We used a goat track which took us to a stone quarry, and then out to the open countryside. There was fruit there: almonds, green and bitter on the outside, white as milk inside — curd-almonds, we call them — and May plums, just as sour and green, which make the mouth dry. We used to gather as many as we could carry and trade them with the soldiers, who gave us army cigarettes in exchange. These were our great resource, one that lasted for a whole year. At that time, men would smoke anything. My uncle had tried vine-leaves sprayed with wine and baked in the oven, eggplant-leaves smeared with honey and wine, dried in the sun, and even artichoke root marinated in wine, also baked in the oven. So for an army cigarette, he would pay up to half a lira. First I fixed the price, asked for part payment, then produced the two or three cigarettes of the day. In the evening they tried to get their money back or looked for more cigarettes: I pretended to sleep and watched them shaking my clothes and going through my pockets. But they found nothing, because I always took care to spend every last penny before coming home, and if I had any cigarettes left on me, I hid them in the umbrella-stand as I came in. Because of the cigarettes I got for my uncle, no one dared fall out with me. When my father got angry at my grasping attitude, my uncle would calm him down, fearing that business might end. He used to wander round the house, forever saying,

'I'll die if I don't have a cigarette!' He would give me a look of hate and then ask me gently if I had one.

Once, a soldier who came from Zara gave me a packet of twenty, of the best quality, for two eggs I had stolen from home; my uncle paid twelve lira for them. By evening, there wasn't a penny left and my father could have killed me. But my uncle came between us to protect me, he had to, or the next day he wouldn't have had any cigarettes, not even after his ersatz coffee, which was when the need for a smoke really gripped him. When they rang the bells for the emergency and started shouting up from the streets the news that the Americans were at Gela, my uncle went into a frenzy, so I raised the price of an army cigarette to a lira. On the third day of the emergency, the school caretaker, passing by, shouted up to my uncle, who was at the window, 'We've chased them away! The Germans attacked at Favarotta, slaughtered them!' My uncle came back in shouting, 'Between the beaches and the sea, the Duce said, between the beaches and the sea!' and he declared that he wouldn't pay more than half a lira per cigarette. The news was false and in the evening the price was re-established at a lira.

Filippo sold his cigarettes to his brother, and to the waiter of the aristocrats' club, who then resold them to the members at a profit. With the money we played at bouncing it 'off the wall' or at heads and tails, or we bought a sickly mush made of carob-beans and every evening there was the cinema.

Filippo had an exceptional gift as a spitter, he could hit ten centimes at ten paces, the nose of a cat as it lay in the sun, or the pipes of the old men who sat chatting in front of the Friendly Society club. I missed the target by a good few inches, but in the cinema it didn't matter, you couldn't miss. It was an old theatre, and we always went up in the circle. On high in the dark we spent two hours spitting down in volleys into the stalls with a few minutes' pause between one attack and the next. The voices of those we hit rose up violently in the silence, 'Son of a bitch!' Silence returned. Several bottles of pop were opened. Then again, 'Son of a bitch!' and even the voice of the municipal policeman came up with menace from that well, 'If I come up there, I'll throttle you, so help me God!' But we were certain he never would.

When there were love scenes, we began to sigh heavily, as if overcome by uncontrollable desire, or we made the sound of sucking lemons, imitating the kisses. It was also a thing that grown-ups did in the circle. This, too, raised protests from the stalls, but with a certain indulgence and tolerance, 'What's the matter? They dying up there? Never seen a woman before? Bastards!' They never suspected that the greater part of that din was made by the two of us, who, during the films' love stories took delight in spitting down on the people who were gaping like idiots.

But the cinema was closed during the emergency. You couldn't go out in the streets without the written permission of the marshal — my father had it for going to the office — so there were only carabinieri and militia in the deserted streets. In the schools, the soldiers lay in their camp beds, playing at *morra* and cursing; they were hungry. The major with the white goatee who commanded them couldn't be found, nor the captain, nor the lieutenant. There was the sergeant-major, who hung about, bored because the bugle wasn't braying out like a soul in torment. None of them had the urge to go to the cinema, when it was still open, because we still had the silent screen, something they found laughable. Now there was no longer even the cinema.

At dawn, on 10 July, they hammered at the bells and the town became as empty as a shell: life had an empty, indecipherable sound, just as if you put a shell to your ear. People were locked in their houses, shops had their blinds down, as if a funeral were passing; there was a murmur of expectancy and anxiety. We went about keeping close to the walls, ducking into doorways to avoid meeting the carabinieri. The town was beautiful like that, empty and full of sun; we'd never heard the fountains sound so fresh and sweet, and there were gleaming aeroplanes rumbling in the sky, which seemed even emptier and more remote. We got the impression that the Americans didn't want to come to our town, so silent and so dead, that they were about to circle round it and leave it like that, anxious and waiting. Up there it was enough for them to look down at it, white and silent as a cemetery.

Filippo's father was a carpenter. He'd been a Socialist, and was often taken to the barracks and held for several days for questioning. Seeing the militia, Filippo always cursed, 'Bastards!' and awarded them the decoration of spit on their backs whenever he could. So he was waiting for the Americans; his father wanted to relish showing everyone those bastards who had him taken to the barracks. Even though my father had never said a word against the Fascists, I was on the side of Filippo and his father, who had a workshop smelling of wood and varnish; with the glue-pot smoking outside on the stove, a sickly sweet smoke which left a taste in my mouth. I was waiting for the Americans, as well.

My mother told me about America, that she had a sister there who was rich and had a large store and four children, one already grown up, a son who might be one of the soldiers we were waiting for. For me, America was my aunt's large store, a shop as full of good things as Piazza del Castello, with clothes, coffee and cuts of meat, and my aunt's son was a soldier who was bringing those good things with him, and he was good at fighting of course, at telling us about the store in America and letting fly punches at the bastards pointed out to him by Filippo's father.

But the Americans didn't come. Perhaps they'd stopped at the neighbouring town and were lying on their camp beds, playing games like our soldiers, calling out numbers, shooting their fingers out from clenched fists, and who cursed, saying that they would end up as prisoners. I spoke to my mother and she gave me all my father's and my uncle's cast-off clothes — even Filippo brought something. The soldiers were pleased with them, and those who hadn't got any set off in search of some. It was something that pleased me too, because it meant that the Americans were really coming.

That day when they'd said the Americans were coming, and there were the two Germans passing instead, the news spread mysteriously through the town. My father and uncle set to, burning their Fascist Party cards, portraits of Mussolini, pamphlets on the Mediterranean and the Empire, and they threw the badges and metal decorations of their uniforms on to the roof of the house opposite. But the next day, equally mysteriously, word spread that the Germans, seriously this time, were driving the Americans back to the sea, between Gela and Licata. The political secretary who, prudently, had stayed at home for several days, came out again, darting glances which, according to my father, were aimed at the buttonholes where the black beetle of the Fascist Party usually was, and if it wasn't, looking at the person directly with frosty reprobation and scorn, as if to say he would unfailingly remember all those cowards who had thrown their badges on to the roof-tops. My father did not believe the Germans would succeed in driving the Americans to the sea, but the glances of the political secretary irked him, so he proposed that Filippo and I should go and look for the badges on the roof opposite, promising a reward of two lira. It was not difficult, but my mother was frightened, cursing the Fascist emblem and the badges: she was able to agree to Filippo climbing onto the roof because, she said, he was more supple and strong, but not her son, who had legs like two sticks and had to take Proton. Filippo felt flattered, but hesitated, while I was keen to do the climb. I asked for an advance, which my father paid, insulting me. We took the ladder and went up on to the roof, with my father directing the search from the balcony of our house, 'You must be blind! Can't you see that one shining, there? To the right, behind you, it's in front of your nose, no, more to the left. . .'.

Barefooted, we walked about the roof, and stayed there even after we had found the badges.

It was a hard loss of two lira for my father because, right at that moment, the Americans arrived, and he had to get rid of them again, this time keeping them within reach, buried in the parsley trough.

We were walking over the roof when suddenly we were surprised by a loud, confused shouting, just as if the radio had been switched on in the middle of a football match, when someone's about to score a goal. The surprise at that clamour exploding in the silence of the town paralysed us for a moment, but we guessed the reason straightaway. We slid down the ladder, pushed our feet into the shoes we had left on the pavement, stamping to get them on — we always had tight shoes — and found ourselves hurtling down the street, while my mother, heartbroken, shouted to us to come back home, that they might shoot, that they would take us away, that there were Negroes, we could be taken anywhere.

There was a huge crowd yelling and clapping in the piazza, but there was one voice which rose above all the others, that of

Dagnino, the lawyer, a tall robust man, whom I used to admire for the way he cried out the Fascist hurrahs, '*Eia, eia, alalà*', who was now clapping his hands and shouting, 'Long live the United States!' People were swigging wine, which was passed from hand to hand over the crowd. Following in their direction we reached the Americans, five of them there were; they wore dark glasses and had long rifles. The parish priest of San Rocco was in his trousers, collarless, pale and sweating; he was talking to the men, repeating 'Pleez, pleez', but the Americans weren't listening to him. They seemed drunk, they looked about them, drawing nervously on their cigarettes. Glasses were filled with red wine, then offered with gentle insistence to the soldiers, who refused them. Dagnino, the lawyer, was standing on one of the club chairs, still thundering, 'Long live the United States!' Filippo's father came to look for us in the crowd and took us away, saying, 'Come on home! Just listen to that bastard shouting, all the swine are out today!' It seemed a good thing to me that even Dagnino was happy to stand there and shout, that he yelled out, 'Long live the United States!' just as previously, from the station balcony, he had shouted out, 'Duce, my life for you!' Dagnino would shout whenever there was a celebration. I couldn't understand why it wasn't a celebration for Filippo's father; he'd waited so long for the Americans, yet he was taking us away, his face pale and drawn, with a hand I felt trembling on my shoulder.

When we came to his workshop, I said, 'I'm off home', and took off. I didn't want to miss anything of the celebration. In the piazza I found that the Americans had managed to make a little space for themselves, but they kept their rifles at an angle, like my father in the country waiting for the calandra larks to pass overhead. The crowd had massed under the insignia of the Fascist Party HQ, trying to make them come away with poles, but they were hooked on to the balcony. They pushed a man up to take hold of the iron railings of the balcony, applauding once he was inside it. The insignia fell down with a crash, and were attacked and kicked and then dragged about the piazza. The Americans watched, exchanging a few words between themselves, taking no notice of the priest who was saying 'Pleez, pleez', or of Dagnino the lawyer, who was no longer shouting, but had come up to the patrol and was whispering something in the ear of the one who had black stripes on his arm, a corporal, perhaps. Then a carabiniere brigadier made an appearance, with four carabinieri; the soldiers' rifles were raised at them; when they were close, an American went round behind them and adroitly unhooked their pistols. Another round of cheers broke out.

'Long live liberty!' shouted Dagnino.

Suddenly an American flag blossomed above the crowd, held firmly by the primary school caretaker, a man who used to walk about the town in his uniform every Saturday afternoon, wearing the red flash of a squad member. When he got annoyed, he kicked the boys in the school entrance hall, but the Head merely said to the fathers who came to protest, 'What can you do? The blessed man's intractable, once or twice he's even laid hands on me! But he was on the March, and the Duce's even made him the present of a radio.' Now he was holding up the American flag, shouting, 'Long live America!'

But the Americans took no notice of the procession which was forming behind the flag. They were speaking to the priest, who told the brigadier, 'They want you to go with them.' The brigadier said he would, and went off with the patrol. If Filippo had been there, we would have followed them, but I didn't feel like going on my own. I stayed to watch the crowd, standing next to the four disarmed carabinieri, who didn't know where to look. They seemed like dogs after a beating.

Then from every side, armoured cars and trucks began to stream in. The crowd opened up, cheering; the soldiers threw them cigarettes, and one took snapshots with his camera of the scuffles that followed.

I don't know why, but suddenly I felt a wave of tears welling up inside me. Perhaps it was for the carabinieri, or for the flag raised above the crowd, or for Filippo and his father alone in the workshop, or for my mother. Then, heartrendingly, almost as if I wouldn't find it as I'd left it, a feeling of anxiety for my home rose up in me. I rushed back up the road, now festive with voices, and when I closed the main door behind me, I felt as if I were in a dream, as if someone were dreaming and I was in that dream, climbing the stairs, tired out, with a tight lump of tears choking in my throat.

My father was talking about Badoglio. My uncle was looking

so beaten he seemed like a bag of sawdust, but he livened up on seeing me come in. He took a packet of Raleigh cigarettes, the one with a bearded man on it, out of his pocket, and loading his voice with gentle hypocrisy, asked me, 'How much would you make me pay for a packet of these?'

I burst into tears. 'Cry!' he said, 'Go on, because the Land of Cockaigne is over for you! Even if I'm condemned to death, they won't deny cigarettes to this man.'

'Leave him alone', said my mother.

II

They put up notices in the piazza. One began, 'I, Harold Alexander. . .' My father said they wanted all guns, pistols, and even sabres, handed in. Another notice said that the soldiers had to keep away from the town, but evidently they took no notice of it, because every evening the little piazza was full of jeeps. The soldiers were looking for women; they took them to the cafés and drank. They took handfuls of money from their trouser pockets, thrust them on the tables and drank from the bottles. They drank with the women on their knees. The women were filthy, obscene and disconcertingly ugly; there was one in the town who was called 'Bicycle' because she walked like someone pedalling uphill, but she seemed more like a crab to me: she passed from one to another, and as the soldiers pulled her on to their knees, they glued the bottle to her lips and she swayed about blind-drunk, drooling obscenities. The soldiers laughed, then they threw her like a sack into a jeep and took her away.

Many soldiers even spoke dialect. In the early days, people thought they couldn't understand a word of it. Perhaps the first ones, from a Texas division, really couldn't, but then, in a café, an American asked for a bottle, pointing it out on the shelf, indicating he wanted to buy it. A youth in the café said to the proprietor, 'Ask him ten dollars for it', and turning round furiously, the American said in dialect, 'He can ask that prick of a father of yours!'

Nourished by dollars with a yellow stamp on them, and by Allied military lire, the local procuring trade was in full swing. Someone procured meetings with the more secluded women, those who would never go in cafés, who were afraid of the public eye, and especially of the already suspicious eye of their mothers-in-law: the women whose husbands were away. The Americans came late in the evening for these women and, in order to clear the piazza, so that no one would know that men

were received in certain houses at that time of the day, the
soldiers plotted heavy firing in the piazza. This was an excellent
ruse suggested by the pimps — so excellent that it was also used
by the black marketeers for loading and unloading their lorries
without being seen. When the shooting started, everyone shut
themselves in; no one even stayed on the balconies for the cool
of the evening. My uncle, who persisted in staying there, or else
he'd die from the heat, he said — because he was so nosey, I
thought — felt a bullet whistle past his ear, and dived back into
the room with a string of oaths. But the Americans' precaution
for protecting the honour of the secluded women was only use-
ful up to a certain point: the women who opened their doors
were known just the same. A quarrel at the fountain, one of
those where violent protests were made about precedence for
getting water, was enough to cause an explosion of accusations
around the town, backed up by day, time and the name of the
pimp.

Filippo and I were extremely well informed: he knew those in
his quarter, and I knew those in mine. But what these women
did with the Americans, what a man did with a woman,
remained a nebulous fantasy for us. That the women undressed
was a fact; we often went to Mattuzzo where there was a large
fountain, to look at the legs of the washerwomen, hiding ourselves behind a bramble. When they noticed us, they chased us
away, shouting that we should go and look at our mothers or
sisters. Perhaps the Americans paid to look at the women without being chased away and also, as in the cinema, to kiss them.

Rousseau would have said we were at the age when there are
more words than things in the mind; and we really did have the
words, even for things we didn't know about and couldn't even
imagine: the most atrocious and obscene words.

A boy our age who brought us boxes of K Rations — there
were sweets and sugar cubes, a pink cheese and biscuits in them
— ended up in tears because we kept on asking him, 'Who gives
you these things? Your mother's American? Have you ever seen
what she does with him?' and we linked the most prohibited
words to imagined gestures. The boy said no, the American
was a relation, his mother didn't do those things. Then he burst
into tears and we left him. The following day he came to find
us again, and brought more K Rations with him, saying, 'Any-

way, the American's my uncle, you shouldn't say those things about her!' but it always ended up in the same way.

So, the Americans wanted the guns in; they said they would give them back later. My father had his name inscribed on the butt of his, a good-quality Belgian gun, which, he said, had no equal. He deluded himself into thinking they would give it back to him, and so he had had his name inscribed on it. Then he produced a pair of pistols I'd never seen before, one of which was as long as an arm, a muzzle loader, and also a rusting sabre; it had no point, but you didn't know what trouble the Americans would have caused if they had found it in the house.

I wanted to go down too, on the day of the handing in. There was an American soldier and the carabiniere brigadier, who wrote down in a register for us: a shotgun, two pistols, a sabre. My father said he should have taken down the make and serial number. The brigadier looked annoyed. He was better off now than before; he went after women with the Americans and, they said, he had a room full of tins of food and cartons of cigarettes. 'You just leave it, and I'll see to it', he said. You could see he was really annoyed.

My father softly placed his shotgun on the pile of weapons. In that moment I think he understood there wasn't a hope of getting it back, and he remained in a foul mood for the rest of that day, the next, and every time shotguns were mentioned. Later on, they returned a shotgun, two pistols and a sabre to him, but only the sabre was any good. The shotgun and pistols were only fit to be sold for scrap.

Filippo had been in the barracks' courtyard for some time enjoying the handing in of the weapons. My father went off and I too stayed to watch. It was like a procession. As soon as they handed in their weapons, the peasants emerged exploding with curses: 'Robbers have got machine-guns now and honest folk not even an old shotgun!' they said. And it was true, there were robbers about. Two were found with muskets and masks, and were paternally pardoned by the American major. He was a fair-skinned, upright man and they said he taught philosophy in his country, but, perhaps, because here anything odd is said to derive from philosophy. The major pardoned the two robbers, urging them to pursue a quiet, honest life of hard work. The interpreter translated with a face which said, 'I give up, you see what suckers the Americans are!' Later, the defending lawyer, who hadn't managed to say a word, cursed Columbus as well, because with their being pardoned like that it was going to be difficult to get the men to cough up their several hundred lira.

But we liked the American major, we used to follow him through the rooms of the Town Hall and he never told us to go away. Every so often he'd look at us and say with difficulty, 'Little Sicilians'. He must have been a good man, perhaps he had children of his own at home in America.

Even the soldier who oversaw the handing in of the guns had a kindly face, chewed gum and smiled; he exchanged one or two words with the brigadier and then remained silently smiling and chewing. Perhaps he was thinking of home, of America, all high buildings and cars, and his mother looking out of a high window. He didn't seem to be aware of us. When he moved to offer us some sticks of chewing gum, we thought he wanted to send us away. Instead, he gave us the gum and said, 'It's good, it's not mint.' He didn't like mint, and neither did I. I said 'Thank you' and so did Filippo. With foreigners, we were able to pass for being polite boys; we even knew how to act like little saints, but this we saved for catechism lessons. The American looked at us, smiling. I said, 'My aunt lives in America.' It seemed the right way to make friends.

'Oh, in America', he said.

'Yes,' I said, 'in Brooklyn.'

'I live in Brooklyn, as well,' said the American. 'It's a big place.'

'How big is it?' I asked, 'As big as this town?'

I knew very well that it was as big as our town, Canicattì and Girgenti put together, and perhaps even bigger, and that it was only a single district of New York, but I didn't want the conversation to lapse.

'Much bigger', he said.

'It's as big as Palermo,' said Filippo, 'I know, my father's been to America.'

'Yes, it's as big as Palermo', said the soldier.

'The sea's at Palermo,' I said, 'and at Porto Empedocle. I went to Porto Empedocle before the war, but I can only remember some boats. Is there sea at Brooklyn?'

'It's near the sea,' said the soldier. 'We can take a car and go there.'

'It is beautiful?' Filippo asked, when I would have preferred to talk about cars.

'No,' he replied, 'it's beautiful here.'

'Do you like fighting the war?' I asked him.

The soldier smiled and said, 'War is an ugly thing, even boys like you get killed. But here it's beautiful.'

Above the courtyard, the sky was like water when washing blue's dissolved in it and the clouds were like foam. The sandstone belltower of the Church of S. Giuseppe seemed like gold.

'Are you coming?' said the brigadier, and the soldier left us without a word.

We came back to the barracks' courtyard the next day. The soldier was sitting in the same place, reading a book and chewing. When he saw us he said, 'Hello', and started reading again. After a while he closed the book, took out a packet of gum and offered us some.

'*Chewing gum*,' he said, 'That's what it's called.'

'And what do you call sweets?' asked Filippo.

'*Candy*,' he said, 'we've got all kinds of candy in America.'

'There's no candy here', I said.

'Not even potatoes,' said Filippo, 'I've forgotten what potatoes taste like. We always ate them when I was little.'

'There's a municipal policeman who sells them secretly. But they're very dear, my father says you might as well buy meat.'

'Oh, yes, meat,' said Filippo, 'there's no bread, and you want to find meat!'

'Why don't you bring us wheat?' I asked the American. 'My father says you throw wheat in the sea.'

'It's not true we throw it in the sea', he said. 'We've no ships to bring it in. When the war's over, we'll bring wheat.'

'Will the war be over soon?' I said. 'My aunt's coming when the war's over.'

'From Brooklyn?' he said, 'She's coming from Brooklyn? But it's a long war, you can't tell when it'll be over.'

'My aunt's got a store in Brooklyn,' I said, 'a huge store. She sent parcels before the war, and put dollars in her letters. She sent me a dollar every Christmas.'

'His aunt's rich', Filippo told the soldier.

'She's got two cars,' I said, 'one's huge, all shining. I've seen it in a photograph.'

'When the war's over, your aunt'll come over with the beautiful big car', said the American. 'I'll come over with the car, too. It's beautiful here.'

'Have you got a car?' I asked, 'What's it like?'

'Everyone's got a car in America. This is mine.'

He pulled his wallet out of a pocket, and a photograph from the wallet. It showed a long, shining car, the man with a hand on the car door, a fat woman in a flowered dress and two children in sweaters; there were trees in the background.

'Your father's not there', I said.

'No, he's not, he's dead', he said.

'I saw a dead man once,' said Filippo. 'He was a German. They pulled him out dead from the aeroplane. It fell near here. I dreamed about him afterwards, he seemed to be alive. I'm not going off to see any dead men again.'

'And what can the dead do to you?' I asked, although I'd never seen a dead man, and I didn't want to. 'The dead are dead, they can't come back. I would like to have seen the dead German. Have you seen any dead Germans?' I asked the soldier.

'Yes,' he replied, 'lots of them, and dead Americans, and English, French and Australians.'

'But the Germans are bad', said Filippo. 'It's better for them to die.'

'Now we're at war, and it's better they die', the American said. 'The Germans are dying and we're winning.'

'Russia's winning, too', Filippo said.

'Oh, Russia?' said the soldier.

'Russia isn't like America', I said.

'Yes,' said the soldier, 'Russia's something else.'

My uncle stayed at home listening to the radio from morning to night.

'The bastards,' he kept saying, 'God knows where they've taken him to!'

'Stop it!' my father sometimes burst out. 'D'you still want to dress up like a clown? Haven't you had enough of all that he's done?'

'What's he done?' said my uncle. 'Italy was respected and

feared. Everything was fine. There was order. Even you dressed up like a clown, and said he was a great man. What's he done to you now, socked you in the eye?'

'And the war he wanted is nothing, is it?' my father replied. 'For you it's nothing, of course, you're right, but there are some people paying for it, you've never even turned a hair. . .'

One evening, Orlando spoke on the radio, saying that the bombardments from Sicily on Calabria were like a ring joining Sicily to Italy, an image that stayed in my mind.

'Orlando's a great man', said my father.

My uncle wrung his hands and said, 'He'll save Italy, he will, an old man in his dotage!'

'Yes,' replied my father, raising his voice, 'that old man's got a head on his shoulders, while your Duce's mad, fit for the asylum, even Bocchini said so: he once secretly told Ciccio Cardella, who's a bigwig in the Ministry.'

'Huh, Bocchini,' my uncle went on, 'don't talk to me about Bocchini! Bunch of traitors!'

My father went on raising his voice, 'Everyone betrayed him! Only you didn't betray him, because how could you with your backside always stuck in that armchair, shouting "Duce, Duce!" on the holidays he ordered!'

'Don't shout,' said my uncle, 'they'll hear you outside. With the office I had they'll come and take me very smartly off to Oran, that's if I ever get there! They're quite capable of pitching me into the sea during the voyage.'

My uncle began to make out that he was ill, and I took advantage of his condition to get some amusement out of it.

I started to sing 'Duce, Duce, we want to die for you. . .' and he would rush up, because I used to go and sing in the garret, saying, 'You little wretch, can't you see I'm involved in it, they'll take me to Oran!' I burst out laughing and he put on a schoolmaster's solemnity, 'Italy weeps and you laugh. Try and understand, the enemy's here, in our very homes. . .'

The American soldier's name was Tony; he was born in Calabria and went to America when he was one. Now he was waiting for some leave and was about to go back to Calabria where he had uncles and cousins in a little village there. The Americans were already in Calabria, the ring of bombardments was over.

I asked him if he loved his uncles and cousins in Calabria, I wanted to know if my aunt and her children would love me and my mother.

'They're poor', said Tony.

'In what way?' I asked. 'We're poor here.'

'They're a lot poorer than you,' Tony said, 'they sleep with their sheep. Their children go around barefoot.'

'Do you send them money from America so they can buy shoes?' asked Filippo.

'Yes, sometimes', he said.

'The war's ending now,' I said with a diplomatic turn, as if everything depended on Tony's decision, 'and the Americans will bring shoes for everyone, shoes and wheat, boatfuls of them.'

'Americans work,' said Tony, 'they work and they've got shoes. They've got decent clothes, good homes and cars. The Italians don't want to work.'

'I want to work,' said Filippo, 'and my father works. It's the rich who take the bread from the mouths of the poor, my father says.'

'You have to work to get rich', said Tony. 'In America, everyone works and gets rich.'

'My father's got an uncle who doesn't work, and he's rich', I said.

'No one works here,' said the American, 'neither rich nor poor. Here it's beautiful for the rich, better than America.'

'I'd like to go to America', I said. 'I'll make some money and then I'll come back. I'll buy a beautiful car and come back.'

'Not me', said Filippo. 'When the war's over there won't be any rich people any more.'

'There'll be more than before,' said Tony, 'and those who were rich will be even more rich, and still no one will want to work.'

'But aren't you driving out the Fascists?' asked Filippo. 'If you drive out the Fascists, then we'll have socialism.'

'We do all the fighting and you create socialism!' said Tony, 'That's some thanks we get. I know who I'd tell about your kind of talk!'

'Who?' I asked.

'Anyone who lives in America', he said.

One evening the bells rang. My mother thought it was fire or danger, but they were shouting in the street that the Armistice had been called. My mother started saying prayers of thanksgiving because so many sons had been saved from death. My uncle paced nervously up and down, and said, 'I want to hear the Germans now, we really needed the shame of this. If the Germans think about it like I do, I'd like to see that Marshal Badoglio, Marshal, my. . . and that other one, half-pint turncoat. . .'

'And what would you do?' said my father. 'You ought to go yourself and carry on the war, it's like something from a puppet show: Honour! Treaty! Friendship! Why don't you go with your shining armour and put things right?'

Taking advantage of the conversations growing livelier, I slipped out. There was a crowd in the piazza in front of the church of Sant'Anna, the only one which hadn't joined in the chorus of bells. The people had wanted the priest to ring them, but at the presbytery window, he said, 'What's there to celebrate? Don't you understand we've lost? Are you so irresponsible?'

It ended with someone losing his patience and firing at the bells. It was one way to make them ring. 'Villains!' said the parish priest, and hurriedly bolted the windows.

My uncle later said that the only men in the town were himself and the parish priest of Sant'Anna.

Tony was tall and blond; my father couldn't believe he was the son of Calabrians, as all the Calabrians he knew were small and dark. My uncle said the Calabrians were blockheads: Italy was a great country, but the Calabrians were blockheads, the Sardinians treacherous, the Romans uncivil, and the Neapolitans beggars. . .

Tony went to mass on Sunday, and at the elevation you could see that nobody in the town was as tall as he was. After mass, where he took communion, we went with him to the café. We asked him if there were churches in America. There were, and the people were religious, more so than here. We asked him what Sunday was like in America. From what he said came the picture of a melancholy day. Whereas for us Sunday was the piazza full of people, stalls and vendors' cries, they looked for solitude and silence instead, going hunting or fishing.

'And what do the children do?' I asked.

'Play,' he said, 'they play all kinds of games.'

'My aunt once sent me some skates', I told him. 'What can I do with skates? When I tried them I almost cracked my head open!'

'Skates are no good here,' he said, 'the streets are bad.'

'What are the streets like in America?'

'Huge and smooth,' he said, 'there's no dust, and at least ten lanes of traffic can run together.'

'In America', said Filippo, 'the trains run underground, and in the air, too. I'd like to go on one, not underground, but I'd like to go up in the air.'

'A train's not an aeroplane', I said, 'I've never heard of trains that can fly.'

'No, they don't fly', said Tony. 'There are overhead rails, and the trains run along them. There are high iron girders and the trains run over the city.'

'Do they run over houses?' I asked. 'What if they fall down?'

'What do you mean, if they fall down?' said Filippo. 'The frames are made of iron. I bet you'd be too frightened to go!'

'I'm worried about the houses underneath. I'd be frightened living in a house underneath a girder.'

'I'm not frightened at all', said Filippo.

'You're frightened of the dead, though', I said. 'You see a corpse and then you're afraid at night.'

'Corpses don't come into it', said Filippo. 'It's true they don't come into it, isn't it?' he asked Tony.

'It's the same thing', said Tony. 'A person's frightened of corpses because he doesn't want to die himself.'

'I don't want to die', I said.

'Then you're frightened of corpses as well', said Filippo, triumphantly. 'No one wants to die and everyone's afraid of corpses.'

'Soldiers are willing to die', I said.

'The soldiers have to drive out the Fascists, and they're willing to die, too', said Filippo. 'My father was willing to go to prison and the soldiers are willing to die, but that's something different.'

'What did the Fascists do?' asked Tony.

'Nothing', I said. 'My uncle was a Fascist and he did nothing, nothing at all.'

'Perhaps they didn't do anything', said Filippo. 'My father was willing to go to prison, my mother says it was like that.'

My cousin found himself in Italy, fighting the war, but from his letter we couldn't make out where he was. He wrote that if he had some leave he would come and find us. There was a letter from my aunt with his, and five or six thousand-lira notes.

'My dear Sister,' wrote my aunt, 'perhaps they'll be sending my son to Italy, and so I'm writing in the hope that you're all in good health, as we are, thanks be to God. I've a thorn in my side with Charlie going off to the war, but I hope the Blessed Virgin will look after him. Things are going well for us: my daughter Grace has married a Jew, but he's a good boy and a worker, too. He's got a barber's shop near our store, but at the moment he's a soldier, too, and the Blessed Virgin will look after him. We didn't want this war, but God won't allow any misfortune in my house, I've promised the diamond ring I wear to the Madonna of our town, and when the war's over I'll come and bring it myself. It should be over soon, America's strong and she's winning. . .'

My mother wept for joy on reading it. She read out the most important news for my father, 'Grace's got married, my sister's promised a ring to the Madonna del Prato', and when my uncle heard about the strength of America and victory, he began to chomp like a cat chewing a dish of lungs. 'America's winning, eh? Cowards! Everyone's forgotten how respected we were, how they used to spit on Italians before. The fasces made us respected abroad. Now everyone's spitting on us again. I'll laugh when this mess is over.' He didn't speak loudly, so as not to annoy my mother, especially at that moment. He was just like a cat with a lung, puffing and panting, but persistent.

I told Tony, 'My aunt's written, she says America's winning.'

'The Fascists are winning,' said Filippo, who was set on the idea, 'the Fascists and the Germans.'

'We're winning the war,' said Tony, 'we'll win the war and I'll go home to America.'

'To Brooklyn', I said. 'Then you'll get the car and come back.'

'Yes,' he said, 'I'll come back. When I don't want to work, I'll come back. It's beautiful here, when you don't have to work.'

Tony left one day in October, a jeep came for him and I almost burst into tears. He made us a present of packets of chewing gum and tubes of sweets; he waved from the jeep and said, '*Goodbye!*' The day seemed long and empty, we passed it in the most violent games.

We went to school reluctantly. Filippo got off lightly, because his father was on the Committee of Liberation and the schoolmaster had been the head of his cadre, but with me it went badly. The schoolmaster sent for my father and said that it was like trying to dig a hole in water. My father ordered me to stay at home and made my mother responsible for any absconding. But I knew it would all come to nothing, because as soon as my father launched on a dramatic speech on the subject of education, my uncle came in with, 'One reaps as one sows. There was education, but you didn't want it. Now children can only grow up like animals!' and that was enough to change the conversation and spark off one of the usual debates.

In the north, the Fascists had founded the Republic and my uncle was glued to the radio; he even had it with him at night. He rubbed his hands and repeated one of Hitler's phrases that went more or less like this, 'At twelve o'clock they think they've won, but at five minutes past, victory will be ours!'

I thought Hitler was like one of those wooden heads you throw balls at, five for a lira, at the fairground. They made my hair curl, those Aunt Sallies. When my uncle mentioned Hitler, I used to say 'Aunt Sally' and if he got annoyed I kept on saying it. 'When America gets him, she'll make mincemeat of 'Aunt Sally', like a cat with a mouse', until my uncle really saw red and I slipped down the stairs. I sang it out once more from the stairs to give myself the excuse of being chased right to the door. My father forgave me for the exit, and I even won a little sympathy as a victim.

In the country, there were robberies and murders every day, there was even a kidnapping, and my father conceded something to my uncle at this point. 'Who's denying the good things he did? You certainly didn't see any of this sort of thing. But you wait and see, things will be better than before.'

'With a democracy?' said my uncle. 'There needs to be a strong government, democracy's like a slippery eel.'

Because my uncle didn't like it, I began thinking democracy was a good thing. Although I certainly didn't risk going beyond the last houses of the town anymore. I saw the hedges full of armed, masked men. One night I dreamed they seized me and, in order not to have me cry out, they put a whole packet of cotton wool in my mouth. When I awoke, my mouth felt dry because of the cotton wool. I started to shout out and my mother came in to tell me that it was still night.

Filippo said, 'They won't seize me. They can keep me a year, but they'll have to feed me, after all, and they wouldn't get a penny', but he was frightened.

The oratory garden gave off the feeling of the countryside, all rustling with yellow leaves. The rural dean now called us more actively for catechism, offering us dry figs and roasted almonds.

In the town the emblems of two parties appeared again. One said 'Social Democracy' with a large sheaf of corn, the other 'Independent Sicily Movement', which had a head at the centre of three legs, bent so as to form a wheel. The 'Independents' were the Separatists who were talked about so much; they wanted a Sicily independent from Italy. My father said they weren't wrong, Sicily had never been treated properly. 'Poor Italy,' said my uncle, 'Italy, I see your walls and arches. . . these vandals don't even leave us any walls! Throwing bombs as easily as they recite the Lord's Prayer. And now this fellow wants an independent Sicily! He's a clown and so are all those who follow him.'

I followed the Separatists, I wore a cockade of two ribbons, one yellow, and the other the colour of curdled blood. 'Degenerate!' said my uncle, seeing the cockade. But it was all great fun. In the evening, we went through town with a paint-pot, together with other young Separatists, writing on the walls, 'Long live Finocciaro Aprile! Long live Independent Sicily! Down with the enemies of Sicily! Industry for Sicily!'

Fed up with always writing the same things, the young boys then started to write, 'Down with those who starve the people! Death to those who sell wheat at 2,500 lira!' and a kind of competition was born from which, the next day, the townsfolk learned from letters a span high and a beautiful bright red, that

Don Luigi La Veccia was a thief and Don Pietro Scardìa, a thief and a cuckold. This was a real game for us, and when, especially, I saw the paintbrush give rise to 'Long live America! Long live the Forty Ninth Star! my Separatist faith became fanatical. I knew that the 'Forty Ninth star' would be Sicily, the American flag had forty-eight — forty-nine with Sicily — we were about to become American!

My aunt wrote all the time, sending letters via her son, who posted them in Italy, perhaps from Naples. He wrote a greeting in English after his mother's letter. However, my mother couldn't reply, she couldn't even write to her nephew in Italy.

'Dear Sister,' wrote my aunt, 'they promise us here that in a little while we'll be able to send letters directly to Italy and even send parcels. I'm getting ready many things to send to you and your husband, and to your son, especially, because I know how much the children are suffering. I've seen photographs that have brought tears to my eyes. God will deal with those who've landed us in this hell. . .'

'And who's landed us in this hell?' said my uncle with satisfaction. 'That paralytic President of theirs who's come pestering us. . . Do you think a paralytic's got any sense? By this time, we'd have had England blitzed and there'd be world peace.'

'Some peace', said my father. 'Some peace we'd have had with Hitler!'

'With "Aunt Sally"!' I said. My uncle couldn't stand me any more.

'This Colonel Moscatelli,' said my uncle, 'God, he makes me sick! And who is he, anyway? Which gaol have they dragged him up from? And Parri! Who's ever heard of Parri? He must have been in gaol. All the scum's coming out now!'

'But they're not ordinary bandits, you know', said my father. 'They've been in gaol for political reasons.'

'They're worse than ordinary bandits', said my uncle. 'Ordinary bandits ask for your wallet, and if you don't hand it over, they'll flatten you with a shotgun blast. But these men have killed off Italy, they're subversives, they want to see the end of the world. Please, don't say another word, The best thing we can do is not talk about it at all. Colonel Moscatelli! *Madonna santissima*, I'm going mad!'

I burst out laughing.

'I can already see what Italy's going to become,' he said, his eyes popping out with rage, 'the Italy of Parri and Colonel Moscatelli and wretches like you: no manners, no feeling! At your age, when I heard the fatherland spoken of, tears came into my eyes. When I heard the Anthem for Youth played, I'd roll on the ground with emotion, I could have done anything listening to that music.'

I saw him rolling on the ground like a donkey scratching itself, and burst out laughing again.

He didn't see the donkey scratching itself in the grass; he saw political damnation in my eyes, and became so furious I thought he really was going mad.

'The Communists!' he said. 'Neither you nor your father understand anything of what's going on. They're coming now. You'll see those murderers arrive right here, burning the churches, destroying families, pulling people from their beds and shooting them.'

My uncle was thinking of himself. He was in bed at least sixteen hours a day. I pictured him being dragged from his bed by the feet — which pleased me — but I wasn't so pleased at the thought he might be shot.

'There's General Cadorna,' said my father, 'you think a general like him will lose control? And then there's the Americans, don't you count on them for anything?' He seemed a little worried himself, now.

'It's revolution,' my uncle said, 'who can stop a revolution? They've got American weapons. God knows how many Russians there are. . . Do you think America will start a war against Russia? These c—— are our business, we must sort it out. I know how it'll end up, I'm going into a monastery, I am.'

The vision of the monastery placated him for a moment. Then suspicion and fury rose up again.

'Some joy I'll have in a monastery. They'll hand me over and have me roasted alive, that lot — full of Christ's Providence, blessings and sung masses — then you go to a cardinal for safety and you find Moscatelli there.'

'Don't talk rubbish,' said my father, 'they caught him while he was with the Germans, getting away.'

'And you talk about the Comunists who burn churches,' said my mother, 'while you go thinking such things — that cardinal's a saint.'

'Saint or not,' said my uncle, 'I wouldn't trust him with a dog. Even if it's not true what they say, he certainly hasn't lifted a finger to protect the weak.'

'The weak', said my father, 'being those who were shooting young men up to the day before. The carabinieri catch a murderer and he becomes one of the weak.'

'They shot rebels,' said my uncle, 'rebels and traitors.'

'Those who obeyed the King's government weren't rebels', said my father. 'There's no way of convincing you of that simple concept.'

'The King's government! The King's government makes me laugh, a King who burrows like a rabbit in the middle of the Americans. You know what I say? To set things right, Giuliano needs to be made king, Giuliano's got more honour than that King of yours!'

'Benedetto Croce. . .' my father began.

'Oh God, must we bring Benedetto Croce into it? I don't give a fuck about him or the books he's written. Nor about Dante Alighieri, nor you, nor the whole of Italy now! I'm going to go into a corner and die, I'll become deaf and dumb, you can count on that.'

'The Americans are disarming the partisans', said my father.

'Oh, they're finally doing something right', said my uncle.

My aunt wrote: 'Dear Sister, here we're still celebrating the end of the war. The Lord's granted my prayers and spared my home and family, my son's in Germany and is fine, and my son-in-law too, who fought in the Navy against the Japanese. We needed this new bomb. America has many scientists who are always inventing something new. Mussolini made a big mistake setting himself against America. He should have remained friends with America: he would still be alive and in charge, because he knew how to lead and Italy was doing fine under him. You can't imagine what effect it had on me learning the way he was killed, it shocked everyone here in America. But we can't know God's will. Anyway, I pray all the time that God will put a stop to these killings going on in Italy. Dear Sister, coming to fulfil the promise I made to our Madonna and to embrace you and our relations is ever in my mind. Now they say we can send parcels to Italy, you can't imagine how much stuff I've got ready for you all, even things to eat, because I know there's hunger in Italy. . .'

'There's a Christian soul speaking', said my uncle. 'It's true Mussolini made some mistakes. But the atom bomb was German, you can only find scientists like that in Germany.'

Like Filippo, I went to private school; we were getting ready for the entrance exams, doing our homework together at his house because his father didn't trust him and wanted to see him studying under his very eyes. 'Just think what it takes me to earn each lira I spend on you,' he used to say. I'd read something similar in De Amicis' *Cuore*. Filippo's father seemed to have hit the jackpot with Parri forming the government; he would tell us about Parri's life and about the adventures of the partisans, which I liked. He read them in the newspapers and books and then he would recount them. There were always other socialists in his workshop, which was like a club. 'If your father had his wits about him,' said Filippo's mother, 'he'd set about looking for a position, instead of staying here nailing tables together and gossiping. With the gaol he's done, even the Council would employ him. He's better at reading and writing than a lawyer.' But Filippo's father liked planing tables and knocking in nails, while he discussed Parri and the partisans with his friends. I liked the trade as well, I'd rather have done it than gone to school, even that type of informal club appealed to me.

My uncle said the name of Parri made his guts turn over. 'Talk to me of Parri,' he said, 'and I can't digest my food. I have to swallow a fistful of bicarb each time I hear about him.'

'And Moscatelli?' I said, 'and Pompeo Colajanni?'

'Don't talk to me about Colajanni,' he said, 'I've seen the damage he's done with my own eyes: in Caltanissetta and Canicattì, he was always talking about Marx and Russia, drawing all the young men about him. What suckers we were not to sling him in gaol and let him die!'

By now I knew my uncle like a pianist knows his keyboard. 'Yes, exactly, what suckers you were, what suckers.'

'No,' he resumed, 'we weren't suckers, the Duce was a good

man, we needed an iron hand instead.'

'They killed Matteotti, though', I said.

'They're always talking about Matteotti! We should have killed thousands of traitors.'

'But they're in charge now,' I said, 'and they'll come and get you and kill you just like Matteotti. You wanted Colajanni dead, now Colajanni will have you taken away in a car and have you battered to death.' I knew the whole story of Matteotti.

My uncle's face twisted up. 'And what harm am I doing?' he said, 'I don't wish anybody dead. Colajanni's an Under Secretary and I stay at home, everyone's happy and contented. You don't let it enter your head to tell that. . . Filippo's father, I mean, that I say certain things, do you? I don't say anything, I mind my own business, even if I see people walking upside down, I've got nothing to say.'

The parcels from my aunt arrived, ten in one month. There were things I had no idea even existed: biscuits that tasted of mint, tinned spaghetti, tinned herring and tinned orange juice; and suits, shirts, ties with wild designs on them and pullovers. There were cigarettes in the pockets and packets of chewing gum up the sleeves. There were even pens, pencils and safety pins. My aunt had thought of everything.

My uncle supervised the opening of every parcel that arrived; he looked, sniffed, chose and gave forth his usual monologue, 'I'll take the cigarettes, you don't smoke them anyway, you only smoke Nationals. I need this pen, the suction doesn't work on mine. This is a good shirt, just my size. . . I could wear this tie, the colours are not too bad. . . perhaps even this suit would fit me, it's too small for you. . .' My father said neither yes nor no and my uncle gathered his booty together and took it up to his room.

'Well,' he said, 'these Americans, eh? They don't want for anything there, they couldn't help but win!'

The clothes my aunt sent for me either barely fitted me, so that I looked as if I were being crucified, or else I swam inside them, but that wasn't so bad because my mother could alter them for me. My aunt couldn't manage to get an idea of me, of my size and thinness; she was buying things for me blindly. Some T-shirts with Mickey Mouse printed on them suited me down to the ground, but there was no way I'd be caught wearing loud blue and yellow shirts.

The town was full of boys in loud shirts and Mickey Mouse T-shirts. The grown-ups were wearing clothes of unmistakable American cut, too: shirts with pockets, ties with chrysanthemums, pinwheels, trumpets, naked women; and the women wore dresses printed in the same style as the ties. 'America's dressing us,' said my mother.

The whole town really was dressed in American gear, and everyone was living off help from relatives in America. There wasn't a single family which didn't rely on a relative there. In one corner of the piazza there even blossomed a moneychanger's stall: a dollar came to be worth nine hundred lira; but my father wouldn't change his dollars, he was waiting for the rate to go even higher.

Everywhere there was trade in American goods: tinned food, bars of soap, shoes, clothes, cigarettes. The biggest business was in medicines. A vial of penicillin was literally worth its weight in gold, as you had to sell a great mound of land to get a vial of penicillin. In the really desperate cases, the doctor would fling his arms up and say, 'What do you want me to say? If you can manage to find some penicillin, I can give you all the hope you want. . .' Everyone knew where to find penicillin and at what price. There were some people in the town who, instead of having cigarettes and tins of meat sent to them, had their relatives send medicines instead, and they made a packet. My father said, 'Tell your sister to send a parcel of penicillin', but my mother wisely said, 'You'd only give it to someone who needed it, and then end up in gaol for your pains.'

My aunt wrote all the time, she sent parcels and long letters with dollars folded in their thin leaves. She always said the same things: the good Lord, the Sacred Heart, the Holy Virgin, her promise to the Madonna, her children, the store, the people of New York.

The school year was almost finished, but I had other things on my mind than school. Everyday there were meetings, scuffles in the cafés, get-togethers in Filippo's father's workshop: Monarchy or Republic, Republic or Monarchy. It seemed like a football match to me, as if the team from the next town had come and a storm was breaking out.

At that time, the King had nominated my father for a knighthood, sending him a handsome diploma accompanied by a letter with someone calling himself Lucifero — a name which startled me — writing on behalf of the King. My father said the knighthood didn't mean a thing to him, he even wanted to return the diploma and letter. 'But,' he said, 'I must give my vote to the King. On principle I'm a Republican, but the times won't allow me to vote according to my principles.'

I wore an ivy-leaf pinned to my shirt, the Republican Party appeared to me to be one and the same thing with the Republic, even my uncle made the same mistake. Now he was against Pacciardi; he looked at the ivy-leaf and said, 'You can wear all the ivy in the cemetery. . . I know you do it deliberately, you know the worry gnaws at me and you do it deliberately.' Then he went on to explain his theory of the shot in the dark, concluding that only God knew if Umberto deserved his vote, after the way his father had betrayed Mussolini, but he could only go ahead and give it, because if the Republic won we'd wake up with the Red Guards by our beds. Great disruptions were always pictured happening about the bed.

My aunt wrote at the time, saying that if she were in Italy she would give her vote to the King. A Republic was a great thing for the Americans, but with so many Communists in Italy, who could say how things might finish.

The Republic won. 'We're lost,' said my uncle, 'wait and see, they'll make Togliatti President yet. It's going to end in trouble.'

'Dear Sister, I still want to come over very much. You say you don't believe me, but I think about it every moment. First of all my husband was ill, now, thank God, he's better than he was before, then we made the store larger, now Grace is expecting a baby in the first days of the New Year. If it's Our Lady's will that everything goes well, I'll be in Italy before 1948, but first of all I want to see how your elections go, everyone's thinking about them here and the newspapers are talking about them. . .'

'They're thinking about them!' said my uncle. 'Who doesn't think first sighs later. They should have thought when there was still time.'

'Dear Sister, I hope the votes don't bring the Communists into power, nor any of those like the Communists who are the enemies of religion and order. Our leaders have got faith in De Gasperi and the Christian Democrat Party. Without De Gasperi, Italy would lose all America's help. We pay heavy taxes and we know our money's being well spent; we're always giving money for Italy, in church and through our organizations, but if the Communists win, Americans' money won't be coming any more, we won't even be able to send parcels. There's a great religious spirit in America, American money mustn't end up in the hands of the godless. De Gasperi is a religious man, I've seen photographs of him kneeling down at mass, and his party will defend religion, and it wants friendship with America. . .'

'Listen,' said my mother, 'even my sister says so.'

'And am I saying anything different?' said my father. 'But if I vote for the Liberals it'll be the same thing.'

'No, it won't be the same thing,' said my mother, 'America only has faith in De Gasperi.'

'De Gasperi sticks in my gullet', said my uncle. 'But it's true that unless votes are concentrated in a major party, we'll be playing the Communists' game. It weighs on me to have to give a vote to De Gasperi, but otherwise it'll just be lost. . . at least it's a party of order.'

'Dear Sister, it saddens me to hear that your husband wants to give his vote to the Liberals, because I've asked Father La Spina, the son of Michele La Spina, our fellow townsman, whom you'll certainly remember; he's a very doctrinal priest and he told me that the Liberals are a long way from God's grace and at certain times they make agreements with the Communists. It's up to you to make him see the dangers of a vote badly cast, for your son's future and for the salvation of his soul. . .'

'Then write and tell her I'll give it to De Gasperi', said my father. 'Your sister's capable of writing even to the Pope for the salvation of my soul.'

'You really must vote for him,' said my uncle, 'at least out of respect for your sister-in-law, who's filled your house with belongings; and there is a danger. Can't you see how strong the

Communists are? Yesterday evening there was a meeting that was frightenïng, there were two thousand people there.'

'. . . and I thank God that He illuminated your husband in time, He should enlighten the consciences of all Italians in the same way. There's great anticipation here: all those who were ready to leave have postponed their departures, even those who already had a ticket. As soon as good news reaches us from Italy we'll set sail, too; we've already packed the trunks.'

'The trunks. . .' said my uncle. ' I wonder how many things they'll bring.'

The day before voting, a telegram came from my aunt, again recommending a vote for De Gasperi's party; my father made some remarks that put my aunt's balance of mind in doubt, but on going out he found that a couple of hundred similar telegrams had arrived throughout the town.

My uncle rubbed his hands together. 'What an idea!' he said, 'It's true, money brings some good ideas with it. You wait and see what effect these telegrams'll have, coming into houses where people only received one when someone died: it'll be as if there really was a death. And some people had better have a good think; if their relatives don't send them anything anymore, it'll be like cutting off barley from the mule, they'll be left eating straw.'

There was only the voices of the cab drivers, shouting greetings and insults at each other as they met, the crack of their whips and the rumble of cabs: the haze of dawn, dawn in a lazy city, where the smell of frying, which circled it like a halo throughout the day, was still faint in the morning breeze; the haze of dawn over the silent houses of Palermo. Via Maquada, then Corso Vittorio Emanuele, and we entered the port, which was already full of voices. Once again, my father checked the time of the steamer's arrival. 'Look, you can just see it,' someone said. We couldn't see a thing, but after a quarter of an hour the steamer was outlined clearly, drawing nearer, it was like someone with a pencil and paints adding something to it after having sketched a steamer on a piece of murky green and blue paper.

When it was near enough to be able to pick out the gesticulations of the passengers, who were so close together I thought they might tip the steamer up like a weight on a balance, my mother started to move about impatiently, waving her hand, saying, 'I'm sure she can see us!' but we were in such a crowd it must have been impossible for those in the steamer to distinguish anybody. It was now so near you could see their faces, the clean-shaven faces of Americans with gold spectacles and big cigars. Names issued from both land and steamer: Turì! Calì! Pepè! There must have been about a hundred Turìs, Calìs and Pepès aboard and as many on land.

My mother recognized her sister when she was ten strides from us, she leaped over the chain and ran to embrace her. My aunt was a fat woman, she wore a dress with huge flowers all over it, and gold spectacles. Her husband was tall, with a smooth, youthful face under his white hair. The girl was small like my aunt, but well-formed and pretty. The boy was rather ugly, or so he seemed to me, perhaps because he was looking hostile, and was still full of sleep.

My aunt told her husband to look after the baggage, my father offered to help him, but my aunt said, 'He won't be long', in a manner that made me think they'd just had an argument, but it turned out it was just her usual attitude towards him. My mother was crying for joy but couldn't get over the fact that she hadn't been able to recognize her own sister among the passengers on the deck of the steamer. My cousin looked at the tears in astonishment, and a little fed up perhaps.

When her husband came back we set off out of the port. My aunt said she wanted to stay in the best hotel. My father said that ours was a good one, but my aunt said, 'It must be the best, and you'll come with us.' So my father told the driver to go to The Palms. My mother was a little dismayed.

In the entrance of the hotel, my aunt sniffed around with her head up, and asked if there was air-conditioning, bath, shower, sockets for electric razors and radio. She wasn't entirely satisfied.

'Is this really the best?' she asked my father. When my father said that Wagner, the Kaiser and General Patton had all stayed there, she was convinced.

I felt my aunt's questions made the porters look at us with some irony: what did my father and mother and I know about air-conditioning and electric razors? The others came from America and knew about these things, they could even afford to live in the hotel for years on end. I felt a little ill at ease.

We went up to our rooms to rest for a while, and, according to my aunt, change; we didn't rest and we didn't have any other clothes to change into. When we met again in the entrance hall, they were relaxed and smart, while we were feeling even more tired in clothes that were creased and smelled of the long train journey. It took almost a whole day to get from our town to Palermo. My aunt began to ask question after question, it was almost as if she had a map of the town in front of her with all the streets and houses on it, and where her finger landed at random, a street or a house, she wanted to know all about the fortunes and misfortunes of the people there. Her husband and children remained silent. Again, I felt the weight of the waiters' gaze pressing on me in the dining room. My aunt was talking about poverty and riches, night and day, and I thought the waiters' look was sending me right back to the dark zone of our miserable town. After a rapid consultation with her parents and her brother, my cousin ordered from a waiter, who spoke American. My father ordered spaghetti with tomato sauce for us, and fish. Seeing ourselves in front of the spaghetti while the Americans had tomatoes stuffed with a dark paste and a piece of white, gelatinous fish with curls of butter round it, we were even more mortified. My aunt's husband called over a waiter with a small patch of black cloth on his white jacket, like a badge, on which a bunch of purple grapes was embroidered. He began talking rapidly and afterwards the waiter brought some bottles, let him look at the labels and my uncle said, '*All right.*' My uncle drank freely, but he was careful pouring out wine for his children, a thimbleful for the boy, half a glass for the girl. My aunt kept her eyes on the operation, then, for our benefit, she launched on a long speech about her educational criteria relating to wine, lipstick and *boyfriends*. In the course of this complicated speech I understood that a *boyfriend* was a schoolmate or neighbouring boy who became the close companion of a girl.

'If I learn she's got a boyfriend, I'll take her out of college and keep her at home.' She looked at her daughter suspiciously and threateningly. The girl smiled. My mother warmly approved, but asked what college she was talking about, a question I also wanted to ask. 'Syracuse', said my aunt. 'If only you knew what it's costing me!' My mother was none the wiser. My father explained to her that 'college' meant 'university' and that Syracuse was the name of the American city which had a university. My mother looked at her niece with a new consideration, full of pride. 'What is she studying?' she asked. Again there was a complicated discussion, but my father illuminated it, suddenly saying, 'Medicine.' The boy however, said my aunt, was a *loafer*, maybe he wouldn't even pass from *high school*, but in the end it wasn't so bad, he could stay at home and look after the *store*.

I had left all that had been brought us almost intact on the plate. I toyed with my fork and didn't eat. I didn't even eat the bananas I liked so much.

My mother suggested that the next day we should leave for home, but her sister said no, they wanted to enjoy Palermo. She remembered how it was in 1919 when she had left for America; now it seemed different and more beautiful, not as beautiful as an American city, but beautiful. She was particularly struck by the new post office building, which she thought was wonderful.

Before ending its voyage in Palermo, the steamer had stopped at Gibraltar, Barcelona and Genoa. They remembered the fruitsellers in Barcelona, the changing of the guard in Gibraltar and in Genoa they had visited the cemetery, talking about it as if it were the most beautiful thing they had ever seen — even the girl said it was beautiful. They wanted to see Palermo cemetery, but were disappointed. The carabinieri in the sentry-box outside the Royal Palace took up more time than the chapel inside; and the airport at Boccadifalco, more time than the cloisters of Monreale, where I could have stayed the whole day. From the scenic view near the cloisters, my father showed me the road Garibaldi had taken coming to Palermo, tracing it in the air for me because a light mist was sparkling over the city and countryside: I had read Abba's *Noterelle* at school, a book I liked very much. My aunt said that Garibaldi was a Communist; my father tried to explain that it wasn't so, that the Communists had taken Garibaldi as a symbol for their election campaign. My aunt cut him short, saying it was the same thing.

We toured Palermo like this for five or six days. I can see the group of us on the Palermo streets as if we were fixed in a photograph blurred by too much sunlight: my aunt, who cut through the streets like the prow of a motor-launch; my mother, tired and silent; my father, livened up a little by the holiday; my aunt's husband, who seemed half-asleep; the boy always sulking; and my cousin, who was beginning to make friends with me and was constantly making comparisons for me between what we were looking at and what there was in America. This group finally found itself in a small, first-class compartment like an oven, in a train heading for the interior of Sicily, making for our home town. My aunt continued to talk endlessly, I sat beside my cousin and, smelling her sweat and perfume, which stirred up an unknown desire and tenderness in me, I fell asleep.

'We'll be home in an hour', said my father. It was already dark. Whenever I put my face to the window when the train stopped, the lights of the towns seemed like crystal buttons on a black dress. As we were leaning against the window, my cousin lightly touched my neck and I wanted to purr like a cat and murmur all the love that was welling up inside me. Suddenly, out of the night, our town appeared: rows of scattered lights between low houses. I wouldn't have recognized it if my father hadn't begun to take the cases out into the corridor. It was a poor town, I thought my cousin wouldn't like it and I was a little ashamed of it.

Looking at the low town from the station, its streets marked by lights, opening out like a fan below us, my aunt said, 'It's still the same.' I thought there was a certain impatience in her remark, a little rancour; or perhaps it was the defensive tone my mother took, saying that it wasn't the same, that there was electric light and new houses and streets, which gave me that impression. My uncle was waiting for us at the station, he had organized a cart for the luggage and the carriage for us. Looking at the cases which the driver had already loaded up, he asked, 'And the trunks?' My aunt explained that they were coming on later. He seemed reassured.

They arrived the next day and my aunt began the distribution of goods, standing in front of the open trunks. 'This is for you, this is for your husband. This is for your son, this is for your brother-in-law. But for me the most hateful things appeared. I was hoping for a 36mm rifle, like one I'd seen at a friend's who had received it from his uncle in America, and a movie camera

and projector, or even an ordinary camera. Instead, there were
clothes and more clothes. There was a battery-operated radio,
for which my uncle showed so much enthusiasm that my aunt
decided to give it to him: it was like a white medicine-box; and
electric razors for my father and uncle, from the immediate trials
of which they emerged looking as if they'd been in the wars.

Then the visits started. All those who had relatives in New
York came to ask if my aunt had seen them, if they were well
and then if there was anything from them. My aunt had a list
that long, she looked for the name on it and told her husband to
pay out the five or ten dollars; all the townsfolk in New York
were sending five or ten dollar bills to their relatives. It was like
a procession, hundreds of people climbing our stairs. It's still
the same in Sicilian towns whenever anyone comes from
America. My aunt appeared to be enjoying herself: she offered
a photograph to every visitor, as if it were a snapshot of their
relatives, of a family group in beaming health, set against a
background in which stood symbolic particulars of that
economic well-being they enjoyed. This one had a *shoppa*, that
one had a good *jobba*, someone had a *storo*, someone else worked
on a *farma*, they all had children at *aischoola* or at *collegio*, and a
carro, and *iceboccese* and a *washatubba*. With these words, which
only a few people understood, although they certainly meant
something good, my aunt sang the praises of America.

The relatives of a certain Cardella came, receiving dollars
from their relatives and gifts from my aunt. She explained that
in New York Joe Cardella was a powerful man: she said that
one day two guys came in and asked for twenty dollars and that
every Friday they'd be back for the same amount. She had the
idea of speaking to Cardella, and the following Friday he came
to the store, tucked himself away in a corner and waited till the
two men showed up. Just at the right moment he came out and
said, 'What's come into your heads, boys? This store's like my
very own, nobody comes here trying to be smart. . .' and the
two of them saluted him respectfully and went away.

'Of course!' said my aunt's husband. 'Cardella sent them in
the first place.'

My aunt shot up as if she'd been stung by a wasp. '*Shurrup!*'
she said. 'You cause trouble every time you open your mouth.
Even if you think certain things, you don't have to say them.

and anyway, it's a fact that all the others who've got stores have to pay, and we never have.'

'Is this Cardella a mafioso?' asked my uncle, who understood certain things like lightning.

'What do you mean, a mafioso?' said my aunt, with a thundering look at her husband. 'He's a gentleman: rich, elegant, and he looks after his fellow townsmen. . .'

'Sure,' said her husband, 'like he looked after La Mantia.'

My aunt nearly burst with rage.

'We're with family here', he said, and told us about a certain La Mantia, who, half drunk, had insulted Cardella. Friends had immediately intervened and calmed them down the same evening making them shake hands and have a drink together. But the next day La Mantia was found lying on the sidewalk with a bullet in his head.

'How you talk!' said my aunt. 'You'll earn a bullet in the head yourself, in the same way.'

'Why don't the two of us go for a walk, out of town,' said my cousin. 'Ugh, what a lot of flies there are!'

They had brought DDT powder with them, but the flies were never ending, you only had to open the window and they entered in droves. My mother was in despair because she could see the Americans were suffering being with us; they barely touched their food because of their concern for the flies which settled on plates, glasses, meat and bread. My aunt cursed the town, saying she'd hoped it might have been different, newer and cleaner; instead, it was worse than ever. There were two sides to my aunt's disappointment: we, her relatives, weren't the starvelings she'd imagined us to be in America, and then the town hadn't improved as she'd hoped. She was expecting to find us in dire straits, to be fitted out with her clothes and nourished by her tins of vitaminized food. Instead, there was no shortage of bread, olive oil, milk, meat or eggs. We had a radio, curtains, and soft beds, But in America my aunt thought of this house, where she had been born, as it was, with a red tile floor, the hard bed, with its bedboards and horsehair mattress, tucked into a dark alcove, the straw-bottomed chairs and the oak chest as the only pieces of furniture. She wasn't conscious of it, but it was a disappointment to find rooms full of light, with elegant furniture. We were not as poor as she thought, nor rich enough so as not to make her and her family feel the lack of those comforts which she said existed not only in her own home, but in all American homes. And there were the flies.

One day, when my aunt was explaining about all the evils that came from flies, my mother, a little crossly, said, 'Nevertheless, you and I grew up with flies, there were more then than there are now, and, thanks be to God, we're in good health.' My aunt didn't mention flies any more for the rest of the day.

I went out with my cousin that day, and then every day, towards the evening. We went down a country road where we met only the peasants coming back home, their faces baked by the sun, their mules loaded with French honeysuckle or rustling oats. They looked at us wickedly because she either held me by the hand — I was as tall as her, even if I still wore short trousers — or else she put her arm around my shoulders, drawing me towards her as if to whisper something in my ear. If a friend of mine caught sight of us and met me on my own the next day, he would tease me; even Filippo teased me, asking me if I got up to anything with her in the middle of the tall wheat. I grew red with shame and anger. 'More fool you if you don't!' he concluded, and added, for good measure, the proverb about Jesus sending biscuits to those with no teeth.

As soon as we were out of town, my cousin took out cigarettes and matches and began to smoke like a chimney; she even made me smoke. She couldn't smoke at home, and if her mother had even suspected she did there would have been a tremendous scene. So, with the excuse of the flies, she'd thought up this afternoon escape. If her brother showed any desire to come, the walk was postponed, because he used to tell tales.

Besides smoking, my cousin covertly drank spirits. She secretly gave me the money and I juggled about to smuggle the bottle into the house, hiding it in the garret, where she went every now and again for a drink. She told me that in America all the college girls drank, and that they always bet on who could drink the most. She once drank fourteen glasses in a row, and it was hard liquor. At the table, my aunt was forever giving her famous speech about wine, finally pointing her finger at her daughter, unfailingly warning her, 'If anything happens to you while you're driving the car, I'll come and bail you out, even if it takes thousands of dollars. But if the police say there's whisky on your breath, I'll see you in the Tombs* without any qualms whatsoever.' The girl wore a face like a patient saint. I liked her, both in her mother's presence, when she was like a town girl, modest and quiet, and when we were alone, when she drank and smoked. I liked her even more when I smelt the cigarettes and drink on her. Because of the sinful images I had formed of women, of their bodies and their love, I thought that those forbidden things, smoking and drinking, were the sweetest and deepest sin.

In the heat of the day, she went about in a light sunfrock, her shoulders blossoming neatly from her dress. When she shaved her armpits with a small electric razor, I stopped to look; she smiled at me in the mirror. Something in that operation disturbed me, there was attraction and repulsion, the sense of a sinful mystery and an even more sinful mystification. Once, my uncle happened to come in while she was shaving; he was in favour of that depilation in the name of hygiene and beauty, and stayed a little while to joke; then he became aware of me and said 'What's the porcupine staring at?' My cousin smiled at him wickedly, while I burned with shame and hate. His mere presence now was enough to annihilate me, I meditated upon plans of revenge, because when he was around, my cousin no longer took any notice of me. The nickname of 'porcupine', given to me by my uncle because my hair stood up like wires, completely destroyed me, and my cousin laughed whenever she heard it. My uncle seemed to have become another person. He shaved every day, smelled sweetly of *eau de cologne* and was full of attention for the Americans, complimentary and amusing in his hateful way, which, however, pleased my aunt a lot. He cursed the flies with them, and said that in Mussolini's day there were none, which, my aunt readily believed. 'There were more then than there are now!' I said. But he turned on me straightaway, 'He's a Communist, bad company's ruined him.' My aunt looked at me with unrelenting horror, while my mother strenuously defended me from this accusation.

My aunt began to grow tired of us, but because my mother

---

* A New York prison — *Author*.

was so fond of her sister, she didn't see the signs of coldness and resentment which were clear to my father and myself. She grew more distant from us every day, counting the days remaining that she had to spend under our roof. Long summer days of flies and dust; a washtub for taking a bath in; nights so humid that if you left the windows open the sheets stuck together, if you closed them it was like an oven. . . Every day she repeated the same comments.

Then the boy, who, among other things, spoke only American, fell into a state of hypochondria. He said that as soon as he arrived in America he would run and kiss the toilets, which great phrase my aunt translated for our edification and continued to quote, drawing the boy, who was always by her side, near to her and kissing him. He may have been a *loafer* at school, but he understood quite a lot.

There were numerous small incidents. My aunt gave dollars away, to be remembered by and to bring good luck, she said. She gave a ten-dollar bill to all our relatives, but once, when my mother suggested a poor relation, a widow with no children who lived on charity, my aunt wouldn't even part with a dollar. Later, speaking of the poor woman, she said that her relatives wanted to ruin her, that they only made her welcome for her dollars, and that they were all spongers. My mother said it wasn't true, but my aunt insisted, in such a way as to suggest that we were spongers, too. On the contrary, it happened that when she offered money to my father for the extra expense, he refused it, and she was a little offended by it.

All in all, we just didn't know how to take her. Every day it was clear that the only person in the house she liked was my uncle. Taking after my aunt, he became a homegrown Saroyan, celebrating America in falsetto, all its good things and good feelings, melting like an ice cream in the heat of his America so rich and full of goodness. The American soldiers had brought a little book with them to teach us about America: *The Human Comedy*, it was called, and I used to think that Saroyan was the Bible. Now I was growing tired of it, it seemed a game to me, one of those delicate games people play after a good dinner with toothpicks and crumbs: Saroyan was the finally satisfied and grateful man, who played with toothpicks, singing the praises of America.

My cousin still came out with me, just the two of us down the country roads. She came up to the garret where I spent much of my day, among the old books and newspapers, not even knowing what I was looking for. Every so often I would pick up a motheaten book with a marbled cover and read *Marco Visconti* or *I Beati Paoli*. I read hundreds of books in those years, even the complete works of Vincenzo Gioberti. But when my cousin came up, I stopped looking about and reading. She sat down on a chest and told me things about America, taking small sips from her bottle. Then she drew me to her and laughed. Each day my hands seemed to become like those of the blind, more aware and lingering. Her body, in my hands, flowed like music underneath the light dress.

Meanwhile, my aunt was weaving a plot of her own. She had already hinted to my mother that, should she find a good match, she wanted her daughter to marry someone from the town, a presentable young man willing to go to America, she wanted a fellow townsman and she would set him up with a store. Then she took a liking to my uncle, and she told my mother she would be happy to take him with her to America, he was so well-mannered and likeable, and would certainly make a good husband for her daughter. Happy to have her brother-in-law taken off her hands, but concerned about her niece's future, my mother said that, without doubt, it was a marvellous idea, but one had to take the difference in age into consideration and the fact that her brother-in-law had never ever worked. He had a good diploma as an accountant, which had succeeded in getting him appointed as an administrative secretary of the Fascist Party, but he had never done anything else. Moreover, he was notoriously incapable of stealing himself, but was happily disposed to allow himself to be cheated of money by anyone. A Party employee had taken advantage of his absolute incompetence with accounts and ledgers to fiddle the books with alacrity. My mother told her all this, but her sister assured her that once he was in America it would be her business to instil in my uncle the desire to work. They consulted my father, who treated it as a joke, 'Are you going to take him with you, or shall we post him on afterwards?' but he became convinced my aunt was serious, and openly presented the negative aspects of the case. My aunt said she would accept the risk.

Then they spoke to the interested party himself, who was overcome, and asked for time to consider the matter. But there was little to consider: the twenty-year-old girl danced before his eyes, he was thirty-five; with a burning desire to see America; she was good-looking and my aunt and America were rich.

It seems that everything was settled within a couple of days. I learned of it as a *fait accompli*, they told me the details later. A walkabout was decided upon to let the town know of the event: my uncle and cousin arm-in-arm, in front; my mother and aunt twenty paces behind; then my father and my aunt's husband. My other cousin, who was still grumbling, and myself, with a black spot of death expanding inside me, went about by ourselves. After a while, I started to kick an empty tin can about, accompanying the walkabout with the sound. My father looked askance at me to make me stop and my uncle, when I sent it right between his feet, said, 'Must you always be a nuisance?' But he was smiling, you could see he was happy, and my cousin clung to him like a cat.

They spent some days getting my uncle's papers together. My cousin had brought hers from America. They were married in the Town Hall, as my aunt had decided that the church ceremony would be held in America, with great fesitivities. The day before the marriage, my aunt said to my mother, 'Listen, you've got one child, I've got four. This house you're enjoying is half mine. Before I leave I want to sort it out: I'll sell you my half.' My mother wasn't expecting this subject and spoke about it to my father. They had no money, so my father suggested a postponement. 'It must be now', said my aunt. 'If not, I'll sell my half to whoever, at a giveaway price, and leave you to sort the mess out.' My father was furious at having been caught by the throat, especially when my aunt threw in our faces all she had done for us. My father, exaggerating, said that when all was said and done, she'd sent us a few rags, all cast-offs. That tipped the balance.

'So I've sent you second-hand stuff, have I?' she yelled. 'That's how you repay all the kindness I've shown you! It was all new stuff, bought specially for you, it cost dollars and dollars, a thousand dollars worth of stuff I sent you!' Her husband silently nodded.

My uncle intervened, saying my father was wrong, and my mother began to cry. In the end they came to an agreement: my father would pay for his brother's ticket to America — in first class, my uncle specified — and my aunt would relinquish her share of the house. But everyone remained hostile to each other and the wedding the following day took place in a funereal atmosphere.

Then they all left for a tour of Italy. They were to take the steamer home from Naples, while my uncle would stay behind and wait to be called by his wife, a matter of a few months. Meawhile, he went away with them on a honeymoon to Taormina, and then to Rome. We accompanied them to the station, my mother crying and crying, saying between sobs that this departure was final, she would never see her sister again in her life. 'We'll see each other in the next one', she said. It was true, my aunt would never visit Italy again, and the thought even upset me. While the diesel train whistled, the sisters embraced each other again, then my aunt turned round from the footplate and said, 'The stuff I sent wasn't second-hand, you know.'

The last thing I saw, while the curve along the trees was swallowing up the train, was the blue glove of my cousin. Without thinking, as if to myself, because I never would have thought of saying such a thing to my father, I said, 'The trouble is, she'll be unfaithful.' I said it for my uncle's sake. My mother looked at me astonished, with reddened eyes. My father's slap left me deaf for a moment. Fortunately the station was empty.

The Death of Stalin

In a dream at daybreak, on 18 April 1948, Calogero Schirò saw Stalin. It was a dream inside a dream. Calogero was dreaming about a great pile of ballot papers. He had signed a thousand of them the previous evening, because the Party had appointed him scrutineer. He was looking at all those ballot papers and then suddenly at a heavy hand placed on them which issued from the sleeve of an old-fashioned military tunic. In his dream he thought, 'Now I'm dreaming this is Stalin', and he raised his eyes to look Stalin in the face. It was a grim face. Calogero thought, 'He's blazing mad, something's wrong', and straightaway he made an examination of his conscience and of the Regalpetra local Party section and found small blemishes: the assistant secretary who had filched some UNRAA sugar from the Town Hall and had not been expelled; the miners' secretary who took money for seeing to certain files. He began to feel perturbed. Stalin spoke with a marked Neapolitan accent and said, 'Calì, we'll have to lose these elections, there's nothing we can do, the priests've won the first hand.'

Calogero thought, 'It's a dream', but perhaps Stalin read the disappointment and sadness in his face. He gave a half smile and said, 'D'you think we won't make it? Today we'll lose, the people aren't ready yet, but just you see if we don't get there!' and he put a hand on his shoulder to rouse him. His wife was rousing him in the same way, saying, 'Calì, it's six o'clock, Carmelo's calling for you.'

Calogero woke up, feeling a black growth knotted inside him because of his dream. While he was dressing, he told his wife to tell Carmelo to come up. His friend came up beaming, dressed up as if for a wedding, and greeted him loudly, 'We'll deal with those bloody priests today!' But Calogero knelt down to tie up his shoes and made no reply.

His wife brought in the coffee. Between sips Carmelo said, 'I just want to see the rural dean's face! Frightening people, saying we've got the noose ready for the hangings! I'll show him the noose all right!' But Calogero, without looking him in the face, said, 'And what'll you show him? We'll need years to get rid of these. . .'

Surprised, Carmelo said, 'What d'you mean? Only yesterday you were betting. . .'

'Yesterday was yesterday', said Calogero. 'Night comes and you can reason it out better: the priests have won the first hand, we're still not ready.'

He didn't want to say anything about the dream, because Carmelo was young and laughed at dreams. Young men like him didn't even bet on the State lottery. Calogero didn't believe in souls in Purgatory, nor did he believe they could give out lucky numbers for the lottery, but he did believe in certain dreams, especially those just at daybreak, which even Dante believed were true.

Calogero had been interned with an anarchist poet, he knew ten or so cantos of the *Divine Comedy* by heart, as well as poems by Carducci and his anarchist friend. It was not the first time he had seen Stalin in a dream, a dream which events later proved to be true. There was nothing of the supernatural. Stalin thought and Calogero received the thoughts in his dream. Even scientists admitted such things.

In 1939, when Calogero read in the newspapers that Stalin had made a pact with Hitler, he had almost had a stroke. He had been released from internment a couple of months previously and had reopened his shop, but not a soul brought him a pair of shoes for resoling or repair. All day he reread the few books he had. The best moment was when the *Giornale di Sicilia* arrived. He devoured every bit of it, even the business notices and the deaths column. It was good to read the news about the Duce inaugurating, receiving, giving speeches, flying here and there, then to comment on it in a loud voice, invoking galloping ulcers and syphilis on that active body or addressing fantastic insults and terrible prophecies to that image, smiling or stern, which the newspaper never failed to publish. No one stopped by his shop for a gossip, only the rural dean stopped by for a moment to commend common sense and discretion to him. Sometimes he added, 'God has great power, that rabid dog will get what's coming to him', and even Calogero, who didn't believe in God, felt completely consoled. The 'rabid dog' was Hitler: the

Osservatore romano, too, made it understood what the dean was saying, loud and clear. Then came the pact, and the dean commented, 'It had to come to this, they've sniffed each other out, like dogs.'

Calogero lost his discretion, thus depriving himself of the daily consolation the rural dean gave him: he started to shout that it wasn't possible, either the news was false or there was something behind it all, and that Stalin was better than the Pope. The dean made a face like someone seeing a hail storm coming in a previously clear sky, turned his back on him, and did not pass by the shop for months.

Calogero really did feel he was going mad at that news. There wasn't a hope that it was false. Then came the photographs, Stalin next to Von Ribbentrop: they looked like old friends. How could it be that Stalin, Comrade Stalin, the man who had turned Russia into a fatherland for human hope, was shaking hands with that delinquent son of a . . .? It was true that old fool with the umbrella had done nothing to attract him to his side, and perhaps Mussolini was right in making fun of a decrepit England; but Stalin could not ally himself with the murderer just for that, unless feigning friendship, he was preparing a deadly trap.

And that was how Calogero first came to dream about Stalin, and in confidence, Stalin told him, 'Calì, we've got to crush this poisonous snake. When the time's right, you'll see what a thrust I'll drive into him.' And Calogero felt calm. It was now as clear as day that Hitler would suffer a direct blow from Stalin, and at the right time.

A friend let him have Dimitrov's speech, the one which said that the USSR would hold back and observe the two Imperialist blocks; which speech Calogero held to be true up to a certain point. According to him, what Dimitrov was keeping quiet about, and could not do anything but keep quiet about, was the fact that Russia was waiting for the moment when the German forces, even if victorious, were at their most exhausted, and then she would attack. He used to imagine the secret preparations: aeroplanes and tanks coming out of the people's workshops, to be placed, camouflaged, in a huge line along those frontiers which Hitler certainly felt were secure. At the most opportune moment, neither too soon nor too late, Stalin would give the signal and, without losing a second, the Red Army would spread out over the mountains and plains of Fascist Europe, as far as Berlin and Rome.

Meanwhile, Hitler was eating up Poland, his army moving out like a nutcracker, and Poland was suddenly crushed. A Poland rotten with its huge estates, thought Calogero, with its heroic working-class and those rotten estate-owners who led cavalry charges against Hitler's tanks, all Poland with a single great heart, long live Poland, heroic but doomed! He wanted to stand in the piazza and shout out, 'Long live Poland!' and he was in tears as he read the latest war news. Even the Fascist journalists seemed moved when they wrote about Poland in its death throes. One of them wrote a piece about the fall of Warsaw which Calogero cut out of the newspaper and kept in his wallet. When Russia moved to take her share of Poland, the rural dean turned up again. He leaned against the door and said, 'You ought to know Mameli's hymn, oughtn't you?' but Calogero didn't understand what he was driving at. He knew Mameli's hymn, even if he couldn't remember all of it; he had it in a book. 'Read it,' said the dean, 'where it says "He drank the blood of Poland with the Cossack", have a good think about it, listen to what your conscience tells you.'

'I've already thought about it,' said Calogero, 'if you want to reason it out.'

'All right then', said the dean.

'The pact, as it's called, of non-aggression, is a complete joke, the right moment will come and Stalin will give such a blow to that son of a. . . he'll be left in smithereens!'

'Boom', commented the dean.

'It's as true as you believe in Heaven', said Calogero. 'The thing can only go like that: Fascism has to die at the hands of Stalin, Fascism and many other things besides, and those who bless the Fascist flags will go the same way, too.'

'Listen,' said the dean, 'we don't bless the flags of Fascism or whatever the devil you like, we bless all those young sons of families who march under them, all the Christian souls who follow them. And then, if you want me to tell you quite plainly, Mussolini isn't the same thing as Hitler, he fears both God and the Church.'

'Let's forget about that,' said Calogero, 'otherwise I'll start to rave like a lunatic. Let me reason it my way, then you can say all you like. Well, Stalin is going to attack Hitler. In the meantime, he's improved his position, he's pushed further towards Germany. Then, and this is the most important thing, he's taken, for the time being, half of Poland, to save her from Nazi oppression and revitalize her, because Poland was old, full of injustice, the proletariat was suffering and the rich. . .'

'Oh, it's true the Poles have profited,' said the dean, interrupting, 'Stalin instead of Hitler, they've really profited, they've really hit the jackpot.'

'Can't we reason it out, then?' said Calogero.

'What do you mean, reason it out?' said the dean. 'If you call what comes from your mouth "reasoning", then reason's dead and buried. Stalin has to attack Hitler, Stalin improves his position, Stalin saves half of Poland. . . it's enough to make a cat lose its taste for milk.'

'In a few months,' said Calogero, controlling himself with difficulty, 'in a year at the most, we'll see which of us can reason.'

'Well, you wait then. . .' said the dean.

He waited, and in the meantime, Russia attacked Finland. In odd moments, Calogero caught himself siding with the Finns, moments that went like this: Finland was resisting and he thought the tiny nation was standing up well, come on Finland, come on Mannerheim! But wasn't he a petty Fascist general? No, not Fascist — yes, Fascist, they were all Fascists around Russia. Whoever resisted Russia and was afraid of her was a Fascist.

'Even Finland must be liberated from the Fascists', he thought, 'and even if they aren't Fascists we must get there before the Germans, establish bases there for the war against the Germans. *Russians bloodily repulsed along the Mannerheim line.* Come on, Finland, petty nation of Fascists, Fascist general. Perhaps Germans are there on a secret mission. Things aren't clear.'

Calogero submitted himself to a trial by self-criticism, in the form of a monologue, but he didn't succeed in avoiding the feelings of sympathy for Finland which blossomed inside him, nor the doubts about the Soviet army's effective power which tormented him. The rural dean rescued him from these doubts; he

wanted to take it out of him a bit for the defeats accruing to the
Russians, but, instead, he stirred up all of Calogero's rational
strength, a flash of lightning in which the obscurity of events
was suddenly dispelled.

'It's all a trick,' said Calogero. 'Stalin's pretending to be weak,
he wants to reassure Hitler, all the Fascists in the world will get
the idea that Russia's weak, and Hitler will be convinced Russia's a little mouthful to be left for last. On the other hand, Russia's strong, and when she really starts to move, Hitler and his
crony won't even have time to say "Amen".'

'To tell you the truth,' said the dean, 'I suspected as much.
It's certainly a little strange, this business.'

Calogero didn't say that up to that moment he hadn't even
had the suspicion of such a game, or that the truth had suddenly
been revealed to him. He savoured his victory sweetly.

'Stalin's the greatest man in the world,' he said. 'To think of
traps like that you need a brain as big as a fifty-pound sack of
flour.'

It ended as it had to end, with Finland ceding territory to Russia.
Immediately after, the Germans took Norway, gaining two
advantages from one move: they placed themselves in a good
position for the attack on England, and they neutralized the
advantage the Russians had in Finland. Perhaps the madman
was beginning to suspect something of Stalin's game. Calogero
held that, as Norway had fallen to the Germans, Stalin would
have to strike. On the contrary, Stalin stayed put, pretending
not to notice anything. The Germans spread out into Belgium
and Holland. 'This is the moment', thought Calogero, but
Stalin did not move.

The good news was that, in England, the old wet blanket
with the umbrella had gone and Churchill, who made a good
impression on Calogero, had come up. He knew that Churchill
was one of the few who had not believed in the joke of Munich.

'He's got the face of a real mastiff', he used to say. 'What with
him and Stalin the Germans will come to regret the day they
were born.' But he was apprehensive about something else, that
Mussolini would not pitch in, that he would remain neutral and,
at the last minute, side with the winners. But by this time the
Germans were in France, and Mussolini thought the war was

won, thus relieving Calogero of any worry over his secret designs. Stalin was keeping quiet, but Calogero could see him in a huge room in the Kremlin, bent over a map of France, stirred and full of compassion, his emotions telling him to run straight to help the French, but his reason bringing him round to a precise calculation of the time and manner of intervening.

Paris fell. Calogero had been there from 1920 to 1924. . . Paris, so beautiful in June. He had lodged in rue Antoinette, spent the evening in a café in Pigalle, or in the Café de Madrid with its orchestra and the man with the lean, intelligent face, who sang in a low voice and told funny stories, the boulevard des Italiens, the boulevard of Montmartre. . . Now there were Germans in the Café de Madrid, Germans marching past in the Bois, in the Luxembourg Gardens, in Pigalle. And the Jews of Pigalle, that Jewish girl who played the violin? Full of hatred and grief, Calogero fretted a whole month over Reynaud's appeal to President Roosevelt.

'They won't make a move, those bloody Americans! Allowing France to die. . . they're dolts, stupid bastards, who don't give a fuck about France and Europe. . .'

'Even Russia's holding back and watching', said the rural dean.

'Russia's another thing,' said Calogero, 'Russia's waiting.'

'And what's she waiting for? She's waiting for Hitler to leave some bone for her to pick, that's what she's waiting for', said the dean.

'We'll see what she's waiting for within a year. Hitler and that pig of ours will be hopping about on one foot when Stalin makes up his mind.'

'Oh yes, within a year: you said the same thing last year', concluded the dean.

On the 1st October 1940, the newspaper carried two important headlines: Serrano Suñer, the Spanish minister and, as far as one could understand, brother-in-law of Franco, was coming for talks with the Duce, and 'Russia confirms that her relations with the States of the Tripartite Pact remain unchanged'.

It was because of the war in Spain that Calogero had been interned for a couple of years. His brother-in-law in America had enlisted in the Brigades, writing him a moving letter about the motives of the war and about his participation against the Fascists, the contents of which Calogero came to learn in the local police headquarters, where they had summoned him in order to know what his feelings were with regard to his brother-in-law. They had read him selections from the letter and then speedily sent him off to Lampedusa. Now it seemed that those two news items on the same page of the newsapaper were making a fool of him, of all his friends in internment, of his brother-in-law, and all the Communists who had died fighting for the Spanish Republic. How was it possible that Comrade Stalin, the man who had made Russia the fatherland of human hope, could continue to declare his friendship to the Fascists, while in the meantime Europe lay bleeding, France had a new government which stank like a sewer, and Spain had a savage general who looked like a parson?

'I go mad just thinking about it', he said to himself. Straight-away, he decided that he must see someone, talk about it, be with people who had the same sentiments as himself for a little while and who, like himself, were certainly suffering. He had to go to Caltanissetta: Gurreri the lawyer was there, and Michele Fiandaca, people who could follow the political world better than he.

Gurreri received him after making him wait half an hour. Calogero didn't recognise him any more, he was bald, his face drained and he was forever wiping a handkerchief over his forehead. He use the formal *voi* and asked him what he wanted. Calogero knew he had stepped right in it.

'Well, really. . . I wanted. . . I don't know if you remember, at the end of the war, in Regalpetra. . . my name's Schirò. . .'

'Yes, I remember, Schirò, certainly I remember', said Gurreri, still wiping his forehead with his handkerchief.

Calogero plucked up courage again, 'You remember what a struggle there was? I was secretary of the local section, the Nicola Barbato Section. That speech you made from the balcony of Lo Presti's house. . .'

'Oh,' said Gurreri, and it looked as if, on opening his mouth to smile, he had found a grain of aloes on the tip of his tongue. He pulled a face. 'All byegones,' he said immediately, 'a waste of time thinking about them. . . Let's come to the present, you've come here for some advice, I take it. . .'

'Well, really,' said Calogero, on hot coals again, 'I've come to you to talk about the situation, to get some clarification, I don't understand very much: Russia's standing still and Germany's crushing half the world. . .'

Gurreri really began to sweat.

'That's exactly it, my friend, Russia's standing still and Germany is conquering the world, and deserves to conquer it. . . What a nation! What an army!. . . but, with respect, my friend, I'm a lawyer, I'm not here to talk politics.'

He rose from his chair, and Calogero rose too, the lawyer placed a hand on his shoulder, gently ushering him towards the door, which he opened, saying, 'Please. . . and remember, I'm a lawyer, just a lawyer.'

Angry and embarrassed, Calogero found himself outside. The lawyer was rooted in the centre of the room, drying off his sweat. 'Scoundrels!' he said. 'For fifteen years I've kept myself to myself, and yet they still persist, they won't be convinced. . . They even send a spy to me, a spy!'

Calogero went up the Corso Vittorio Emanuele, asked the whereabouts of Via Re d'Italia, which he could not find because, after so many years, Caltanissetta seemed like a new city, but in fact nothing had changed. He found the small, dark doorway, the winding staircase and there was still the smell of boiled cabbage and rotten eggs. Michele Fiandaca was at home, where he worked as a watch-repairer. His children were making a hell of a noise, but he was undisturbed, bent over his small apparatus with a lens attached to his eye.

After his meeting with the lawyer, Michele Fiandaca's welcome encouraged Calogero. Michele's wife was a pale, silent woman, who immediately prepared ersatz coffee for her husband's friend, while Michele took out cigarette papers and tobacco. They began by asking each other news of their comrades in internment, then Calogero entered into the heart of the matter.

'I went to see Gurreri,' he said, 'I wanted to ask him what he thinks of the situation, but he was in such a fright. . .'

'Yes, he's become like a maniac', Michele explained. 'You should see him walking down the street, he walks as if there were a pack of hounds after him. . . There's nothing we can do now. He sees the situation in just one way: if the Federation secretary summoned him to give him a Fascist Party card, he'd have a great celebration.'

'And how do you see the situation?' asked Calogero.

'What do you want me to say? I'm worried. But it certainly can't end up with a bunch of killers ruling the world.'

'And Russia? What's Russia going to do?'

'Pompeo says that before six months are up Russia will launch herself against the Germans. Do you want to talk to Pompeo? We see each other every evening. If you can wait till then, I'll take you. Pompeo's all right.'

'I know,' said Calogero, 'I know he's all right, I'd like to meet him, but my wife doesn't like being alone at home at night, I promised I'd be back home this evening. It's enough if you tell me what he thinks. Within six months, then, he says?'

'Yes, he knows how to explain the situation well. It's a pleasure to hear him reasoning it all out. If it wasn't for him I'd feel like one of those stray dogs that curl up into a ball and die. He gives me courage, he's always so calm. . . And then there's another lawyer, the one from the Populist party, he's all right, too. We sometimes see each other.'

'And this lawyer who talks about Russia, does he think she'll launch herself against the Fascists?'

'He thinks the same as Pompeo', said Michele.

'Good!' said Calogero. 'I want to tell the rural dean, he's always talking to me about that lawyer, I want to tell him what he thinks.'

'We get on well with the priests here, as well', said Michele. 'We agree so much it's a dream.'

'Old sea dogs', said Calogero, 'can scent which way the wind's blowing and hoist sail: they always want to land on their feet.'

'What interests us now is to increase our numbers, to get all the anti-Fascist forces together. We'll deal with the priests and the bourgeoisie later. Can't you see Stalin's game?'

'It'll be a great thing,' said Calogero, 'in six months' time, when he thrusts himself at them, the Fascists will look complete fools.'

'And meanwhile, the capitalist forces are dying, too. Stalin will be the only one to win this war. Never mind Napoleon,

Stalin wouldn't have given a fuck about him, either!'

To break the back of Greece, Mussolini sent soldiers without shoes; but there was snow in Greece and a population that did not want to have its back broken. Spring came, and the Germans; they and the Italians reached Athens together. Yugoslavia was occupied as well; a cloth of mourning covered the people of Greece and Yugoslavia. Six months, a year, then finally Russia entered the war, or else it was Germany who attacked her, Calogero was not quite clear. The fact that German troops were rapidly advancing into Russian territory like a pair of open jaws, engulfing regions larger than the whole of Italy, with Soviet armies in them who surrendered, meant nothing to Calogero. It was one of two things: either Hitler had anticipated the Russian attack by several days and had therefore upset their plans, or it had been Stalin who had attacked, but with very few troops, as if for a small border incident, and thus the Germans had been drawn by magnet into the vast Russian territory, like Napoleon's French army, and then they would be beaten and annihilated. After some days of indecision, Calogero was certain that Stalin had purposely opened the doors of Russia to the Germans.

Calogero's shop was now beginning to be frequented again: a student, a corn-broker, the Consortium warehouseman and the sacristan from the Matrice, who only left the conversation for his regular ringing. The dean was worried: one afternoon he had surprised him stretched out on a chest in the sacristy, looking at the line of portraits of the Matrice deans, all of them, from 1630 to date, singing in a low voice, 'Down with the priests who act as spies, the secret police and the bourgeoisie!' He decided to train a new sacristan. Calogero felt happy with these four, who agreed with Stalin's strategy, so passionately divulged by him, without reserve. He had dreamed of Stalin again, but it had all been confused: there was snow everywhere, birch trees whistling in the wind, and men swarming across the snow in broken lines. Then he appeared, but in an extreme dissolve, Stalin's face with its knowing look, smiling.

Calogero had read *War and Peace;* in his imagination, Stalin's days were like those of Kutuzov in the novel. After a month of war, Stalin had assumed command of the army. Calogero pictured councils of war in the peasants' cottages, with the generals looking confused and worried in comparison with the knowing serenity of the man, with peasants' brown bread and honey in front of that smiling, paternal man. Certainly, with each news of the Germans' advance, Stalin was thinking, 'Well, let them race on! This is the one-year-old's race!' lighting his pipe and taking satisfying puffs. In August, when Mussolini asked Hitler for the honour of sending an army into Russia, Calogero thought, 'Poor young men, like mice in a trap', and Stalin, ironic and compassionate, must have been thinking the same thing.

In November 1941, the Germans came to a halt before Moscow, Leningrad and Rostov. Calogero said, 'Now the heavens will open, wait and see what happens now!' But up to May 1942 nothing happened. The Germans took up their advance again, remaining stationary around Moscow and Leningrad, but beginning to move towards the Caucasus. Calogero wasn't troubled by it, 'The one-year-old's race continues', and he made the forecast that it would not be six months before the implacable Russian counter-offensive would be released.

'Winter has to come', he said. 'Let winter come and then see what happens to the "anti-Bolshevik crusade". Stalin will deliver you the German army packed up like a barrel of pilchards', and he prayed for a terrible winter, an immense blade of cold to raze the hitherto victorious army from the face of the Russian soil.

Already in autumn people began to hear about the numbers. Before Stalingrad — and it could not have been otherwise for a city which had taken its name from Stalin — the Germans halted. Then the counter-offensive began. The Russians formed a great pincer movement, steadily pressing together with half a million men inside. Calogero felt for the Italian soldiers freezing in the snow, cursing the bloody fool who had sent working class sons from the lands of the sun to die in those freezing plains.

The Italian army, together with the German one of Marshal Von Paulus, was crushed. The Germans went into mourning when Von Paulus surrendered, but straightaway word was secretly going round concerning Von Paulus, about an understanding with the Russians. Calogero considered the possibility of a Communist revolution in Germany. According to him, the war could still drag on for months, or even years. But Russia had already won at Stalingrad, nothing could stop the victory of Communism in the world now.

The Americans were already in Regalpetra when it became known that Mussolini had been arrested in Rome. The news seemed to come from another world, as already, for the previous ten days in Regalpetra, people had been giving vent to their feelings against every sign of Fascism with chisels, fire and spittle. Calogero felt a little sad, seeing Federation spies and local Fascist leaders in frenetic anti-Fascist zeal, going round with the Americans, whispering denunciations; to satisfy them, the Americans took away the political secretary, the mayor and the carabinieri marshal. Calogero judged the Americans to be *di prima informativa,* people who thought the first comer was right. The Russians would have reacted differently. To round off his indignation, the carabinieri sergeant came to tell him that the Americans didn't like the meetings he held in his shop. The Americans perhaps knew nothing about the meetings, but they certainly didn't please some of their go-betweens.

In an indulgent moment, Calogero cut two portraits of Stalin out of an American magazine, and put them in handsome frames, hanging one up in the workshop and the other in the bedroom, next to the Madonna of Pompei, which his wife had on her side of the bed. 'Oh, that's your father, is it?' she commented, bitterly, but seeing him turn ugly she said nothing more.

The rural dean's reaction was more violent, and they came to hard words. The portrait in the workshop could be seen from the other side of the piazza. The dean, who had not set foot in the workshop for a while, came over, full of curiosity, then shaking with rage once he had made the image out, he asked, with feigned innocence, 'And who is it?' Calogero replied that it was the greatest man in the world, the man who would change the face of the world, the greatest and most just man.

'He's really handsome,' said the dean. 'Looks like a cat with a lizard in its mouth.'

'He's not Rudolph Valentino,' said Calogero, patiently, 'and even if he does look like a cat, I'm glad you've noticed. Now you know what end you've got coming to you! If Stalin's the cat, someone's got to be the lizard it eats.'

'My cat died', said the dean, 'from the nasty habit of eating lizards, they stuck in his gullet, he foamed at the mouth like someone having a fit, and became as thin as a rake.'

'This is a different kind of cat', said Calogero. 'This one can digest the big black mistake as well.'

'The cat to eat up the big black mistake — if you mean what I think you mean,' said the dean, 'has yet to be born. And you can rest assured that it never will be! But let's leave aside cats and big mistakes. You get rid of the portrait, I'll come and bless the workshop and then I'll give you a lovely painting of St Joseph the Carpenter.'

'No,' said Calogero, 'let's do it like this: you give me the St Joseph and I'll put him next to Stalin, he's a worker-saint and won't look out of place. In return, I'll give you the portrait of Stalin I keep by the bed and you can put it in the rectory, but next to a good saint, not someone like St Ignatius or St Dominic of the Spanish Inquisition, understand?'

'Lost wretch of a soul!' shouted the dean crossing himself repeatedly. 'I want to see you when your toes point up, face to face with the judgement of God. I'll deny you the sign of the Cross!'

'I'm touching wood,' said Calogero, quickly grasping his shoemaker's knife, 'because when you priests speak, there's only one thing you can believe, and that's that you never fail to bring bad luck.'

'Animal!' said the dean, upset, and he departed.

In Sicily, Committees of Liberation were born, while on the mainland the anti-Fascists were still locked in combat; they died under torture, were hung or butchered: the Germans were like rabid dogs. But in Sicily there were the Americans, and the Committees of Liberation played at forming local administrations, then disbanding them — they even toyed with purges. There were political parties, and each party had two representatives per Committee. Calogero was certain that a place on the Committee was coming to him, but instead the Party sent the postal official, who used to wear the Fascist Party sash, and a sergeant of the Fascist Militia. He felt bitter for a while, but later thought that, like everything the Party decided, there had to be a good reason for their choice. They made up for it by nominating him town councillor responsible for public works; he had some good projects, but there was not a lira in the public coffers.

The Russians, meanwhile, were pushing forward and the dean was worried, impatiently following the advance of the second front, that of the English and the Americans. But because there was a prophecy by S. Giovanni Bosco relating to the horses of the Russian army, which would one day water in the fountains of St Peter's Square, he was also prepared to resign himself to the designs of Providence.

'If it is God's will, the Russians will come down as far as Rome; it will be glory for the church to win these new barbarians over to the faith.'

But Calogero was nursing the opposite hopes. Stalin was coming down into the very heart of Europe, bringing Communism and Justice. Thieves and usurers were trembling, and all those spiders who wove the world's riches and its injustices. In every city that the Red Army reached, Calogero imagined dark swarms in flight: the men of oppression and injustice convulsed with animal terror; while in the light-filled piazzas the workers mobbed Stalin's troops. Comrade Stalin, Marshal Stalin, Uncle Joe, everybody's uncle, protector of the poor and weak, the man with justice in his heart. Calogero closed every reasoning out of the things wrong with Regalpetra and the world by pointing to the portrait, 'Uncle Joe'll take care of it', and he thought it had been he who had invented the familiar nickname, which by that time all the comrades in Regalpetra were using. On the contrary, all the farm labourers and sulphur miners in Sicily, all the poor who believed in hope, used to call him 'Uncle Joe', as they once had done to Garibaldi. They used the name 'Uncle' for all the men who brought justice or vengeance, the hero or the *capomafia*: the idea of justice always shines when vindictive thoughts are decanted. Calogero had been interned, his comrades there had instructed him in doctrine, but he couldn't think of Stalin as anything other than an 'Uncle' who could arm for a vendetta and strike decisively *a baccagliu,* that is, in the slang of all Sicilian 'Uncles', against the enemies of Calogero Schirò: *Cavaliere* Pecorilla, who had sent him into internment; Gangemi, the sulphur miner, who had refused to pay him for resoling a shoe; and Dr La Ferla, who had distrained him of over two hundredweight of wheat to pay for an operation on his groin, which a butcher could have done better.

Calogero looked at the photographs of the meeting at Teheran and Yalta of Roosevelt, Churchill and Stalin: there was no question that the first two were great men who knew what they were doing, but they were thinking only about the present; Stalin, on the other hand, was playing for tomorrow, for all time, playing for Calogero Schirò and the whole world. When Stalin put a card down, that card was good for Calogero Schirò and the future of the human race. Roosevelt and Churchill were thinking about the war to be won, the world freed from the black threat, and about the navies of England and America making commercial networks all over the world, while Stalin was thinking about the salt miners of Regalpetra, the sulphur miners of Cianciana, the feudal peasants and all the people who were being bled to death in their work. Overcoming Germany wouldn't mean a thing if the people of Regalpetra and Cianciana had to continue living like animals.

Following the vicissitudes of the war, Calogero had put his passion and imagination into what General Timoshenko was doing. He believed him to be Stalin's right hand man: Stalin thought, and Timoshenko struck, a general of the people. Timoshenko had a head as solid as a block of wood. 'You could chop meat on it', said Calogero affectionately. He was a shrewd, suspicious, obstinate peasant, risen from the ranks. During the Revolution, his comrades had elected him an officer, and now he was a general and was not to be made into stuffing by the Germans. The first good news from Russia carried his name. There were other Russian generals, the one who resisted at Leningrad, then the one at Stalingrad, the one at the Don, but Calogero saw the fortunes of war rotating around Timoshenko as around a hub. There were other Russian generals, with goatees, but frankly Calogero didn't like people with goatees, people like De Bono, Giurati and Balbo, all the Centurions of the Fascist Militia he had known: a man who wore a goatee had to have some defects. Timoshenko, on the other hand, was shaved like a piece of polished leather, like a conscript just arrived from the regiment. That was it, he had the face of a peasant conscript, of a man called to arms to defend the kolkhoz, not that of a professional general — a professional general, that was a fine thing to be! Calogero had been a cavalryman in the army, and along had come a general with a goatee who, passing along the review, had stopped to see if the stirrups shone underneath as well. If they did not, he screamed out in indignation and distress. He would have liked to have seen that general during the retreat from Russia, turning up the stirrups to see if they shone underneath. Timoshenko was a man to look in his soldiers' faces, not at their stirrups, a man, to be sure, who made jokes with his soldiers, crude peasant jokes. And those peasants, slow and heavy as oxen, were blocking the Germans and crushing them.

Calogero knew all Timoshenko's exploits by heart, the strongholds and cities recaptured, the eulogies and decorations which were his due. He thought, 'In a hundred years' time — let's hope Stalin's death's a long way off — Timoshenko's the man to take things in hand', and he imagined Stalin had already decided on and secretly made his will for such a succession.

Instead, the war ended and no one talked of Timoshenko anymore. Other generals were seen photographed beside Stalin, and Timoshenko's name was forgotten. Once, Calogero asked for news of him from a Communist MP who had just come back from Russia, who made as if it was the first time he had ever heard the name. Then someone told him that Stalin had sent some generals right out of the way, almost in exile: perhaps Timoshenko was one of them. For the first time Calogero had the suspicion that someone had whispered bad advice into Stalin's ear, and he spoke about it to someone on the provincial secretariat, who had made an ugly face, then, with affectionate patience, had explained to him how that was impossible and that suspecting it, even in good faith, constituted a very grave error. Calogero thought no more about Timoshenko.

On 18th April 1948, Calogero had that dream, and the next day the election results proved it to be true. Calogero was so sure, he didn't even want to go and listen to the radio bulletins at the section's club. His comrades, who, listening to his latest forecast on the morning of the 18th, had first called him a bird of ill-omen, later agreed that it was all a question of reasoning. Calogero didn't tell a soul that Stalin had given him the forecast in a dream.

He used to look at Stalin's photograph, and every day he saw even more an X-ray of his thoughts, like a map which continually lit up at different points, now Italy, now India, now America: each of Stalin's thoughts was a world event; Stalin made his moves on the chessboard of the world and Calogero, through some mysterious revelation, knew them before Stalin made them. So that, while *Unitá* said that South Korea had attacked North Korea, Calogero knew that, for once, it was as the Fascist and bourgeois press had it. It wasn't that he had had another dream about the events in Korea, or that he had foreseen that something had to happen there, or even that he knew there was such a place, but he was positive Stalin had had to make the move, if only to see how the Americans reacted. They rushed straightaway to South Korea's defence, it was a test that had to be made. Stalin knew now that if he attacked, the Americans would rush in; it was time to talk peace.

'Peace is working for us,' said Calogero. He became a partisan for peace, collecting signatures for it, and against the atom bomb, and he wore Picasso's dove in his buttonhole. To tell the truth, he did not understand all the great fuss about Picasso and his dove – he could draw better doves himself, with a use of shade so that, in the half light, they seemed real. When Picasso drew Stalin's portrait and the Party said it wouldn't do, Calogero was pleased about it: 'Certain things have to be said loud and clear, Picasso'll be a good Communist, but he's not the painter for us, he ought to paint his portraits for the bourgeois suckers who'll pay him for them', he said. He formed the conviction that Picasso was playing at making suckers of the rich and the Americans, and as far as that went, it had to be said, Picasso was succeeding like God himself.

Each day the newspapers gave him new facts to think about and discuss; his workshop was like a club. When someone who had it in for Communism came along, Calogero felt at home. He winked at his comrades as if to say, 'I'll see to it, now. Leave it to me, I'll have him for breakfast!' and he would begin the attack gently. But he always ended on a rough note, 'It's not everyone who can follow a line of reason. With Fascists and clericals, it's like taking a hammer to a brick wall, they've got such thick heads!'

In fact, the Fascists and clericals who stopped by the workshop for discussions were prudent, with all those Communists around. It was always Calogero who began the insults; he would discuss things very calmly until Stalin's name came up, but as soon as the other person incautiously mentioned his name, the discussion would begin to take a turn for the worse. With the rural dean, who brought up Stalin's name straightaway, Calogero felt as if he had a cancer growing in his stomach – the more so in that the dean was now in control, the town was his, and the fears of 1945 a long way off. The dean would look at Stalin's portrait now almost with compassion. 'Certainly, he must account to God,' he said, 'But perhaps Providence will make him account to men, as well; perhaps he's not destined to die in his bed.'

Calogero sprang up to blast out a more explicit hope for a violent death for all the ecclesiastic hierarchy, starting with the sacristan who, from being a Communist, had now become a pillar of the Christian Democrats.

The last person to learn of Stalin's death in Regalpetra was Calogero. He was up late that day, it was past nine when he went down to the workshop, and he was at work for a couple of hours when he began to feel uneasy because none of the usual crowd had turned up. As it was a sunny day, although a little windy, he thought his friends might have gone out into the country or were enjoying the sun on a walk, so he wanted to go out himself. While he was locking up the workshop, feeling a strong desire for sun and ease, he began to think malicious thoughts about his friends who, through no fault of their own, were unemployed. Naturally, they were becoming used to their leisure, and were having the time of their lives. But he only thought that way because his friends had not come to keep him company that day.

At the section's club, the flag was out with a black ribbon on it, and Calogero thought some comrade or other was dead. Inside, the comrades who came to his workshop every morning were sitting around the table in silence. Seeing the circle of their hands on the table top, Calogero thought they were about to

call the spirits up, and was about to say something jokey, but he
held himself back because of the flag with the black ribbon on it
outside.

'Who's dead?' he asked, and they looked at him incredul-
ously.

'Where've you been?' said one, 'Stalin's dead.'

Calogero felt his knees trembling, the dean's ill omen flashed
like lightning through his head. Immediately he asked, 'Did he
die in his bed? How was it?'

'It was like this', said a comrade, 'he had a stroke.'

The dean had once listed for him all the tyrants who had died
a violent death, which, according to him, Stalin could not
avoid. However, at the end of the day Stalin had died like a
good paterfamilias. Calogero pictured the serenity of that death,
a wreath of silent suffering surrounding the great man who was
dying. But at the same time, it struck him that the news might
be false; knowing certain journalists who were capable of it, he
asked,

'Is the news right? How did you come to know about it?'

'The radio,' they said, 'the newspapers.'

Calogero said nothing more. Well, so Stalin was dead. His
ideas were alive, irresistibly advancing through the world, no
power could stop them, but Stalin, who had carried them forward for twenty years, was dead. Now came the judgement of
history. But Stalin was history itself. The judgement of God.
Let's say that God does exist, that he holds a black book and a
white book, that he holds the scales of justice in his hand. Well,
what has Stalin given, if not justice? And to those whom he
couldn't reach to bring justice, didn't he bring hope? Faith,
Hope and Charity. No, not Charity, only Faith and Hope. And
justice. Stalin has squeezed pain from men, he walked with the
stride of revolution, the stride of blood and violence, but a
revolution is a revolution. Christ brought a new world which
dripped with blood – Calogero had read *Quo vadis?* Those
people didn't kill, but they had themselves killed: it was the
same thing.

'See how I start thinking about religion! I only have to find
myself in front of a corpse to start thinking about it. If I think
about my death, I don't see anything – God, a second life,
nothing. I see the coffin, the grave, someone who'll remember

me as a good comrade, and I'll be just a skeleton inside a coffin when all the world's socialist. But someone else's death makes me think about religion! When my mother, who believed in God, died; when I hear the bells ring for some child who's died; when I saw all those corpses after the train crash. But Stalin's got nothing to do with it, it's ridiculous to think of a man like that having a nice little soul with wings! It's we who carry Stalin's immortality, all the men living on the earth today, and all future men.'

These thoughts went round in his head, but disjointedly, as if he had a fever, like malaria, when you put all the blankets over you and still feel cold, at the same time you feel thoughts and memories turning into a white-hot delirium, you want to fight back, get hold of something solid, anything, the bed, the window, a tree: but that object has already melted in the delirium.

And so, without saying another word, Calogero went home. Seeing him so upset, his wife said, 'I bet that pain in your hip's come back again.' 'Yes,' he said, bitterly, 'you win, it's my hip again. Get the camomile ready.'

As there were certain faces he didn't want to see, Calogero didn't go out of the house for a couple of days. He didn't even want to talk about Stalin's death with his comrades: their memories and hopes were linked to Stalin, as in a close, personal relationship, as in friendship. He thought his feeling was a little different from that of the other comrades, but from the speech Togliatti made in Parliament he understood that all Communists had that same feeling, that Togliatti spoke for them all, finding words for the sorrow of all comrades. Calogero repeated his words and a lump came into his throat, 'Last night Joseph Stalin died. Mr President, I find it difficult to speak. My soul is burdened with anguish for the death of a man venerated and loved above all others, for the loss of a teacher, a comrade, a friend. . . Joseph Stalin is a giant in thought, and a giant in action. . . History will bear his name above all others for the military victory over Fascism. . .'

They were words which came straight from the heart; Calogero could hear Togliatti's voice broken with tears as he pronounced them. Not only was a very great leader dead, but a friend. Those who called Stalin a tyrant made you laugh: there wasn't a single Communist who didn't think Stalin's every thought and wish had been reasoned out and matured inside his own self. When Stalin decided something, it was as if every comrade had decided it together with him, face to face, talking like old friends, with the bottle of wine and packet of rolling tobacco on the table. All over the world, reactionaries performed contortions spying on Stalin's underhand designs — the dark plots he wove (as they said in the newspapers). But on the other hand, the comrades saw it all quite clearly: Stalin was like a card-player with his opponent in front of him and his friends behind him, who, before putting a card down to play, holds it high up for his friends to see, but not his opponent, and every time it's the right card.

Stalin was now next to Lenin, embalmed in the great mausoleum in Red Square, which had resounded in a symphony of glory for three days. What a great man had died! Lenin, too, had been a great man and after Lenin came Stalin. The thought of succession disturbed Calogero a little. Certain newspapers were already looking forward to a struggle for power, but even if there was one, only the best man could win: hadn't Stalin perhaps been right about Trotsky? But of course a man like Stalin couldn't have died without having organized things in the most solid and secure manner. Beria or Molotov? Calogero would have put his money on Molotov.

Instead, Malenkov's name came out; of course, Stalin had designated him and Calogero understood perfectly what his reasoning was. In opening the succession to someone still young, Stalin was killing two birds with one stone because, being young, the longest possible continuity in power was assured and that, moreover, in the hands of a man who had been brought up totally in the school of Stalin. Looking at Malenkov's photograph, Calogero said to his comrades, 'He'll be a good little dog, Stalin's little puppy, a good pedigree puppy.'

But things started to happen that Calogero couldn't begin to explain: the doctors who had plotted to poison Stalin were released; Beria, Stalin's right hand man, was arrested and condemned as a traitor; than Malenkov was substituted by Bulganin. A general, and he had a goatee. Calogero confided in a friend, 'My heart feels as black as pitch, I can't take this Beria business. If Stalin's harboured a traitor all these years, it means a lot of traitorous things have been done. And now this general. . .' But he thought they might be going through a period of adjustment, a power struggle, as the bourgeois press said. He had a strong feeling for Khruschev; after the early reshuffles, he would take hold of the rudder with a sure hand.

Calogero had already arrived at a calm and trusting vision of what was happening in Russia, when the visit of Bulganin and Khruschev to Tito again unsettled him into a state of worry and suspicion. The Twentieth Congress came: he read and heard the speeches about errors and against the *cult of personality*. He agreed with the speech against the *cult of personality*, but the idea that it alluded to Stalin escaped him. Then he heard it said quite clearly: Stalin had made mistakes, power had gone to his head, and he had given the order for dreadful things. The campaign for the local government elections was drawing close and Calogero was invited to stand as a candidate, but he refused. They ordered him to do it for the good of the Party, but, ironically, he appealed in the name of *overcoming the cult of personality*, the personality which the candidature would impose on him. By now he felt less like going down to the section's club, he felt he'd lost everything — like someone with a sack of coins he's earned with sweat and blood, who's told they're no longer currency, they've no value any more — and he made an effort to re-examine past events, to find out where the *errors* lay. But what errors? A vast country like Russia, with so many regions and so many races, a country without industry, full of illiterate people: and now it was a great industrial nation, full of workshops and schools, a united people, a great, heroic people. Russian soldiers had reached Berlin, they had struck a mortal blow at Fascism. Poland, Rumania, Hungary, Bulgaria, Albania, half of Germany, and China: the idea had made progress. Where were the errors? Perhaps Yugoslavia had been an error, throwing Yugoslavia out of the Cominform. . . 'However, I don't like Tito, he's got the face of a dictator, a dictator like Mussolini or Peron.' But time could still see Stalin right.

An MP who had come for a meeting, on learning of Calogero's attitude, wanted to speak to him and went to find him in his workshop. In other days, Calogero would have been happy for the attention, but now he felt embarrassed and annoyed. The

MP told his comrades that he wanted to speak to Calogero alone; as soon as he saw them going away, Calogero felt even more unhappy.

'Listen,' said the MP, 'I know that recently things have upset 'you, they're really serious things, we've all been disturbed by them, I've gone through moments myself. . . But you must realize, you must reason. . .'

'Let's reason it out', said Calogero, cheering up. An invitation to reason always put him in a good humour.

'Look,' said the MP, 'it's like someone who thinks he's in good health, he goes about saying he's got a constitution of iron; he works, goes hunting, enjoys himself; then one day, he runs into a doctor – you know what doctors are like — he fixes him with a stare, then, off-hand, he says "Ever been for a check-up?" and the man says no. The doctor looks at him again, worried. "Come along tomorrow," he says, "I want you to have a check-up." The man begins to get ruffled and says, "I'm fine, what's the matter?" and the doctor says, "Nothing's the matter, but come along tomorrow." And the next day he goes along, the doctor X-rays him, looks at him, listens to him, analyses his urine and his blood, then he tells him he's got a tumour, it'll have to be removed or within six months he'll be dead as a door-nail. The man won't have it, says he's fine, enjoys good health, but they put him on the operating table, put him to sleep and slit him open. "Well," says the doctor, "now you're all right! You had a tumour as big as a baby's head and you didn't feel it." Well, that's how we've been, we had a tumour and we didn't feel it, they've removed it without us feeling a thing, and we still don't want to believe it was there in the first place.'

'The tumour's a good parable,' said Calogero, 'but I don't go to a doctor unless I feel something inside me, and when they slit me open I don't want to be asleep, I want to die with my eyes open.'

'That's all right for a real live tumour,' said the MP, 'but this is different.'

'It's not different,' said Calogero, 'Because if I'm asleep, who's going to tell me if they've really cut out the tumour? I know I was fine, and that's enough.'

'Listen, we really did have a tumour, and we'll slowly come to realize it. Think about certain trials, think about what happened with comrade Tito, the business with the doctors. . .'

'If there was a tumour,' said Calogero, 'I know that tumours reproduce. I didn't see the first one they lifted out, but now I know that other tumours can grow inside me, I've got my eyes open and I'm frightened. You know what happens to someone who's ill like that: I've never known anyone recover from tumours.'

'Christ!' said the MP. 'Let's leave off talking about tumours, it was just a parable, like. . .'

'Well, I liked it,' said Calogero, 'and I want to reason it out.'

'No,' said the MP, 'let's leave tumours be. I can tell you, I've suffered as much as you, and felt I was going mad, you must believe me. I've been through moments. . . But let's not talk about it. I just want to say one thing: Stalin's dead, he made errors, but Communism's alive and it won't die. And anyway, it's not as if we're saying that Stalin only made errors, completely the opposite, he also did very great things.'

'I remember Stalingrad,' said Calogero, ' and the advance towards Berlin. I cried for joy when the Russians reached Berlin.'

'Yes, they're pages of glory, and who can rub them out?' said the MP. 'But we also need to consider the errors.'

'I'll think about them', said Calogero, and again he said, 'I want to die with my eyes open.'

'That's right,' the MP admitted. 'But meanwhile, don't neglect the Party, show yourself down at the section's club — you know how our enemies speculate.'

'I know,' said Calogero, 'they're like grave-diggers waiting for a corpse, but this time we're serving up the occasion to them like manna from heaven, they're having the time of their lives.'

'It couldn't be avoided,' said his comrade.

'Maybe so', said Calogero. 'But there's one thing I know, that when someone dies, thief, murderer, or whatever he was, they put up a plaque about his benevolence and his virtuous life. I could show you some in the cemetery, I'd tell you the real story about each one of them, one by one. And we're doing the exact opposite.'

'It's not the same thing,' said the MP, 'we have to tell the truth, even if we pay dearly for it: the better we succeed in seeing the errors and distortions of the past, the more we guarantee for the future: history is truth and we are the party of history.'

'Those are true words', said Calogero.

Since Stalin's death, the dean had not touched on his usual tale about the tyrant — the dead are still the dead — and had taken up a different line in his discussions with Calogero, instead. But after the local government elections, despite his having given Stalin up, one day he brought Calogero some pages of a newspaper. First he showed them to him like a packet of sweets for a little child, saying, 'Do you know what's written here? The whole of Khruschev's report, the one where he speaks about Stalin, secret stuff. I can lend it to you if you like.'

Calogero made a face and said, 'It'll be the usual fabrication, it makes me laugh how secret business ends up in a newspaper. I bet it's a parish magazine.'

'No,' said the dean, 'It's *Espresso*, one of those magazines which has done you Communists some good turns.'

'I've heard of it,' said Calogero, 'it's a Radicals' thing.'

'Well, read it', said the dean. 'You won't lose anything by it, then you can tell me what you think.'

Calogero launched into reading the report. At one point, he spoke, 'You see how far these American bastards'll go, it's a complete fabrication.' But he went on reading it avidly, cursing away and reading. If it was true, there were things to bring you out in a cold sweat, but it was all invented. He finished reading it when his wife called him to come and eat, but he didn't hear. He went out to buy *Unità* in order to find a denial of the publication. There was nothing. He went back home, swallowed four forkfuls of pasta, and told his wife he was going out and would be returning by the last train in the evening.

He bought the *Giornale di Sicilia* at the station, and straight away his eye fell on the news that Stalin had murdered his own wife. 'Well, that's it, they'll be saying he ate his children next, and where will that bring us?' And in that moment he was no longer angry with *Espresso* or the *Giornale di Sicilia,* but with those who had set the match to the powder-keg.

He arrived at his destination as if he had travelled in a dream and went in search of the MP who had come to try and convince him before the elections, finding him in a café, joking with some friends. Calogero thought, 'It's all false, this chap wouldn't be joking if there really was a skeleton in the closet.'

The MP recognized him, made him sit down beside him and began to ask news of the town. Calogero brought the discussion round to the report published by *Espresso*, saying what he thought about the delinquents who had invented it. The MP became serious.

'Perhaps it is invented,' he said, 'but personally I'm convinced it's true. There's ninety-nine per cent probability it's true.'

Calogero felt his head beginning to spin.

'How d'you mean "true"?' he said, stammering. 'Stalin, then, was more or less just like Hitler. . .'

'It's a bitter pill', said the MP. 'He'd become like that towards the end. But you mustn't think that Stalin could have distorted the nature of the Socialist state. . .'

'No,' said Calogero, 'even Khruschev says so. But I don't understand any more.'

The MP launched into an explanation, speaking with much clarity, and Calogero was convinced. But a thorn remained: Stalin had been a tyrant, just as the dean had said, worse than Mussolini: a mad and violent tyrant, like Hitler. And what if it had been Khruschev who had invented it all, not the Americans; Khruschev and that general with the goatee, and those others around them? No, it wasn't possible. Well, then, it was all true.

Calogero showed the MP the *Giornale di Sicilia*, 'And this other news?' he asked.

'Comrade,' he said, putting a hand on his arm, 'I shouldn't be surprised at anything. Of course, they'll paint it bright red, but it's possible they're telling the truth.'

There was a circular room, resounding with victorious music. He felt that music in his guts, he seemed to be in the body of a huge violin; there was the coldness of deserted churches, a subterranean and far-off light. Stalin was in a glass coffin. Calogero was looking at his hands, which looked dry and hard, like wood. He put his face close to the glass in order to have a better look at that black thread running around Stalin's wrists. He straightened up, thinking, 'That's how women are, my wife's put a rosary on him without my knowing.' He couldn't be certain, but he had the feeling that Stalin had died in his house.

Then he saw a huge hand placed on the glass of the coffin, Stalin was alive, saying, 'They couldn't have killed me off better than this, twice. . .' But the voice had become a murmur, because Calogero, scuttling sideways like a crab, was rushing away towards the door. He hit his elbow against the door and found himself awake because of the pain, panting and sweating. A clear thought came to him, 'They've killed him, I'll resign tomorrow', but he plunged into sleep again.

He woke up badly, his head hurting, his dream still glimmering. He wanted to grasp hold of it to remember it, but couldn't manage it. He plunged his head into a basin of cold water and felt better. He had an aspirin and two cups of coffee. The words of the comrade MP were unwinding in his memory. Things were like that. Stalin's dead, but Communism lives. And Stalin, up until the victory of the war, had been a great man.

He had been in his workshop five minutes, when the rural dean came in. Calogero looked at him in hate.

'Have you read it?' asked the dean. 'Cast an eye over your conscience, and tell me what you think.'

'I've read it,' said Calogero, 'but I don't feel like talking about it. I've read it, and that's enough.'

'That's how you take it, then, is it?' said the dean. 'You should tell me what you think, if you've got the courage.'

'All right,' said Calogero, 'well, I think about it in a special way. . . I'll say this: we'll admit it's all true. And I'll say this: there was his age, he began to do odd things, took off on some ugly whims. I remember that Don Pepé Melisenda, who was eighty, once went out into the street naked. And Caruso, the Solicitor for Oaths, you'll remember him, of course, who cut the plaits off his maid because she wouldn't go to bed with him. He even took against his own children and wanted to skin them alive, and even you know what a good man Caruso had been. It happens that way. Think a little about Stalin, whose brain was beginning to crumble with always having to think about the benefit of mankind: at a certain point he became eccentric.'

'Oh, so that's how you reason it out, is it?' said the dean, ironically.

'I reason it out exactly like that,' said Calogero, 'and I'll say this: you need a little compassion, he's still thy neighbour.'

The rural dean gave a turn as if he were about to have a major fit, passing a finger inside his collar on account of the blood rushing to his head. 'Thy neighbour!' he shouted. 'Now you come out with a story about "thy neighbour", since when have you ever thought about him?'

He went away waving his hands in the air, as if to shake off the memory of the terrible thing he had heard.

'Forty-Eight'

FORTY-EIGHT, *sb. Disorder, confusion. 1. From the events of 1848 in Sicily. 2. To make a 'forty-eight', to end in a 'forty-eight', to profit from the 'forty-eight',* fig. to cause confusion, to end in confusion, to profit from confusion.

— Gaetano Peruzzo, *Sicilian-Italian Dictionary*
Printed by Amato, Castro, 1881

Translator's note:

The Congress of Vienna established the Bourbon Ferdinand IV of Naples as King Ferdinand I of the Two Sicilies. In January 1848 there was a revolution in Palermo, beginning as a popular insurrection then spreading throughout the island, with a demand for a new and more liberal constitution. Ferdinand II granted one at the end of January, but conducted a successful coup in May, regained power in Naples and subsequently reconquered Sicily. Again in April 1860 insurrection spread from Palermo. The Expedition of the Thousand sailed under Garibaldi's command, disembarking at Marsala in early May. Despite scant preparation of the force, almost the whole of Sicily was conquered in under three months, due to Garibaldi's skill and the existing ferment. Garibaldi set up a provisional government under the direction of his associate Francesco Crispi; after their initial enthusiasm, the peasants were disappointed by the failure to partition feudal estates.

My father looked after Baron Garziano's garden, two stretches of land opening out in a fan around the space where the mansion rose. It was land which yielded water if a stake was driven in, dark and thick with trees, so dark it seemed like two in the morning among the trees and earth, even if the sun was scorching down enough to flay you alive. It was as cool as a grotto, with a sound of running water which sometimes sent you to sleep, or sometimes frightened you, and there were birds which called out gaily, then sudden silences torn by the cry of the jay. The Baron called it a garden because there were also magnolias there and trees from India whose trunks seemed like a mass of ropes, with rope-like branches which hung down to plant themselves in the earth; and in the small semi-circle around the house there was also a border of rose bushes which, in May, lit up with huge roses which lost their petals straightaway. The Baron called the house a 'mansion', but it was huge and ugly, like a farmhouse from the garden side, and just as ugly from the side which gave on to the road, but with two naked women in sandstone standing on either side of the main door and Gothic corbels supporting the balconies.

My father was the best pruner in town; they came from the neighbouring ones to ask for his help with the vines and olives, but the Baron paid him three *tarí** a day all through the year, so he couldn't go and work for others without the Baron's permission. Besides the three *tarí* a day, the Baron gave him the house we lived in, next to the mansion, and a plot of land for his own use, where he planted tomatoes, which my mother made into large quantities of paste to sell to the people from Palermo who came for it at the end of every summer. It was a good place, we couldn't complain about our life there. The only thing my father did complain about was the coach; he had to drive it every Sunday, as had been established in their agree

* Double carline of the Kingdom of Naples — *Trans*.

ment: to look after the garden, maintain the stores and be in service with the coach on Sundays. My father liked the coach, he loved horses, but to have to dress himself up in the long jacket which buttoned right up to the collar and the small hat, round as a cheese, made him extremely uncomfortable. The Baron went out in the coach on Sundays to go to mass, at midday, and to go visiting or drive along the coast in the afternoon, and on Sundays my father was like a horse troubled by flies: he made mountains out of molehills, got annoyed at nothing and called down the saints from Heaven — those with which he was most familiar, such as San Rocco, whose parishioners we were, and Santa Venera, who protected the town. He got very angry with the Baron, too, calling him 'this bastard' or 'that bastard' according to how far away, in his rage, he imagined him to be. But when the Baron came down, my father stood next to the open door of the coach with his hat, which, from its original black, was turning green and was really ugly, held in his hand. Behind the Baron came his wife, Donna Concettina, all rustling, with a black and gold Bible and mother-of-pearl rosary in her hand, then behind her their son, Vincenzino, thin and restless, in the suit which the Baron had had made for him, reminding the tailor to take into consideration the fact that he was still a growing boy. But Vincenzino hadn't grown very much afterwards. When the three were already in the coach, the door still open, with my father by it, Donna Concettina would put her head out and call 'Cristina!' then again 'Cristina!' and Cristina would come flying down with her white missal and rosary of green beads, always with something out of place or missing and Donna Concettina would go into a frenzy, peremptorily asking the Lord why he should have sent an orderly person like herself such a daughter, whose head was neither in Heaven nor on earth. My father would ungraciously slam the coach-door shut, leap up into the seat and the coach would rattle over the court-yard gravel, echoing down the entrance to the house as it went out on to the road at a brisk trot. The moment it came out of the main door I sprang up on to the rear wheel axle, without my father noticing, and so arrived at church, leaping to the ground a second before the coach stopped.

Sunday, for me, was a good day, because I enjoyed the drive, curled up behind, going to church or along the coast, or going on the round of visits the Baron made. Only Cristina knew I used to ride behind the coach, though my father perhaps suspected as much. If someone shouted to him as the coach passed, 'Master Carme', give a crack behind!' he didn't give it, thinking perhaps, that I was there. But usually the coach drivers did give several cracks of the whip behind the coach, precisely for the boys who used to climb up there. Cristina knew, but she never told; we were playmates in the garden, and on Sundays we continued our play in that complicity, I clinging like a crab to the coach and she knowing I was there, her eyes searching for me as she got out.

Donna Concettina deemed my company pernicious for Cristina, who always came back hot from our games in the garden; her mother feared she might get a pain in her lungs, from which a son older than Vincenzino had died; and she came back muddy, with flakes of mud even in her plaits, with tears in her clothes and scratches on her hands; and each time she was more badly behaved, either in the answers she gave or the peevish silences she kept. Donna Concettina used to say, 'Each time you mix with that boy, you come back like a devil. But I'll stop your noise, I will, I'll send you to the Sisters' boarding school.' But she never took her to the nuns and at the age of eight Cristina didn't even know her vowels, even if she did go to mass with her missal. I knew how to read print, because my father taught me in the evenings. He knew how to read and write better than the Baron, having had himself taught by a priest when he was grown up.

Once Cristina brought home a live lizard that clambered about, attached to the stalk on which we'd caught it: Donna Concettina gave a moan and fainted. They put her to bed with her feet raised up and rubbed vinegar on her temples. Donna Concettina's eyes went wide with fear even if she saw a lizard or gecko on the wall, so you can imagine the effect of a lizard suddenly wriggling about in front of her. It was decided that Cristina would go to the College without delay, and they took her there in the coach, with myself as usual behind. They left her as the sun was going down and less than an hour after the Angelus the Baron went to bring her back. Once home, Donna Concettina had begun to fret: how empty the house seemed without Cristina, who could say if the nuns would give her her

egg cooked exactly right; so the Baron, cursing, had the coach
hitched up again and went to bring her back, complaining
meanwhile to my father, 'What face can I put on for the nuns? I
can say my wife's mad, that I can say.' And it was true that,
with regard to things concerning the house and religion, Donna
Concettina was a little mad. Perhaps she believed more in the
Devil than in God, because she thought she saw him
everywhere and in the most diverse forms. She didn't use the
world 'Devil' but 'temptation': every ugly and furtive animal
that might walk this earth was 'temptation', every stalk or twig
which might give an itch or a tear, and each part of the body,
apart from the hands and the face, that might be naked. Finding
herself in the presence of temptation, Donna Concettina
repeatedly crossed herself and recited a short prayer at great
speed in order to squash or weaken it. She did the same thing
when temptation, in the form of a curse or obscenity, issued
from the Baron's lips: a remedy which, in truth, had an effect
on the Baron such that his curses and obscenities only multiplied
and became the richer.

Because temptation frequently housed itself in the Baron,
Donna Concettina saw herself constrained to render more in
prayer and almsgiving. She gave her alms to the Bishop's
Revenue, however, never directly to the poor, who, dirty and
badly clothed as they were, had temptation's flame smouldering
in them. She said her prayers at every hour of the day, and even
at night, the Baron's desires permitting. Every afternoon, at the
sound of the Ave Maria, she gathered all the women of the
household together in a huge, empty room — including my
mother — in order to recite the rosary. It was a thing that happened in all the nobles' houses then, but Donna Concettina
insisted on it with particular strictness. She sat on a high-backed
chair with a cushion, the women on straw-bottomed chairs
arranged in a semi-circle; she began the rosary and the women
responded in a chorus of murmurs. In winter, we children went
as well, but because of the unease we felt with the Baroness, we
stayed in a corner of the room, silent. Very quickly, sleepiness
and the cold made me numb, veiled in a sleep ornamented by
the arabesques of the women's murmurs, until I came back to
my senses at 'Glory be to the Father, the Son and the Holy
Ghost, as it was and as it ever shall be, for ever and ever',

because the voices then became clearer. The Gloria finished each decade of the rosary, there were fifteen decades in all, and the women seemed to show relief at every decade completed. On certain afternoons, Don Vico, the parish priest of San Rocco, came to preside over the session and the high-backed chairs became two, with Don Vico wheezing the rosary in a husky voice. At the end of every decade he made a noise in his throat like a goat and took some snuff. The sound he made caused an outburst of muffled laughter in our corner, and Donna Concettina would cast a withering glance our way, saying 'It's temptation that's taken hold of you, say your Ave Marias or I'll have you given a thrashing with the whip' and we began a murmur, which, to the mistress, seemed like a prayer.

At rosary time, the Baron went out to the club, my father accompanying him as far as the door, then going to collect him with a lighted lantern after two in the morning had struck. This service was not in the agreement, but my father did it perhaps because he found he enjoyed playing the part of protector, because at two in the morning the Baron became a mouse; shadows and rustlings made him start suddenly and at each jump my father asked him, in a steady voice, 'What's the matter, your Lordship?' The Baron would collect himself and say, 'Nothing, Master Carme', I thought I saw a movement over there.' My father would raise the lantern and a dog or a cat or even a person going about his own business loomed out of the gloom. 'The fact is', the Baron would say, trying to justify himself, 'that night's a dreadful thing, everything evil happens at night.'

When my father told my mother about the fears the Baron showed every night, he said, 'He's right in saying evil things happen at night, those letters he sends to the Intendant are written at night,' for no one could get it out of his head that certain arrests made by the police were inspired by the letters sent by the Baron via someone he could trust, to the Intendant in Trapani.

It was 1847 (my memories go back no further; perhaps I can recollect my farthest memories in sensations — a smell, a taste, a snatch of song — but I can't hold on to them), the year in which they shut Cristina up in the Collegio di Maria for a few hours, but then there are so many other things that happened towards the end of that year which remain in my mind. One day, clear and gold, in the Indian summer, the news ran about that a steamship full of police and soldiers was in port. I ran to the harbour and saw the soldiers disembarking — there were so many of them the steamship seemed like an anthill crawling with ants. Along the harbour road the townswomen watched them in silence, some of them crying. On land, the soldiers unburdened themselves of rucksack and rifle, and joked among themselves; they nodded towards the women and laughed, but to the children they called out 'little beggars', in their heavy Neapolitan accents.

I didn't like those soldiers. I went home to tell my mother what I had seen, but she showed no surprise, saying that they had been expected for some time. I asked why they had come. 'They've come to arrest evil men and take them away', she said.

'And who are the evil men?'

'Those who steal and kill,' said my mother, 'and the King's enemies, who're even worse.'

'Are there enemies of the King in our town?' I asked, because I knew there were people who robbed and killed.

'Even in our town', said my mother.

'Who are they? How are they enemies of the King, if the King lives in Naples?'

'All I'll say to you', said my mother, 'is that you go and waste your father's time — perhaps he won't mind — but not mine, I've got so many jobs to do that the game of "questions" is the last thing I need!'

My father was making graftings near the crossroads, with the Baron looking on, leaning on his rattan cane with the gold knob. I went up to them, because the Baron didn't make me feel ill at ease, as his wife did, and said, 'The soldiers have arrived, they're disembarking.'

'Oohh. . .' said my father, getting up.

'What d'you mean "oohh"?' said the Baron. 'Let those who ought to say "oohh" say it. Remember, the thorn that doesn't prick is soft as silk.'

'I was saying "oohh" for the kidney that's giving me trouble', said my father, 'I got up and said "oohh".'

'Ah, good!' said the Baron, 'I thought you were saying it

because of the soldiers.'

'The soldiers', said my father, 'are the arm of the King, and the arm of the King knows what it has to weed out.'

'Correct,' said the Baron, 'correct. This evening there won't be a weed left in the whole of Castro, you'll see. Meanwhile, I'm going into town to see the officer, perhaps he's a friend of mine.'

As the Baron disappeared through the trees, with a last gleam of the gold knob, my father said 'oohh' again, and smiled at me. Then he said, 'That bastard.'

I asked no questions.

Towards midday, the Baron came back in the company of the soldiers' commanding officer. He was tall and blond and wore a handsome uniform. Straightaway there was a rummaging in the henhouse and in the kitchen, they even called on my mother to lend a hand. The Baron had small, marble-topped tables and chairs put under the lotus tree, and Pepé the servant, in the striped jacket he wore when there were guests, brought out the coffee pot and cups. The coffee steamed; it was a beautiful day. The Baron twisted happily about in his seat, so that it looked as if someone were tickling him. Cristina and I watched from the height of an olive tree.

'Who's that man?' I asked in a whisper.

'He's a friend of the King', said Cristina. I thought the answer correct, because if he had come to arrest the King's enemies, then he had to be a friend of his. But I couldn't see how the King could have friends and enemies: he lived alone in a palace, which was all gold and pictures, with the queen and the prince. I believed the King didn't have to eat like we did, because eating made you go to the toilet like we did, and that a King should go there was the last thing I would ever have believed. I mentioned it, blushing, to Cristina, who laughed and said no, he certainly didn't go, because the King wasn't made like we were.

Meanwhile the Baron, raising his stick to point out the window, was saying, 'You'll sleep in that room tonight, I'll have it prepared for you. Do you know who's slept there? Try and guess. . . Del Carretto, the Minister. . . In '38, when he came with His Majesty's retinue. . . Oh yes, he was my guest.'

'Oh', said the officer.

'My guest, yes. . . And the other Minister, Santangelo, too, later on. Illustrious people have passed through that room.'

Donna Concettina came out and the officer got up, took her hand as if to twist her by the wrist, but delicately, and kissed it. I was spellbound by the gesture. I said to Cristina, 'Go along there, then he'll kiss your hand. I'd like to see your face if he does.' But Cristina said that she couldn't, because that day she and Vincenzino had to keep out of the way; the Baron didn't even want them at the table when there were guests. They played a game there of looking into each other's eyes to see who would be the first to laugh, but as Vincenzino was funnier, because of the effort he made, Cristina always lost. It was a game which made the Baron irritable, and if there were guests as well, then things became worse; once the Bishop took it badly and the Baron said afterwards that he felt his face fall through the floor with shame.

The officer was talking about a theatre in Naples, when Pepé came to say that lunch was ready. They got up, the officer put out his right arm like a jug handle, Donna Concettina slipped in her hand, which peeped out of the sleeve of her dress like a mouse's nose, and with the Baron continuing to chatter away behind them, they set off.

At sunset, after they had eaten their rations in front of the Monastery of St Michael, the soldiers dispersed in an orderly way through the town, in groups of five or six, led by a gendarme or soldier. In every street and alleyway, you could see police and soldiers in position, with others knocking on the doors. As I started home, a patrol fell in behind me. I lengthened my stride, but the heavy tread of the soldiers was hard on my heels and I began to feel frightened. I slipped in through the main door, forcing myself not to turn round. I went along the entrance and then looked: they were still there, on the threshold, pursuing me with their sure, heavy strides. I shouted out, 'Ma, oh, Ma, they've come to get me! The soldiers! They've come to get me!' My mother came out in alarm, her hands white with flour. I threw myself on her and began to cry, because the soldiers were now in the courtyard, and one of them said to my mother, 'What's this little beggar so frightened of us for, then?' My mother didn't reply. Then, in a different tone, he said, 'Guastella, Giuseppe, son of the late Bartolomeo. It's that gentleman we're looking for.'

'And who might that be?' said my mother, but immediately afterwards she said, 'Oh yes, I understand, you want Pepé. I'd forgotten he was called Guastella, we call him Pepé Sweep-and-Drink, it's a nickname', and she called out in a loud voice, 'Pepé, oh, Pepé. . . you're wanted!'

My fear had passed. I saw Pepé come out in his striped jacket and a rag in his hand, as my mother was asking, 'And what do you want with Pepé?' But the soldier paid no attention to her, he looked at the paper in his hand, then looked Pepé in the face and asked, 'Guastella, Giuseppe, son of the late Bartolomeo?' Pepé said yes. 'Good,' said the soldier. 'Let's go.'

Pepé's face was white and drawn, his eyes glazed like a corpse. Again, the soldier said, 'Let's go.'

'Let's go where?' stammered Pepé. The soldiers made a circle round him, one pointed his rifle at him.

'Where?' said the soldier. 'And how should I know where? Maybe to the Favignana.* Anyway, it's sure to be some nice place or other', and he laughed.

'Me? To the Favignana?' said Pepé, bewildered. 'What wrong have I done to end up in the Favignana? I wait on Baron Garziano, I work, I don't even put my face out of doors, I work like a dog all the hours God sends.'

'Well then, it's a mistake. They've made a mistake', said the soldier, with a face that clearly said that he thought there was no mistake.

'Of course it's a mistake,' said Pepé, 'it's a mistake, and I'll come with you and get the thing sorted out.'

'Listen,' he said to my mother, 'do me the favour of calling my wife, so she can bring my jacket and cap.'

My mother ran off, coming back with Pepé's wife, who was throwing up her hands and shouting, 'What a blow, in my own house! Bad luck had to come, I knew it! Last night I dreamed about sweets, there were so many sweets I wanted to throw up. . . I knew it, sweets are bad luck.' But Pepé made an impatient gesture and said, 'Oh, stop it, give me the jacket, I'm going and I'll be back. It's all a mistake. If I'm longer than half an hour, let the Baron know.'

---

* Prison on the island of the same name, off Trapani — *Trans.*

Half an hour went by. Humid night hung limply about us. My father returned, and in tears, Pepé's wife told him what had happened, imploring him to go in search of the Baron, who was neither at home, nor at the club. 'If we can find the Baron, Pepé'll be saved from prison', she said. You could see my father already had a clear idea of the situation; I knew how to read his face: he didn't think Pepé could be saved — but he went off in search of the Baron. Some time later, he returned with him, the Baron waving his stick about, saying, 'It's unbelievable, an honest man like Pepé, to say nothing of the affront! The affront, yes Sir, as if to say that I keep a thief or a murderer or I don't know what in my service. I'm going right now, they'll hear from me, oh yes, they'll hear from me!' To Pepé's wife, he said, 'You keep calm. As sure as there's a God above, I'll be right back with Pepé.'

He went away, still waving his stick, my father after him.

They came back after about an hour, the Baron no longer waving his stick about. He placed himself in front of Pepé's wife and said, 'My girl, things are not as simple as they seem. . . Er, yes, it's a complicated business. . . that infuriating man, your husband. . . Well, let's forget about it. . . A man like me being taken in. . . Such a good man, Pepé, and what a worker. . . punctilious, precise. . . And then you learn that, at night, Pepé, while others were sleeping. . . Well, that's enough, I don't want to talk about it. . . They're taking him to Trapani now. What has to be cleared up will be cleared up, I'll see to it. It's not as if the Turks had got him. He's sure to come back, that's certain. . . But there's one thing I do want to say, my girl, and you must think on it, tonight: all that glisters isn't gold. . . Pepé wasn't the man he seemed. . . bad company, excesses. . .'

'But how could he?' said my mother, 'if he never went out of the house?'

'Shut up, you,' said my father, 'His Lordship the Baron knows things he can't tell to us, things he's learned about just now.'

'That's it,' said the Baron, 'that's exactly it. I've learned things I certainly can't tell you. That's enough, now. Goodnight.'

Pepé's wife began to whimper.

We went home after having convinced Pepé's wife to get herself off to bed. The fear of what had happened kept me awake, I was shivering. My mother said, 'Oh, poor Rosalia, what bad luck!' But my father was grim, 'Oh, the poor fool you are! What bad luck?'

'Are we just dogs?' protested my mother, 'I feel for the misfortunes of others, I'm not like you. I won't be able to eat a thing tonight, or get a wink of sleep, that's how I am.'

'My feelings are for Pepé,' said my father. 'As for Rosalia, I know what I'd do to her, flog her till she bled and then rub salt in her like a sardine!'

'What's the poor girl done?'

'Listen,' said my father, 'I can keep my eyes open, and I see things — all manner of things — but I keep them to myself. This evening, when you were saying to the Baron what a good man Pepé was, and I told you to shut up, there was a reason for it. I don't want to end up in the Favignana, like Pepé. If I have to go to gaol, I'm not going like Pepé anyway: I'll kill that bastard first and then I'll go, if at all. Pepé, as I knew, and now you know too, had to end up there, because the Baron wants to carry on the affair he's been having with Rosalia, without any trouble. Now you know, but if you tell, I'll rip you in two, I don't want to end up like Pepé.'

They carried on speaking, but I was already sleepy. In my dreams I heard the soldiers striding along, and I saw Pepé's face. Then I was shaken by knocks at the main door and the dogs barking. My father went to open it, it was the officer who was coming to stay the night, Pepé had prepared his room before they took him away; linkmen and police had accompanied him. The Baron came down, in a gay mood, with a light in his hand, to meet him.

The following day, we learned the names of those taken by the soldiers, thirty-four in all. Of course they hadn't taken Vito Lacruna, who lived in the mountains, coming down to town every so often to squeeze money from those who had it and to kill the odd poor soul. However they had taken two enemies of the King (and of the Baron, my father said): Napoli the Chemist, and Alagna, the Doctor. They had found stuff that came from Malta in their houses, printed matter and letters. Once, when I had pierced my thigh on the sharp point of a gate, Dr Alagna had given me stitches. While he was doing it, he

said, 'This young chap's all right, doesn't cry, he's got guts.' It
was true, I didn't cry. He was a likeable man. I knew the
chemist, too, he always gave me a sweet pastille when I went
with prescriptions for Donna Concettina.

I went to the harbour to see the steamship leave. There were
women along the quay, bringing bundles of linen and things to
eat for the prisoners. Rosalia was there, too, with her bundle.
The prisoners were chained together on deck, the soldiers
watching them. Every so often, with the muzzle of their rifles,
they prodded anyone who was cursing more than the others.
On the quay, other soldiers took the women's bundles, had
them say the name, which they then shouted out to their mates
on the boat, the bundle passing from hand to hand to reach its
destination. As soon as the prisoner received it, he waved his
chained hands so that his relatives could see he had it. Then,
from below, they called up 'Guastella' and Rosalia's bundle
made its brief journey, the soldiers passing it along repeating
'Guastella!' and thus I saw Pepé, sitting behind the others. As he
came forward with the bundle in his hands, Rosalia called out,
'There's something to change into, I've brought you all new
things, and there some cigars the Baron's sent you, and some of
the fine wheatbread you like.' But Pepé lifted the bundle up,
opened his hands and let it drop into the sea. Everyone shouted
out in amazement, then there was silence. Pepé shouted, 'You
should've brought poison, because if I live I'll tear your heart
out, and the heart of that. . .' A soldier gave him a blow in the
ribs with his rifle-butt and he was silent. He remained leaning
against the ship's rail, lost, his eyes running with tears.

I can still see him like that, even after so many years.

(I can write these memoirs while I find myself in hiding, alone
in a house in the country in the region of Campobello. Faithful
friends have offered me this escape from arrest, while carabinieri
and soldiers look for me in Castro. As then, Bourbon soldiers
and gendarmes, and carabinieri and soldiers of the Kingdom of
Italy, in Castro and in every town in Sicily, are arresting the
men who are fighting for the future. I regret having escaped
arrest, but being old and tired, prison frightens me. Writing
seems a way of finding consolation and repose, a way of finding
myself again, beyond life's contradictions, finally in a destiny of

truth.)

Rosalia stayed shut in the house for two or three days, receiving visits as if she were in mourning. Even the Baroness came to comfort her, telling her all manner of things about God, and that temptation had certainly taken root in Pepé's heart, for which the hand of justice had taken him away. Rosalia nodded assent, admitting that her husband had seemed a changed man during the past couple of months, and what he had shouted to her from the steamship clearly showed that he had lost his senses as well. 'Keep an honest woman,' said the Baroness, 'and set your heart at rest. If God wants to forgive him and protect him, he'll come back; if his sins are truly black, then he'll get what he deserves', and so leaving Pepé to God's wisdom, she advised Rosalia to take at least a couple of raw eggs, because even refusing food was the fruit of temptation.

Rosalia certainly had no need of Donna Concettina's exhortations to take sustenance, for when she came out to take up her usual round (the poulterer, the baker's, the wash house, and in the afternoon, the rosary, and the small talk with the other women of the household) she was as pink as a peach and moved like a goldfinch, vibrant and bright. She had blue eyes and dark hair, a generous body and was always laughing with a high trilling sound. Donna Concettina should have heard the triumphant peal of temptation in that laugh; it was the laugh in which the Baron had lost himself. Cautiously and furtively, when the Baroness thought he was shut in his study doing the accounts or writing letters, he would go down to Rosalia's house and stay there until rosary time. First Rosalia came out and went up to the Baroness, then out came the Baron like a cat that's successfully raided the kitchen; he disappeared through the trees in the garden, reappearing on the opposite side to call for my father to take him to the club. It was now an everyday occurrence, but it couldn't continue so smoothly. Rosalia began to dress well, too well, in the Baroness's eyes. On some days she wore more gold than the Madonna of Itria, and she had a dove-grey silk dress which made her look very beautiful. Donna Concettina began to have suspicions; not, poor thing, about her husband: only the sin of thinking (as she called it) that Rosalia might be doing evil things in order to get her gold trinkets and beautiful clothes. So she began to put pressure on her husband to turn Rosalia out of her house, seeing that Pepé was no longer there and the house had been given in return for his service. But the Baron resisted, saying that he hadn't the heart to throw the poor young thing out on the streets, and he appealed to Donna Concettina's feelings of Christian charity. It was precisely 'Christian charity', which the Baron had never shown in all the eighteen years of their marriage, which gave the Baroness a definite clue.

One day, from the height of the walnut tree in which we were sitting together (I would never have told her what I saw the Baron doing, because of my father's threats), Cristina saw her father entering Rosalia's house so silently, and looking about him with such a terrible expression, that she thought he was playing a game, and afterwards, in her innocent excitement, she told her mother. Donna Concettina drew the necessary conclusion. She didn't give vent immediately, but the next day she took up watch and a few minutes after the Baron had gone in, she went down to knock on Rosalia's door. Silence, as if Rosalia had gone out. But the Baroness knew that was not the case. She started knocking again in fury, then she took a rock and started raining blows on the door which seemed like thunderclaps. My mother came to the door, my father ran over from the garden, the groom came out, the maid, Vincenzino and the priest, who in that moment was giving a lesson to Vincenzino and all the children, five or six of us, including Cristina. The Baroness gave an order to my father and the groom, 'Break down that door immediately!' But they knew who was behind it and made not a move. Stupidly, the groom said, 'Rosalia's not there, she's gone out. The Baron's gone out, too.' Donna Concettina began to shout, 'Ah, both of them gone out! Now I know what you are, you're all bawds, bawds, all of you!' At which point, having so lost her head as to utter words which, in the mouths of others, would have had her crossing herself, in tears she continued to bang on the door with the rock. Cristina, and then Vincenzino, began to cry as well. The priest came forward, took the rock from her and pointed out the innocence of Cristina and Vincenzino, which should not be defiled, but evidently he hit the wrong note, for rancour and pity spread through her for her children and herself, a furious pity. The priest thought of another one, 'These are matters which dignity requires to be resolved in a different way — a different place perhaps, seeing

we're in a courtyard? Matters which require enlightened counsel, a holy mind which counsels and gives help. Let's go to the
Bishop. I'll come with you myself, only the Bishop can say how
you should act.'

They were words which calmed Donna Concettina, but on
the Baron inside they had the effect of a ferret entering a bur-
row: the rabbit darts out to end up in the net or under the
hunter's blow. Struggling into his jacket, the Baron came out,
red with shame and rage, swooping down on the priest, shouting, 'That's wonderful counsel you've given her, just the sort a
sod of a priest like you would give! I'll whip your backside and
you'll go to the Bishop on a stretcher, you will! And you're
dismissed, yes, dismissed. Go and teach Latin to Mariantonia
and Pietro the greengrocer's daughters and all the other tarts
you keep in the presbytery, sodding. . .'

'Yes,' shouted Donna Concettina, who, surprised by the exit,
had been turned to stone, 'yes, I'll go to the Bishop. I'll go
straightaway! Filthy, excommunicate adulterer, you are! Adulterer, adulterer!' She continued repeating the word, perhaps
because she found a balance in it between the invective on which
she had launched, and the dignity she had to maintain.

'If you make a move to go to the Bishop, I'll kill you,' said
the Baron.

'Kill me, then you can marry that. . . Oh, God, give me the
strength not to speak. . . Enough! Kill me!'

The Baron thrust himself at her with his hand raised, but
everyone pressed round him to keep him from her. The Baron
being surrounded, Donna Concettina profited by it to run off to
the Bishop. The Baron realised this and violently tried to tear
himself away from the hands that were holding him. But the
hands grasped him more tightly. He relaxed, and they let go,
but it was too late to catch up with the Baroness, because the
Bishop's palace was nearby.

'That's a great service you've done me! I'm dismissing you,
all of you.' He turned to the groom, 'And you, you stupid
oaf. . . the Baron's gone out, Rosalia's gone out. . . not to say
that I'm sure one of you's been spying on me: if I ever get to
know who it is, I'll kill him with my bare hands. . . with my
bare hands. . .'

Rosalia didn't hear, she had silently closed the door.

Donna Concettina came back from her talk with the Bishop looking like a martyred saint: she walked along with her eyes gazing up and gave people to understand that from silence and from God she would draw strength to carry her cross, and that therefore no one, much less the Baron, should go near her. The Baron was still recriminating, but was more resigned, and from the way in which he turned to my father and the groom, it was understood that their dismissal had been revoked. But the apparition of his wife froze him: she passed by without deigning to give him a look, disappearing down a garden alley with the priest trotting after her.

The Baron instructed the groom, 'Call Don thingummy. . . what the devil's his name? . . . sod of a priest. Call him for me, and if he doesn't want to come, tell him I'll come and fetch him myself and slaughter him like a young goat!' The groom ran off, coming back with the priest who was trembling all over.

'Bravo!'said the Baron. 'I must drink your health for the counsels you give! That to my wife was worth your own weight in gold. The counsel of a real. . . You really picked that one out of the basket. But now I want some counsel myself: should I kill you or should I kill myself?'

'Your Lordship,' stammered the priest, 'I didn't know. . . It seemed the best counsel in that moment that would. . . I wanted to get the Baroness away from the door, you were trapped, I wanted to free you. . .'

'Oh, you freed me all right!' said the Baron. 'You really freed me, you great. . . Now, not only have I to clear things up with my wife, but with the Bishop as well. God knows how he's taken it.'

'If you want to know, the Bishop was amused, he wanted us to describe the whole scene for him. We came to the point where you came out and as soon as his name was mentioned, he burst out laughing, I swear it, he laughed until there were tears in his eyes. . .'

'Oh,' said the Baron, his face furious, 'so he laughed, did he?'

'I swear it', said the priest again.

'And you,' said the Baron, putting his face so close to the other's that their noses were almost touching, 'do you think there's anything to laugh at in what's happened.'

'Me? I would never even allow myself. . . Laugh? It seems

something more for tears.'

'Tears? Well why not cry? Who's stopping you?' said the Baron, shaking the poor priest with one hand. 'Cry! At least you can give me that satisfaction for all the damage you've done.'

'Oh, but what damage? You did the damage yourself,' said the priest, plucking up courage, 'by taking temptation by the arm.'

'Christ!' said the Baron, deflating before the priest's sudden reaction. 'Now you're talking like my wife! Temptation. . . Eighteen years she talks to me about temptation, and in the end I fall. . . temptation!'

'Now you're reasoning like a Christian', said the priest. 'You fell into temptation, and now you must pull yourself out. The Bishop will help you, you can count on it.'

'That's where the damage is: he'll help me, and I know how.'

'Well, what do you want?' said the priest, being perfectly frank, 'That the Bishop — God forgive me — should be your pimp?'

'That's enough,' said the Baron. 'Tell me, instead, everything the Bishop said.'

'He said he would take charge of things and would settle them in the best way. You shouldn't worry about it.'

'You're joking! Who's worrying? Things couldn't have gone better! I'll have a little celebration I'm so happy. The Bishop laughed about my personal affairs, he's promised to sort them out. . . I'm home and dry!'

The Bishop had the Baron call on him that evening, and must have given him a terrible scolding, because the Baron came back spitting blood, venting his anger on his employees. The consequences of his meeting with the Bishop were seen several days later: the Baron retired to the Monastery of St Michael for a week or so for prayer and spiritual exercises, Vincenzino went into the seminary, and Cristina to the Collegio di Maria. Rosalia, however, remained where she was, and was more arrogant and full of song than before.

Before going to the monastery, the Baron called for my father, making him a handsome speech, decorated with 'We're both men, you follow me. . . You're the only man I can trust', and he charged him with looking after Rosalia, 'Because,' he said, 'alone like she is, she's a creature who could let herself fall into despair.'

Relations between Baron Garziano and the Bishop of the Diocese of Castro, Monsignor Antonio Calabrò, were close and continuous. The Bishop, the Baron, the King's Judge and the Sub-Intendant together formed a quartet of mutual understanding, unanimous in their secret decisions, which the police then translated into unhappy fact. So it came naturally to a Castrese (or Castrense, as the local historian Gaetano Peruzzo would have it), if he was in trouble, to wish on one of the four, or all four together, instant death, cancer and phthisis. Through the Monastery of St Michael and the Bishop's Revenue, the Bishop had a good third of Castro's landed property in his hands; the Baron had another third; and the remaining land was divided into small estates and State demesnes which, slowly but surely, the Baron was usurping, without otherwise raising the alarm of the Civil Decurionary, which should have been protecting them from such private usurpation. The Civil Decurionary had the powers which the Town Councils have today, but the decurions were nominated by the Sub-Intendant, who occupied the position that a Sub-Prefect does today (the one in Castro now makes me long for the Bourbon Sub-Intendants); the King's Judge did what the Magistrate does today; but the Bishop, however, did what Bishops may no longer do. As regards the administration of justice, I must add that the citizen on whom the arm of the law landed had very little likelihood of proving his innocence. If he succeeded in doing so before the King's Judge (to whom the accused was entrusted for judgement which had to come more from conscience than the law), and was declared innocent, he still had to reckon with the police, who could keep him in prison at their discretion, even for years at a time. Because of this, arrest was feared more than death itself, and the peasants sang about it in those terms in the words of a lament.

The Sub-Intendant and the King's Judge in Castro did what the Bishop wanted, and the Bishop often consulted Baron Garziano, or, to put it crudely, the Baron spied and, with alacrity, reported to the Bishop certain conversations held in the club and in the evening meetings at the Chemist's. Sometimes they were innocent conversations, about prices or the bad weather or about the Festival of Santa Venera, but comments, unfinished sentences and looks of understanding cropped up which the Baron immediately noted and catalogued. And when there really was nothing to report, he was helped by an evil imagination.

When the Bishop and the Baron had big fish to fry, getting into trouble people who were not without connections, they by-passed the Sub-Intendant and the King's Judge and went over their heads to the Intendant in Trapani or the higher authorities in Palermo or Naples. Among my papers I have letters from the Baron and from the Bishop addressed to the Lieutenant-General, which came into my hands by chance in June 1860 in Palermo. Those of the Baron (there are five or six) all begin and end in the same way: 'Excellency, it is a public scandal to allow the enemies of the King to be in control by trampling on the Royalists. . . It would be worth watching over and breaking that tie'; those of the Bishop, on the other hand are stylish, subtle and insinuating, sometimes fairly dripping with heartfelt goodwill towards the designated victims: 'With all our distress and compassion, in order to guarantee and protect minds from pernicious, disturbed ideas. . . the Government showing foresight, according to its custom, we beg to inform. . . addressing ourselves, as well, to the same end to the Ecclesiastical and Lay Superiors.'

The thing the Baron most feared in the world was losing the Bishop's favour; therefore he went off to do his spiritual exercises, which he did every year, but this time, so to say, out of season, and for his own exclusive benefit; because every year the exercises were held during Lent for all the gentlemen of the area together. He went off to the monastery and every day my father brought him word of things in the house and in the countryside, but what interested the Baron most came out at the end of the meeting, with a question he used to ask with an absent-minded air, 'Er. . . Wait. . . there was something I wanted to ask you, but I've forgotten. . . Ah, yes, what does that creature say? Is she upset? Is my wife leaving her in peace?'

Donna Concettina was leaving her in peace, so much that Rosalia had taken heart and even, in spite, sang:

Ammàtula tu spicci e fai cannola
ca lu cantu è di marmaru e nun suda★

meaning that the Baron belonged to her and Donna Concettina
was uselessly spending her time combing and curling her hair:
the Baron would remain, like the statue of a saint, in marble
indifference to the artificial charms of his wife. To tell the truth,
she did curl her hair a little, but certainly not to make the Baron
perspire with love: she did it out of the habit of years, at least so
as not to see any temptation present in the curling iron.

The Baron left the monastery, as Christmas was approaching.
The garden was a tangle of bare branches, only the olive trees
shook their leaves in the wind. The town seemed deserted, it
resounded to the breathless sound of the sea like the soundbox
of a guitar, a sound which woke me up at night, bringing dreadful thoughts.

Donna Concettina made a clear pact with the Baron: Rosalia
had to go — 'Either she goes, or I do' — and the Baron settled
her in a small new house not far from the mansion, going to see
her there every day, which no longer caused a scandal. His wife
no longer concerned herself with it, it was as if the Baron had
been cancelled from her life completely, she wouldn't speak to
him nor even look at him: the things she had to say to him, and
those rarely, she said through Don Vico, my father or one of
the servants. Coming back from the monastery, the Baron had
found his wife in the salon, sitting in the middle of a sofa, with
Don Vico and my father standing. At the main gate the groom
informed him to go straight to the salon, which he entered,
waving his stick about, as happy as if nothing had ever
occurred. But that silent picture froze him. Without looking at
him, Donna Concettina spoke to Don Vico, 'Tell his Lordship
the Baron that that woman must leave this house, either she
goes, or I do' and Don Vico gave him the message. With an
amused look on his face, as if he were allowing a joke to be
played on him, the Baron said, 'What, are you still thinking
about that? It's water under the bridge, Concetti', let's forget

---

★ 'You beautify yourself and curl your hair in vain / Because the Count is
marble and does not sweat (for you).' — *Trans.*

about it. It was temptation, you know how temptation works, it burrows in like woodworm, a weak man gives in to it. . . then you repent, you know. . . let's forget about it. . .' But Donna Concettina, still looking at Don Vico, said, 'It's either she or I, tell that to the Baron, and that I shall no longer be speaking a word to him.'

'Listen,' said the Baron, changing expression and coming forward a step, 'listen, I'm a good man, and to prove how much so, it's enough to say that I've borne with you for eighteen years, but don't make me lose my temper, or I'll lose the grace of God and turn into a beast, a beast!'

Unmoved, Donna Concettina asked Don Vico, 'What did he say?'

Don Vico translated, 'His Lordship the Baron says that his goodness must not be given a severe trial.'

'You want to soften the thing', said the Baroness to Don Vico with a touch of disgust; she turned to my father, 'Master Carme', tell the Baron quite clearly that I will not turn into a beast like him, but will go back to the Bishop. And I'll write immediately to my brother so that he may do what he must in Naples, and talk to whom he must there, to put my affairs in order. That woman must leave and he, for the rest of the days that God gives me, must no longer speak to me directly. What he has to say to me he can say it to you and to Don Vico or whoever he likes, but he must no longer speak to me.'

'What a theatrical scene!' shouted the Baron, and stormed out. But he immediately saw to Rosalia's removal and never again spoke directly to his wife. He knew her too well to delude himself that her feelings might change. 'She belongs', he said, 'to a family of blockheads, from whom God save us. Heads you'd need to cook for a week to get a drop of soup!' But there was one of those heads, very near to that of Ferdinand, one which could whisper to the King good words or bad words, which the Baron respected and feared.

On 16th January 1848, the Baron went out as usual to go to the club, but he came back straightaway, pale and agitated, calling for my father, and ordered him to have the main door closed with crossbars and poles and to open it for no one, 'Those inside are inside', and even to fire if certain faces showed up. 'What faces?' asked my father, who didn't understand.

'The faces of those. . . you follow me?. . . the people against me: the people who go to the Chemist's, who want to turn the world upside down. . . you follow me?'

'But what's happening?' my father asked.

'What's happening, dear Master Carmelo, is that the world is coming crashing down, you can't understand things any more, we're lost!'

'But how?'

'What do you mean "How"? It's the revolution, can't you understand? There's revolution in Palermo, in the whole of Sicily, and right here in Castro, they're already moving about in the piazza, people are huffing and puffing like bellows to set things alight, people we should have clapped in gaol some time ago. . . But the bad weather won't last for ever, the King's certain to be thinking about it. . . you'll see. . . Come along with me, in the meantime we'll go and inform the Baroness.'

Seeing her husband so upset, Donna Concettina asked my father, 'What's happening?' The Baron told my father, 'Inform the Baroness that on the 12th of this month in Palermo they started a revolution, and after that, in the rest of Sicily. Now the news has arrived in Castro and the rabble are on the move.'

'Revolution!' shouted Donna Concettina, as usual speaking to my father, 'There's revolution and you calmly come and give me the news as if it were a baptism, while my children are out of the house? You don't give a thought for them, you come back home and, as if it were nothing, tell me there's a revolution! Oh, my poor children. . .'

'Your Ladyship,' said my father, confused, 'really, I've nothing to do with it. . . The Baron came rushing back, told me to close the main door because there was a revolution and then he told me to come up with him. . . and here I am. . .'

'Do you suppose, perhaps, that I am angry with *you*?' said the Baroness. 'What I say to you, you must repeat to the Baron, word for word.'

'Have you forgotten?' intervened the Baron, ironically. 'Revolution or no, in this house we always have to act out the farce, dear Master Carmelo. Come on, repeat what the Baroness has said, then I'll give you my reply and you can pass it on to her. The farce, the same old farce. . .'

But they were hammering on the main door in fury. The Baron's face suddenly changed from the congested colour of anger to that of a drumskin, Donna Concettina gave a flutter of fear and fainted, but neither the Baron nor my father took any notice. The blows on the main door sounded sinister in the silence of the house. The Baron went out and came back with a brace of pistols, one of which he gave to my father, and said, 'Go and see who it is, but don't open the door. Even if it's my mother come back from the grave, you do not open that door. If it's those people, then give them a shot from the pistol without any fuss. . . or rather two. . .' and he gave him the other pistol.

'If his Lordship the Baron will permit me,' said my father, 'I think the idea of shooting is sheer stupidity: like poking a straw into a wasp's nest. I won't fire unless they do.'

'Do as you like,' said the Baron, sinking into a chair, 'do as you like, but go and see who it is.'

My father came back saying it was the Sub-Intendant. The Baron gave a start and shouted, 'And what does he want? Does he have to come to my house right at this very moment? If those brigands are looking for him and come with him as far as here, they'll be killing — God forbid — two birds with one stone. They'll get him and they'll get me, there'll be carnage, carnage! I'm going to leave him outside the door, it's every man for himself!'

The knocking continued. My father said, 'If you will permit me, I'd say that it was worse to have him outside, someone may pass, see him and tell the others. . . better to bring him in.'

'Yes,' said the Baron, 'you're right. Better to bring him in.'

As soon as my father had opened the door a crack, the Sub-Intendant slipped in like a mouse that scents a cat approaching. 'You took your time opening up!' he said. 'This isn't the time to take things at your leisure!' He went up at a brisk pace, wiping off his sweat, and it was a cold afternoon.

The Baron was waiting for him at the top of the stairs.

'They're looking for me', announced the Sub-Intendant, anxiously.

'Oh, they're looking for you, are they?' said the Baron. 'That's really consoling news. So they're looking for you!. . . They're looking for you, and you come to my house, so that if whoever's looking finds, they find you and me together.'

'But I came', said the Sub-Intendant, who hadn't expected such a welcome, 'because you're a friend, you've always declared your friendship, that your house was mine and many other considerate things. . .'

'Well, and who's denying it?' said the Baron, softening. 'My house is as if it were yours. . . The fact is that you are a single man, you don't have a family. . . I, on the other hand, have got a woman in the house, who, as soon as she saw one of those faces appear, God forbid, would pass away. . . And I have children, you understand. . .'

'I understand', said the Sub-Intendant.

'And so,' continued the Baron, 'you can go to the Bishop's. You'll be putting yourself in a safe place, no one will come looking for you there. I'll look after things here as best I can.'

'What you say is very true,' the other agreed. 'You are the very soul of kindness, but the fact is that I've already been to the Bishop's, and he gave me a worse welcome than yours. You know how he dismissed me? With these exact words: "Go, my son, and stay peaceably at home. Flight speaks of guilt. No one will do you any harm because you haven't done any yourself. He who does no evil has no fear." So here I am, as you can see.' The Sub-Intendant made a face like a child about to burst into tears.

'He's a real saint,' said the Baron sarcastically. 'So we're to be the dogs' dinner! I didn't really expect this.'

'There's more yet. Going out, Father Giamusso, who came with me to the door, whispered to me that the Bishop couldn't wait to send me away because he had to receive the Committee. . . the Revolutionary Committee, you follow me?'

'A Bishop starting a revolution?' said the Baron. 'Christ Almighty, my head's in a whirl. . . I don't understand anything any more. . . there's nothing to believe in any more, neither God nor the Saints. . .'

Donna Concettina, who had come round, told my father, 'Tell the Baron to speak like a Christian soul, and that instead of standing there complaining and cursing he should occupy himself a little with his children, who are out of the house, poor little creatures. . .' and she began to cry.

The Baron went blind with rage, and shouted, 'Tell that old

fogey that with a Bishop starting a revolution, they're better off where they are and I'll speak as I like and I want to curse all night long, I want to curse all the saints in the calendar, one by one. . . and I'll do it to annoy her. . . that's why I'll do it, yes, that's why. . .' He picked up an almanac from the table and began to read out the names of the saints, giving each one a blasphemous attribute.

The Sub-Intendant snatched the almanac out of his hand, as Donna Concettina fainted again.

Later, when a little calm had returned, the Baron and the Sub-Intendant thought it would be a good idea to learn what was happening in the piazza, and charged the groom with going out to spy. He came back after a couple of hours, by which time the Baron had already begun to worry they might have killed him for the simple reason that he was in service in the Garziano household. However he came back in a merry mood, smelling of wine, saying that the town was celebrating and some friends of his had invited him for a glass of wine. He reported confusedly that there was a portrait of the Pope in the piazza, with so many lights around it that it seemed to be day, and that everyone was shouting 'Long live liberty, long live Pius the Ninth!' and the King's arms had been pulled down and chiselled off. There were many honourable gentlemen with rifles on their shoulders and many of the ordinary people were drunk: but everyone was making merry, as the gendarmes and soldiers had disappeared.

The Baron plucked up courage again, became obsequious with the Sub-Intendant and ordered supper. 'Tomorrow,' he said, 'as soon as it's dawn, I'm going to the Bishop. I want to see clearly where we fit into what's happening. If we have to start a revolution, then we'll all start it, don't you think so?'

'I am the King's representative,' said the Sub-Intendant, 'and I'm not starting any revolution. Tomorrow I'm going to try to get to Palermo. My superiors'll tell me what to do.'

'But, of course,' said the Baron, 'it's your duty to. . . Nor am I willing to give an inch as far as the King's concerned. All right, let's have a revolution, but the King is still the King. Let's pull down the coat-of-arms with his lily, but I'll carry that coat-of-arms in my heart for ever. . . In Palermo, I hope you won't forget to remind your superiors of my loyal feelings to the King and his officers. . . And the hospitality I offer you in this moment comes from an open heart, believe me. . .'

'I thank you', said the Sub-Intendant frostily.

But it was fated that night that no one in the Garziano household would get any sleep. My father was about to go to bed, telling us about the evening's events, when the main door resounded with blows. 'Ah, ha!' said my father. 'This time the storm's come in earnest, and it's my damned luck to find myself in the middle of it!' He dressed again, opened the door to go out and found the Baron and the Sub-Intendant standing there like two ghosts, waiting silently for my father to come out. They hadn't dared to call out for fear that those outside would hear.

'Excellent, Master Carmelo!' said the Baron, in a whisper. 'You understood we needed you, excellent! Look, you must go and see who it is, but without opening the door. . . and if it's those — you know — say the Baron's not in, he left this very evening, you can even pretend to confide in them or betray me, say I've gone to Fondachello, say the bailiff sent for me. . . Well, anyway, you don't need me to tell you, say whatever you think's suitable. . . but for pity's sake don't open the door. . .'

My father came back and said that Father Giamusso was at the door together with another person whom he didn't recognize; Father Giamusso said he'd been sent by the Bishop. 'Open the door at once', ordered the Baron, letting out a sigh of relief. But then an awful suspicion came to him. 'No, wait a moment, how do we know there's nothing behind it? The Bishop and the revolutionaries are one family now. . . So, let's do it like this: you keep the pistol in your hand and go and open up. Make sure there are only two people, and then open up. We two will place ourselves so that, if they enter with evil intent, we'll lay them out as dead as dogs. . . Right, now off you go.'

But Father Giamusso and Don Cecé Melisenda were bringing a consoling message: Baron Garziano was being called by the newly-formed Civic Committee, of which the Bishop was Chairman, to become a part of it. Naturally there had been violent opposition to the Baron's name, but the Bishop had appealed on behalf of his gentle nature, his noble birth and to the trusted civic sentiment of the opposers, and had won the day.

'What a great man he is, our Bishop', said the Baron. Turning to the Sub-Intendant, he said, 'What was I saying? The Bishop's goodwill could do no less for me, and what he does, cherish it, it's always done well'.

'To tell the truth. . .' began the Sub-Intendant.

'I know what you mean, I understand and commend it', said the Baron. 'But you see, you can't leave the fate of the town in the hands of a group of bunglers. You must intervene, partici-pate. . . defend gentlemen of honour against underhand actions and abuses of power. . . And then, to tell the truth, things were beginning to go wrong: everyone was starting to betray the King, poor thing, they were making a fool of him, everyone was pulling the blanket to his own side of the bed. . .'

'I'm off', said the Sub-Intendant.

'And where are you off to?' asked the Baron, surprised.

'To give myself up to the revolutionary committee, so they can send me off to prison or string me up from the lamp-post in the piazza. Yes, I'm off.'

'Well, if that's how you feel about it,' said the Baron, 'What can I say? If you're happy, everybody's happy.'

The Sub-Intendant looked him fully in the face for a good minute, then brusquely he said, 'Goodbye.'

The following day, the Pope's portrait was marched round again. A procession formed, starting from the Bishop's palace, with the Bishop leading, giving his blessing, smiling and raising his eyes to the balconies, which were so crowded it looked as if they would overflow. On the Bishop's right was the Baron, dressed in subfusc, with two or three Papal decorations; on his left was the Baronet, Don Cesare Melisenda, a man much esteemed for his charitable works, to which he dedicated himself at the sacrifice of his patrimony, and of such politeness in agree-ing with everyone that the liberals had him for a liberal and the Bourbons for a Bourbon. Behind them came the rest of the Committee, twenty or so people, then the Guilds and their stan-dards. The procession halted in the Piazza, the Bishop came to the balcony of the Town Hall to bless and smile. Then Dr Amato gave a speech, which was all against the Bourbons and the police; he remembered the citizens of Castro who were in prison and hoped that they would soon return free men, and he spoke of liberty, quoting lines from famous poets, and ended by declaring his love for the town of Castro and for all Sicily. After him, Canon Liotta came up to speak, and said that the people of Castro deserved praise for the moderation, good sense and harmony they had displayed in exemplary fashion. It was a sure sign for a better future — such, perhaps to give a lead to the whole of Sicily — and he concluded that only the fear of God and love for one's neighbour could give true happiness to the Sicilian.

The taverns swarmed with people well into the night. At the club they held a celebration with music.

A few days later the town was moved by the news that Napoli the Chemist and Dr Alagna had returned. There was a procession of visits to the houses of the two men. They were thin, their eyes glazed as if they had a fever, but they had to embrace and kiss almost the whole of Castro, one by one, and tell each and every one about the torments they had suffered, the prisons, their guards, their cross-examination, the food and lack of sleep. Even the Baron went, but he was received, so people said, with undisguised coolness. The Baron began to show signs of worry and went out of town for a few days to see how things were once the two had been enrolled on the Committee.

Nothing new happened, so, reassured, he came back and participated in the Committee's sessions, but during a discussion about the militia — whether it was right to have them in the new Civic Police, and the Baron was of the opinion that it was — Dr Alagna said, ironically, 'And why not, seeing we have Bourbon spies on the Committee?' In all innocence, and shy as he was, Don Cecé Melisenda, a man who didn't understand tricks and subterfuges, rose up sharply, saying that for the honour of each and all it was necessary to name names, and so clarify if there were spies on the committee, or only liars. Fearing names would be named, the Bishop stood up, opening his arms out like a crucifix, and, in Latin, invoked peace, declaring before God that he would assume the weight of all the sins of the Committee members and of all the citizens of Castro. Then he turned on Don Cecé, avoiding coming up against Dr Alagna.

'Really,' he said, 'I didn't expect a Baronet like Don Cesare Melisenda, beloved among all the beloved of this Diocese, to come to this august assembly and sow dissension. On the contrary, we must do our utmost to lay waste the seed of discord, so that a good harvest can be raised for the nourishment of the beloved people of Castro and as a reward for our labours.' Tears came to Don Cecé's eyes, he felt abandoned in his guilt, and ran to kiss the Bishop's hand and beg his forgiveness. Dr Alagna smiled in an amused way.

The Committee voted to establish the National Guard, a body of young gentlemen of honour, with handsome uniforms of black velvet and rifles with damask straps and silver arabesques on their stocks; they looked very smart seen in the processions and ceremonies. But as far as ensuring public order was concerned, to a large degree the National Guard left that duty and honour to the old body of the militia which, for its part, as it was composed of thieves and murderers who found it convenient to be on the right side of the law, formed a very good link with the brigands infesting the countryside. The gendarmes were no more, having made off at the first news of revolution, and the King's Judge had disappeared with them. So that those wanted by the law had come back to town, a few at a time, from the open country where they had been hiding out in bands. Even Vito Lacruna had come back. They said he wore a belt of plaited leather, to which he added a copper stud for every soul he succeeded in killing, and it already weighed more than six pounds. Not that he showed himself much around the town, and whoever did see him, hooded and wary, so that it seemed he was carrying night around with him, only managed to recognize him because of the fierce, anxious flash of the whites of his eyes. But his presence was felt in every house through the whole town; his vendettas and robberies were recounted in the evenings when the howling of wind and sea, the creaking of a shutter, the bang of a door or the snapping of a branch, carried all the evil and fear in the world.

One evening, the dogs were barking furiously and growling in a threatening manner. My father knew that growl; when the dogs were like that it meant they had seen someone in the garden, they were trained on him ready to pounce if he made a movement. Silently he opened the door, after having doused the light, rifle at the ready. A voice said, 'Call your dogs off, or

as sure as there's a God above I'll plug them with lead. It's
Vito. . .' My father calmed the dogs and opened the door. He
knew Vito Lacruna well, and moreover, had always respected
him. Jokingly he said, 'Dogs will be dogs — why didn't you
come to the main door, like a good soul?'

'Since when have I looked for the straight path?' Vito joked
back. 'I could have come by the main door, seeing as the Baron
invited me, and as there's no longer a single gendarme or spy
who's interested in what I do. But I always like to come from
an odd direction.'

'Good to see you again,' said my father, as he had to say
something, 'And speaking like a brother, it would be even
better if you could see your way to taking to the right path. If
the law's forgotten about you, then forget about the life you've
lived yourself, set yourself in the right direction, go back to
work like you used to do. . .'

'Carme', said Vico, 'you think it doesn't occur to me, sometimes? I spend whole days thinking about this wasted life of
mine, and I get such a longing for home I want to be a cat by
the fireside. But certain things in life are like the rosary; you say
the first decade and if you don't finish, it doesn't count. I've
started my rosary, and I want to come to the end: that's how
that bastard, fate, wants it.'

His voice trembled, then with forced jollity he said, 'Well,
let's go and see the Baron, because if he wants what I suspect he
wants, I'm going to squeeze him like a lemon.'

'What do you suspect?' asked my father.

'In my trade, my friend,' said Vico, 'I've become like a father
confessor: I hear confession and give absolution, and I keep it all
in my belly, so that it's turning rotten on me with all the evil it
holds.'

One evening, there was a hellish shooting between militia and
bandits, right in the centre of town. It seemed as if they were
setting off fireworks in honour of Santa Venera: musket balls
whistled until dawn, all of them scattered in the air, against windows and balconies. Not a militiaman or a bandit suffered so
much as a scratch, so far as anyone knew. A militiaman fainted,
and was as rigid as a post for twenty-four hours; someone on
the Committee proposed giving him a medal.

But isolated shots were heard every night, they blossomed, unreal, as if from night's malignant essence, and they were shots that usually hit their mark. The nocturnal police, that is to say, the two nightwatchmen and the linkman, instead of doing the rounds of the town, usually stayed in the guard house of Trapani Gate to keep the guard company, conveniently in four for a hand of cards. When they heard any shots they set off to see what might have happened. They walked along with the lantern lit, talking loudly among themselves, perhaps to give themselves courage, or give whoever had fired a warning to steal conveniently away. Then the light from the lantern's aperture would come to rest on the murdered body, the nightwatchmen would kneel down in curiosity to identify it, making pitying comments or giving their unreserved approval, as if before a legal execution. Then they would stay there, watching over the corpse until dawn.

On the night of 2nd February, two in the morning having struck some time before, Dr Alagna was killed in that very manner. He was walking home from the club, suspecting nothing, accompanied by the boy carrying the lantern. A shot came from the corner of an alley, and hit him in the heart. The boy stood there with his lantern raised — he carried it like that to give a greater circle of light — but a second shot struck it out of his hand. Afterwards, he said he didn't even feel the jolt. Shouting out, he flew away to call out the gentlemen who were staying late at the club; which gentlemen remarked on the death of Don Nicolò Alagna with a feeling of unanimous regret. The following day there was a gala funeral. From the skill exhibited by the criminal, one shot for the heart and one for the lantern, the whole town recognized the hand of Vito Lacruna. But as to the reasons Vito had for killing a man like Dr Alagna, the conjectures were many; my father's naturally was the most correct. Perhaps Napoli the Chemist, the Bishop and a few others came close to seeing the thing clearly, but they were very careful what they said about it.

Vito was master of the town: he came up with an order to the Committee to pay him, in hard cash, five hundred ducats, or he would burn it down. In the Committee meeting to decide about the demand, those who were against didn't speak, because to have done so would have meant getting a gala funeral. Don

Cecé Melisenda spoke, putting forward the case for dignity and morality, which at that time were worth about as much as an old bean, but Don Cecé counted for so little on his own that Vito Lacruna wouldn't have wasted a cartridge on him, had he known he was against the payment. The speech which the Baron made in favour of the payment made a strong impression on the majority: the Bishop said it was good sense itself speaking from the Baron's lips, and although he agreed in principle with Don Cecé Melisenda, given his fatherly anxiety and preoccupation, he could do no less than advise payment. It was an admirable thing to keep faith with the principles of morality and dignity, but sometimes heavenly worth was acquired through sacrificing those principles to the common good, and to the love of one's neighbour. So Vito had his five hundred ducats, and kept away from the town for a good month, livening up the neighbouring ones, however. Then he came back to ask, more modestly, for two hundred ducats, which the Committee again decided to give him. Then he was killed, perhaps by one of his men; they found his body in a haystack, with half his face blown away by a shotgun. But the town continued to live under the threat of bandits until April 1849, when those whose debts were too heavy to pay again took refuge in the countryside and those who secretly pulled the strings stayed in town to act as agents and mediators, and to collect the 'respect' owing to the *men of honour*.

My schooling was with the priest who had taught my father to read and write. He was very old, but energetic in giving blows with a slim, whistling stick of olive, which left marks. His blows hit my head and hands at every error I made, so that after a few months of school I was like an Ecce Homo, and my mother had to baste me with warm oil every afternoon. Then, warm oil not being enough as my hands were already beginning to ulcerate, she bandaged up both my hands and head. I looked like someone back from fighting the Turk; my classmates gave me a nickname and played jokes on me. To make up for it, Don Paolo Vitale, as the priest was called, contented himself with making the stick whistle past my ears, but sometimes, involuntarily perhaps, he hit me right on the ears with such a painful effect that tears come into my eyes even now just thinking about it. But, in spite of everything, I retain happy memories of Don Paolo. The little he taught me has been a good foundation for all that I've learnt and done, because not only did he teach me to read from an alphabet, to write a letter and not get confused over figures, he also taught me to find faith and companionship in nature, books and my own thoughts.

He lived in two empty rooms, as small as monastic cells, next to his parish church, which was the poorest and most out of the way in the whole town. It had been given to him precisely as a punishment for the open-mindedness and freedom which, according to his superiors, he showed as a liberal who had links with the exiles and English in Marsala, from whom he used to receive newspapers speaking of world and home affairs, and which he used to translate for friends in Castro. But, in truth, a liberal he was not: his love of freedom was born from seeing the people suffer, their freedom was in having bread — the struggle to enable them to read books and to open schools seemed absurd to him. To those who met at the Chemist's he said, 'You'd have the people eat print, while what they need is bread', and the liberals listened to him pityingly.

For himself, he could even do without the news which the English newspapers brought him; he was satisfied with Virgil and Giovanni Meli and the memoirs and sayings of Guicciardini, Lottini and Sansovino, which he often read and elucidated for me from an old book. But above all, he said the Gospels were all he needed, and as he had learned to know men from Guicciardini, so he had leaned to love them from the Gospels. 'And it's a difficult task,' he said, 'learning to love them after having come to know them well.'

He was very lean, had a thin, white face, with an ever sharp, intense look below heavy eyelids. He thought well of me, despite the blows he gave me with the stick. He believed in it as a necessary tool of education and perhaps he wasn't wrong. When lessons were over, he behaved to me as if I were grown-up and let me stay with him in the garden, which was no more than a few square yards of ground, and told me about flowers and herbs, about the seasons and hours, and about the diseases which attacked plants as they do the bodies and feelings of men. He also talked to me about the real revolution; he thought the one they were having was a way of changing the organist without changing either the instrument or the music, and the poor were still there pumping away at the bellows. Because he rarely went out of the house, and after the events of January not at all, he used to ask me ironically, 'What are the revolutionaries doing? Have they started distributing their books?' But he didn't really expect me to give him any news, the questions were a means of giving vent to his feelings against those concerned and against what was happening. 'If there really was a revolution, the revolution I'm talking about, all those on the Committee, the Bishop, the Baron, and even Napoli the Chemist, would run and hide away in priestholes. Even whoever seems to be best of those gentlemen keeps two kinds of bread in his house: fine white bread for his family, and bran for the serving boys. They treat dogs like human beings, but treat the human beings who work for them worse than dogs. And they've the face to talk as they do, tyranny must be vanquished, liberty. . .'

Five or six members of the committee were working furiously for change; the others followed the efforts of the innovators for the reorganization of order and public finance with scepticism and almost with commiseration, implacably saying no to every new proposal, finding the right string to tug to have it fall miserably to the ground, so that revenues were reduced to a paltry sum, the Customs and Excise no longer functioned, and both town and country were infested with criminals.

But the provision of public entertainment had solicitous attention from the whole Committee. A band was eventually given permanent establishment, with a salary for the leading bandsman and the acquisition of instruments and uniforms. Plasterers and painters were called in to decorate the town's theatre, built twenty or so years previously, modelled on the one in Trapani, but permanently unused until then, to the cost of about one hundred and fifty 'ounces'.★ Between January and July, the Committee had about a hundred sessions, and on the whole they didn't manage to pass more than ten legislative measures destined to be carried through: the instituting of the National Guard and the band; the decorating work for the theatre; planting trees along the sea front; hiring four new

★ Gold coins minted by Charles III in Palermo — *Trans.*

employees, and the removal of a wooden mortar from an out-of-way villa to the Town Hall, in silent procession through the town with speeches full of blood, fatherland, sacrifice and fire. Another celebration was held when the Bishop went on an official visit to bless the National Guard. Then, as every year, there came the festival of Santa Venera. The month of June spread out like a glowing blanket of fire over town and sea, the town bubbled with festivities: the white stalls of the nougat and sorbet sellers, the red flesh of the watermelons cut up for sale in half-moon shapes on the tables, the glazed earthenware flashing in the sunlight, all seemed one with the sun, with the rumble of drums, the voices and the explosions of the fireworks.

The nuns had put forward Cristina's summer holidays for the festival. She came back thinner and more thoughtful, and seemed to have become one huge pair of eyes. At times, from her look, I had the impression of seeing, like a bird's wings fluttering up from a trap, the madness of Donna Concettina. By now she knew many things about religion and she used to talk about hell, which I didn't believe in. Whenever I did anything wrong, my mother would say, 'You'll go to hell with your shoes on!' and I was a little worried, primarily because of the shoes: goodness knows what sufferings I imagined went with them. Once I asked Don Paolo, who smiled and replied, 'Well, there's a yes and a no: either you behave yourself, or get used to walking barefoot.'

I came to the opinion that no one really knew about the business of hell and shoes and that it was better not to think about it. However, Cristina wanted to have me do so and discuss with me whether, if one had to end up in hell, it was better to be in the flames or in the ice. Because the sun was flaying us alive, I opted for the ice. You had to pay tuppence for two pounds of ice: I would have liked enough to have a bath in. But whether it was ice or fire, I didn't like talking about hell, so that it wasn't the same with Cristina anymore, I only liked playing at blind man's buff with her, which they had taught her at school.

After the festival of Santa Venera, the Committee worked with alacrity preparing the elections for the Town Council. All those citizens who could read and write and wanted to register were entered on the electoral roll. My father didn't want to register, but the Baron said that if he didn't he would take it as a personal affront, so my father decided to go along. In all, there were three hundred citizens registered on the roll and they had sixty councillors to elect.

Voting came in the first days of July, in perfect tranquillity. Those elected councillors were fifteen priests, twenty or so people linked to the Bishop or with open Bourbon sentiments, ten master artisans, well known to be indebted to, or economically dependent on, those who were in turn linked to the Bishop, so there were no more than fifteen councillors noted for their liberal sentiments, either hazy or firm. To make a more concrete and effective appraisal, the Council's composition was approximately the following: thirty gentlemen or members of the bourgeoisie; five nobles; fifteen priests and ten commoners. At the first session of those nominated, Baron Garziano was elected Chairman, with forty-nine votes for and eleven abstentions; and to the other posts were elected Canon Mantia, with thirty-seven votes, Napoli the Chemist, with thirty-six, Vitanza the Barber, with forty-four, and fifty-nine votes for Don Cecé Melisenda. Results which, if you look at them for a political interpretation or one reflecting interest groups, you risk not understanding a thing. Knowing the town, I would swear that the Baron didn't get the nobles' vote, the Canon that of the priests, and the barber that of the commoners and so on. The unanimous vote for Don Cecé can be explained by the fact that, in plain words, Don Cecé was considered a nobody: all prayers and kindness.

The Council's work began with considering the nomination of a temporary rector for the Jesuit church — 'so that the holy sect should not be lacking there, nor all that was previously carried out by the dissolved Society of Jesus' — following on which it was decided to celebrate a solemn triduum to avert drought and to grant an interest-free loan of 1,200 'ounces' to the Bishop's Revenue — 'seeing that, because of the unhappy times, the said Revenue cannot collect its incomes, nor withdraw from its account, which the Government has decreed shall not be touched.'

All three proposals came from the liberal group and the Council passed them unanimously. The Baron, Don Cecé Melisenda and Vitanza the Barber exultingly took the news of their deliberations to the Bishop, who said coldly, that, yes, he thanked the Council, 'But', he added, 'with my usual sincerity, I ask you: do you know what this means? It means, if you will excuse me, throwing beans down to catch the pig.'

'What beans?' asked Don Cecé, confused. 'And, with all due respect, what pig? With Your Excellency's forgiveness, I can't see either beans or pig.'

'Dear Don Cecé,' said the Bishop, 'you see the world as plain and smooth as a marble balustrade: you don't understand underhand things, you're like a fresh rose. . .' and he spoke some words in Latin about worms and snakes that hide and crawl in things that appear to be good.

'If I haven't forgotten the little bit of Latin I learned in the seminary,' said Don Cecé, 'Your Excellency is now talking about snakes and worms: I should first like to have the meaning of the pig and beans interpreted.'

'What can we do with Don Cecé here?' said the Bishop, turning to the Baron and Vitanza, in a tone that was both joking and commiserating. 'What can we do with the infuriating man? We'll tell him plainly and simply, so that he'll know how to act in the future. Well, then, I am the pig. . .'

'Your Excellency!' protested Don Cecé.

'. . . I am the pig — let me finish — and, with today's decision, the Council has done nothing other than throw a pile of beans down for me. If the pig eats our beans, as certain of your friends on the Council are thinking, the pig'll be ours. But, on the contrary, I say this: the pig will eat your beans, but he'll never allow himself to be caught by you. There you are, my dear Don Cecé, there's the proverb interpreted for you well and truly, according to our situation.'

'Your Excellency,' said Don Cecé, 'when I understand something, I understand it well: if you think it's like that, then I, as an obedient son of the Church, can draw the right conclusion, and tender my resignation. I'll leave the Council, I don't want to, excuse me, carry on holding the candle for those who are trying to dig the earth from underneath our feet.'

'You speak like a saint,' said the Bishop, 'but the fact is, if you leave the Council and the Baron leaves it, and Vitanza here, and all the God-fearing men leave it, into whose hands will the town's affairs fall, I'd like to know? Well? Come on. . .'

'That's the point', said the Baron.

'But', said Don Cecé, 'for my own edification, I want to see things clearly. Your Excellency wanted me to participate in the Council, therefore I find myself on it in the certainty that, in seeing to the interests of the town, and those of Sicily, there's no distinction with regard to our religion and the interests of the Church. But, if Your Excellency now says there is, two and two make four, and I'll resign.'

'"Be ye therefore wise as serpents"', quoted the Bishop. 'Do you understand? "Be ye wise." Those were Christ's words, my dear Don Cecé. You, on the other hand, forgive me, throw yourself about like. . . like. . .'

'. . . a bull in a china shop,' said Don Cecé, turning red.

'I wouldn't have ventured to say it', said the Bishop.

'And why not?' marvelled Don Cecé. 'It's true the bull has horns, but on that account I'm as untroubled as a homely nun, and then, horns or no horns, it's a worthy animal, but the serpent, Gospel or no Gospel, is an animal — I hope Your Excellency will forgive me — that turns my stomach. . .'

'We're talking about all the beasts in the ark', said the Bishop, 'without getting the rabbit out of its hole. . . Now I've come out with another one, and for goodness' sake don't start philosophizing about rabbits now. . . Let's talk in concrete terms, then. As a Catholic, and you've never given me any reason to doubt your faith, you are about to defend the just rights of the Church, as distinct (exactly, as distinct) from the interests, let's say, of the State. . . And I 'll give you an example. If the Government, as seems likely, orders the confiscation of all the gold and silver to be found in the churches and monasteries, if the Government gives such an iniquitous order, what, as a devoted son of the Church, would you do?'

'I've already heard some talk about it,' said Don Cecé, 'and it has given me some unease, but then I reasoned it out like this — I could be mistaken, but it seems clear to me: the whole population, rich and poor, as a sign of their faith and acknowledgement, gave the gold and silver which shines on our altars. The Church, which is the mother of everyone, would be giving back the presents she has received in love and charity, in order to save the lives and liberty of her children.'

'Well done!' said the Bishop. 'It's a pleasure to hear your line of reasoning! But you spin it out walking backwards, like a master rope-maker, and you can't see the mouths of hell opening up before you. Since the ree-vol-oo-tion,' he said, mockingly exaggerating all the vowels of the word, 'I hear you saying certain things that, if I didn't know you as I do. . .certain things that. . .'

'I may be mistaken', said Don Cecé, but without humility.

The Baron and Vitanza grinned pityingly, and the Bishop, who thought he knew Don Cecé after so many years of close contact, and how easy it was to bring him to repentance and tears continued to pressurize him, alternating irony and disdain with fatherly persuasion and sweet words. But all three were greatly mistaken, because that day Don Cecé, like all shy and docile people, was having his one terrible moment of intolerance and rage. The Bishop was saying, 'But this, my dear Baronet, to have thought that the Church would start a revolution, and one against the most worthy and legitimate principles, is a sin to be confessed. And to think that all that is ornament and honour in the house of God could be thrown away like that, on behalf of a cause which, apart from the illegitimacy from which it springs, is a very poor thing, like all human vicissitudes, when compared to the glory of God. . . Governments pass, my dear friend, but the Church remains. . .'

'Your Excellency,' interrupted Don Cecé brusquely, 'the light is beginning to dawn, you have put your finger right on the spot: that's the problem, the Church remains. . .'

He made a slight bow and left. Their faces were masks of astonishment, fixed on the gilt door which Don Cecé had closed behind him.

Thanks to Vitanza the barber, whose business had a large clientele, the whole of Castro knew of the incident, blow by blow, the following day. Those friends who were most curious and went in search of Don Cecé learned he had left for Marsala.

When the order came to confiscate the treasure from the churches, the Bishop had a few vessels and candelabras handed over, asking that their value should be ascertained and he immediately bought them back. Don Cecé no longer showed up at the Council meeting and didn't even frequent the club. He was considered to be mad by everyone, including the liberals.

The Bishop enquired solicitously after his mental state to all and sundry, expressing his regret that the awful fate of losing his senses should have happened to such a pious man; but most were of the opinion that, pious man though he may have been, Don Cecé had never had any sense at all.

But the encounter between the Bishop and Don Cecé, even though everyone put it down to sudden or congenital madness on the part of the old gentleman, opened up cracks in the Council which had hitherto gone unnoticed; cracks which then deepened and became unstoppable. The Baron went around to all sides proclaiming he was keeping his position at personal sacrifice, merely to impede the hot heads of the Council and stop them from doing just as they pleased. The meetings became more lively, but inconclusive; pointed comments came from the liberals' seats, aimed at those of the clergy and the 'moles', which made the public present in the hall howl with delight. But everything came to a stop with the nomination of the inspectors for the public works, street lighting, Customs and Excise, provisions and brokerage. Life became totally blocked by inspections, to such an extent that the tenders for the contracts for the Customs and town lighting remained blank, because no one wanted to get himself into the difficulties which the contract specifications promised, as they were both detailed and lengthy. There was a feeling of the transitory in the air, a feeling that such a confused situation could not last long.

The usurpations of State and common land had reached their greatest extent, both among the peasants and shepherds and, especially, among the gentlemen who formed part of the Council, and an investigating commission was nominated to check up on them. But the commission, once it discovered the extent of the usurpation, could do nothing more than propose legalizing them with contracts and rents of a token payment. The gentlemen immediately had contracts drawn up, but the peasants and shepherds thought it would be better to continue exploiting the land without them.

Food prices rose sky-high; security of life and possessions in both town and country was completely lacking; public education, despite the Council's declaring they had it continually at heart, remained what it was. To the good, there was the fact that the liberals' group was beginning to take note of the problems and attempt to resolve them. They had become toughened by the opposition they had met, and the political ideal, which had been vague and uncertain in them before, came to assume such a power that it even distracted them from their sectional interests. And one could say that, for the minority of the Council, the idea of the revolution came to maturity exactly in the moment in which events were running headlong towards the reaction.

After an unhappy winter of hunger and murder, a frail spring came. The countryside, having been abandoned after seed-time, threatened catastrophe. The Council no longer met. The Bishop had had his palace barricaded, there were matttresses and tables at the windows for protection, while the liberals spoke openly against him, publishing caricatures, derisive verses and insults. But the people, however, were beginning to hate the liberals, and flocked to the churches on Sundays to hear the sermons against those who, not having any fear of God, were the authors of the people's suffering and of disorder. Almost the whole of Castro was hoping for the return of the old order.

Then, finally, on 25th April 1849, the news came that order was returning. The Bishop had it first by courier, then he sent for the Baron to give him the news, instructing him as to what he should do in the Council. The Baron called his councillor friends together and, from the club, they moved over to the Town Hall, followed by the priests, nobles and gentlemen, all of them men who were visibly happy, or at least relieved. The liberals, on the other hand, left the club to withdraw to their homes; three of them, however, followed the Baron, white with fear.

From the height of the Chairman's bench, the Baron briefly imparted the news to the Council and concluded, 'God willing, the tomfoolery's over.' They all applauded. It was at this point that Don Cecé Melisenda came into the hall, and sat himself down. The Baron dictated to the secretary, 'This day the Civic Council met spontaneously, without any invitation from the Chairman, in the hall of the Senatorial Palace, having understood from voices at large that the Capital has sent a commission to Prince Satriano declaring its obedience. Wishing to correspond with an equal demonstration, the Council declares its desire to concur with the same motion passed in the Capital, declaring in the same way its obedience to the commended Prince Satriano.' He said it all on one breath, as if reciting it from memory. The assembly bestowed a long applause on him, and the Baron rose up to thank them with bows. Then again he said, 'The tomfoolery's over.' From his seat, Don Cecé calmly said, 'If what is over is tomfoolery, then all those clapping their hands for you are fools, and you're the prize fool of the kingdom.'

'What? What's that?. . .' said the Baron, and they all joined in an uproar against Don Cecé. But the old man, self-possessed and standing upright, his stick pointing in front of him, walked up to the secretary and said, 'I have some rights on this Council, and I want to use them, even if they only serve now to earn me a spell in prison. Now, write down what I say, because I want to sign it straightaway and leave.' He turned his gaze on them all and, in a firm voice, dictated, 'Sir Cesare Melisenda of Villamena wishes to dissociate himself from the decision taken by the majority of the Council to present its terms of obedience and those of the town of Castro to Prince Satriano, and likewise wishes to declare his allegiance to the principle of liberty which the Council unanimously applauded at its first session.' He signed the margin of the minutes book next to his declaration and went away.

'Fucking lunatic!' shouted the Baron after him.

As if by magic, the King's Judge, the Sub-Intendant, the gendarmes and the militia reappeared in Castro, as if nothing had ever happened, perhaps with precisely the order of pretending to ignore it all — the events and the people who were compromised by them. Right until autumn, there wasn't the least sign of reprisal, the police even appeared to be better mannered, the Sub-Intendant smiled at everyone — and even played cards with Napoli the Chemist. Then a column of troops arrived and the disarming of the National Guard was ordered, but the action was symbolic, only the massive presence of the troops caused any fear. The National Guard handed in their rifles, and a moment later they had them again under their new title of City Guards. The symbol of Trinacria was chiselled off the front of the theatre, and the Bourbon lily set in its place. Lilies reflowered over the doorways of the public buildings.

The Bishop brought an action against the town, denying 'the individuals of the same town the right to gather wood on the estates pertaining to the Bishop's Revenue.' The Town Council, almost to a man, became the Civic Decurionate, only Don Cecé Melisenda, for whose insanity even the Sub-Intendant and the King's Judge felt sorry, and the two liberals who had fled to Malta, were missing from it. All told, it couldn't have gone better. The troops almost crept away on tiptoe, taking with them a dozen criminals captured in the countryside. The town heaved a sigh of relief.

According to the Baron, public affairs were now sailing along merrily, but the wind was still bringing inclement weather over his personal affairs: there was Donna Concettina, who never spoke to him; Rosalia, who cost him a fortune and was, perhaps, unfaithful to him; Cristina, who wouldn't go back to boarding-school, and Vincenzino, on the other hand, who wanted to remain in the seminary and become a priest. The Baroness supported Cristina's reluctance to go, and was happy about the vocation which had been revealed in Vincenzino, continually going to the Bishop, to spite her husband, exhorting him to foster and nourish the vocation of her son. The Baron, through an interpreter — as always — said to her, 'You'll drive me as mad as Don Cecé with this tale of your son's vocation. One of these days I'll go to the Bishop and tell him plainly: you and he have rigged this farce up about his vocation, the poor boy's a tortured soul in your hands.' Without ever forgetting the interpreter, Donna Concettina replied, making the Baron see red, 'Tell the Baron he should go and tell the Bishop plainly, I would like to see him do it, I really would.'

'I've got too many thoughts in my mind', said the Baron. 'I can feel them jumping about like crickets, in my sleep at night. As soon as I'm dropping off, zap! up jumps a thought, and I find myself wide awake.'

'They're the crickets of temptation', murmured Donna Concettina.

The three-way discussions — father, mother, interpreter — on the subject of Vincenzino's vocation gave Cristina as much entertainment as if she were at the theatre. She loved her mother and enjoyed seeing the Baron always get the worst of it; all the more, in that by now, she was convinced the Baron was on the path to an infernal destination, on account of his kept woman and the vocation he was hindering. Once I asked Don Paolo Vitale if the Baron really was destined to end up in hell, but he shook his head and said, 'He won't go to hell, he'll find a way of making his peace with the Good Lord at the last moment.' And in fact, the Baron did die like a saint, with all the sacraments, leaving legacies for parishes and charitable institutions in his will. In his last years he established a Friday alms-giving: each poor person who presented himself at the gate was given two *soldi*,★ and he sometimes came to distributing five *lire* in a single day.

But in 1849 the Baron enjoyed perfect health, he had a robust constitution, being a great eater and a moderate drinker. He was a passionate hunter, he went round his estates on horseback, especially during the harvesting, and almost every day he found time to call on Rosalia. He didn't worry about hell, indeed, putting it plainly, he said that at a pinch, he could just about believe in purgatory, but hell he thought was a fairy tale for coarse people: a good fairy tale to keep the rabble in subjection, and he thought it might have been invented by Dante Alighieri. 'He wasn't all there, because of his fury at having been driven out of town. . . set himself the task of frightening people.' But Donna Concettina — without, however, ever having read it — was convinced that there was divine revelation in Dante's work.

Vincenzino was insistent, supported fervently by his mother. He didn't want to come out of the seminary even for the holidays, fearing the Baron would put him under lock and key to make him lose his vocation. He had become as tall and white as a candle, his head swaying down from his long neck so that it looked as if he was awaiting decapitation.

'He's a dead man', said the Baron. 'They'll have him wear himself away with their penitence and prayers. They'll put it into his head he must become a saint, and he'll starve himself to be one the sooner! And he'll be one, oh, yes, he'll be one. . .' On the other hand, Donna Concettina was of the opinion that he was simply growing: everyone in her family was like that when they were in their growing period. Vincenzino didn't take

★ The twentieth part of a *lira* — *Trans.*

after the Garziano side of the family, who became solid-looking in their adolescence; he was like Donna Concettina's brothers, father and grandfather in everything: physically, they were delicate, with delicate feelings — old Spanish nobility, who had given the Kingdom men of letters and devotion.

'I don't give a fuck about the delicate natures of your tribe!' said the Baron. 'I don't want my son to be a saint or a philosopher! That was a fine reward for that uncle of yours, when he went and got himself crucified by the Chinese or the Indians or whoever the devil it was! And don't talk to me about that other relative of yours, the one who's written all those books in Latin, it makes my head spin just to look at them. He was mad, just as sure as there's a God in heaven! Doesn't he say in a book we should all share everything together: houses, land, animals, women? You can't get madder than that! Let's forget about that. I want my son to be like me, I want him to go hunting, to look after the estates, eat like a lord, and to like women. . . and by the way, that relation of yours had a good idea in sharing women around . . . It's the only good thing that's come from anyone in your family!'

This was the last straw for Donna Concettina, she gathered up everything into her dress, as if there was a mouse under her feet, and ran away. The Baron enjoyed a moment of satisfaction, then he looked worried, perhaps at the thought that he had said too much and that Donna Concettina, in her exasperation, would end up reporting the insults from the Baron to her brother, a man of great prestige at the court. Out of the house, the Baron boasted and gloried in the brother-in-law he had at the court. 'My brother-in-law's written to me that the King. . . I'll write a couple of lines to my brother-in-law. . . If my brother-in-law puts his mind to it, it's done. . .'

In January 1850, a small event occurred which distracted the Baron from the difficulties of his private life. On a frosty blue day, sailing in a line along the coast, a huge squadron of the British navy passed by Castro: its masts, flags and the movement of the men on board could all be clearly seen. For the liberals of Castro, it was a decisive show of strength by the British Government, which, in the previous months, had cut off relations with the government in Naples. In the English newspapers you could read opinions of the Bourbons and accusations against them evidently inspired by the tempestuous relations between the two governments. Incautiously, the liberals showed their joy over the demonstration. The English were well liked in Castro for what they had done for the wine industry in the neighbouring town of Marsala; they were known for being upright and liberal-minded, men of few words and trustworthy behaviour. Seeing the naval squadron passing by, then fantasizing about an act of intimidation, if not of war, against the Bourbon government was, for them, one and the same thing. But so much were they mistaken in counting on others' help that the British certainly gained an advantage from the warning cruise, while the liberals of Castro ended up in prison.

A few months later, a regiment of troops came to Castro, along with fifty or so gendarmes, led by a man famous throughout Sicily for his hatred of the liberals and the tortures he used on them. After that of Maniscalco, the name of Lieutenant Desimone meant prison and death, he being the right-hand-man and brutal executioner for Salvatore Maniscalco. I remember him as I saw him that day, which must have been one of coming spring because I remember the bitterish smell of almond flowers in Baron Garziano's garden. He had a vinous nose, a gaze which seemed to skim over things from his pig-like eyes and short, uncertain legs underneath his barrel chest. He was cheerful, bursting out laughing, clapping the Baron affectionately on the shoulders in his laughter and poking him in the stomach with the gesture of a shared secret. The Baron laughed, too. They drank wine together, and laughed. Lieutenant Desimone drank nothing but wine. When the Baron suggested coffee, he burst out laughing, 'Coffee, you said? You want to give me coffee? D'you know what I call it?' He whispered something in his ear, and the Baron doubled up with laughter. 'Give me wine, as God commands, because wine is the drink of the angels.' The Baron ordered a couple of carafes from the servant, specifying the 1837 vat.

Over their wine, intimacy grew between Baron and Lieutenant; they talked about the enemies of order in Castro and then about women. The Baron was for those of Trapani, while Desimone swore for those of Palermo, who, without a doubt, were greedy for money and full of whims, but they were the fieriest he'd ever known. They agreed about the women of Syracuse, the Baron had known one, and also the Lieutenant: 'But she was a wonderful woman, my dear Baron, you'd smack your lips over her. . . like something Greek. . .' 'That's the right word,' seconded the Baron, 'Syracusan women are like something Greek. . . The one I. . . you follow me. . . she was like a statue, a perfect statue, and she did some things for me, things. . .'

That evening I saw the eleven liberals they arrested, leaning against the wall of St Michael's monastery inside a semicircle of soldiers and gendarmes. Their hands were chained and then they were all chained together. The lantern's unstable, flickering light brought out of the shadows now the face of Napoli the Chemist, now that of Don Giuseppe Nicastra and others whom I didn't know well: faces that seemed feverish or petrified with fear. Beyond the hedge of soldiers were the townsfolk. Word was going round that the prisoners were to be shot, the people had heard and silently crowded in front of the monastery. But Lieutenant Desimone only wanted to have his joke; after a couple of hours, he led the prisoners away to the gendarmes' barracks and then, satisfied, went back to the Garziano mansion to tell the Baron about the joke and to have a good supper.

In his *History of Castro,* page 187, Gaetano Peruzzi, Esq., states that 'there are clear indications that the arrests of 1850 were inspired by Monsignor Calabrò who, as if in a plot, was very close to the King's Judge and a notable person of the town, whose name will not be mentioned, because out of love for his country, and to make up for his unhappy past, he did all he could, in the events of 1860, to help the cause of Garibaldi.' And by those clear indications, all the citizens of Castro recognize Baron Garziano as the name of the person whom Peruzzi doesn't mention. Peruzzi adds that the Bishop 'was moved to his plotting by the behaviour of us youngsters, who, heedless and derisive of things religious, absented ourselves from every kind of pastoral ceremony and gathering: and the small demonstration of jubilation at the passing by of the British Royal Navy served to further our arrests, with all the appearance of a just reason.' This statement is strengthened by the fact that the families of the arrested men turned to the Bishop, rather than the authorities of the Crown, for clemency; and that the Bishop, while protesting that he wasn't connected with the arrests, let it be known that letters of contrition on the part of the arrested men would be welcome and that he would, perhaps, try to intercede. Some of the men were convinced by their families to write to the Bishop, and they obtained a kind of reduced trial, which separated their lot from the harsher one of those who had refused to write. Nevertheless, those eleven arrested men plunged as many families of Castro into anxiety and ruin. Whole fortunes flowed through the hands of judges, lawyers, police, gaolers and mafia bosses (who ensured protection for political detainees inside), and the most beautiful girls with large dowries were sacrificed in marriage to old judges and functionaries. The marriage of the daughter of one of those arrested in 1850, Don Vito Bonsignore, to an elderly judge on the Trapani Tribunal is still remembered in Castro: a young girl of fifteen or sixteen, who I thought was like a delicate, untouchable magnolia flower. So far can family love go beyond the right and permissible in Sicilian towns.

The years passed. For the liberals of Castro, shut up in the cells of Favignana prison, famous for their horrors, the measure of the season was their aching bones and a painful skeleton inside worn-out flesh, a skeleton cracking from the deathly cold; to others, more amenable to asking for clemency, the measure of long days was the sound of unfamiliar bells, the bells of Castelvetrano or Girgenti, which brought melancholy and desperation and tolled the hours of the milder suffering of internment; others still measured out their exile in Malta by the rhythm of the printing presses, from which issued manifestos and pamphlets destined to cross the stretch of sea to Sicily — so near that on clear days you seemed to be able to touch it with your hand — but which separated them so implacably from it.

Time passed more mildly for Baron Garziano, and perhaps even the very troubles he passed through in his family life served to give his existence that touch of dramatic transfiguration he needed for it to have some flavour. Among other things, Rosalia had a baby boy, and this fact, which further poisoned Donna Concettina's existence, gave the Baron a youthful arrogance and a certain lack of concern about the continuing vocation of Vincenzino, as he was perhaps nurturing in his heart a plan to legitimize this other son who, according to him, was so like him that he seemed to come out of a small mould taken from his own features.

Cristina, meanwhile, became more beautiful and distant, ever more distant for me, as she no longer played outside and didn't even come down into the garden; Donna Concettina felt the breath of temptation in her flowering, and for that reason was never more than a step away from her. I saw her nearly always at the window of what Donna Concettina called the 'work room', bent over the lace pillow which blossomed with vivid flowers under her hand: her delicate profile weighed down upon and as if scraped back by the bun of her golden hair. I had a vague feeling of love for her: she seemed weak and empty like an ear of corn that comes up seedless. Although she was there throughout the day, she lived in me as if in the essence of memory, recollection and melancholy, a slender, graceful ear of corn which gave no bread. It was said she might already be promised to a man in Castelvetrano, a handsome man twice her age and very rich. I felt a certain relief in thinking that, once she married, she would have to leave the town, and that I would never see her again and would always remember her just as I saw her at the window, with the profile of a slender young girl, ethereal as a new moon.

By now I was reading many books, hiding myself away in remote corners of the garden to read, and because of the passion I had for reading and thinking about books, I was becoming absent-minded and lost in my own thoughts. My father began to think that reading was poisoning me, and he gave me lectures full of old saws and proverbs: 'Better a live ass than a dead scholar', 'The lame ass enjoys the way' and 'The best youths go to the Vicaria'. This last proverb, of recent coinage, referred to the feelings of hate for the Bourbons which were growing in me, because the best of Sicilian youth lived on those feelings, and the Palermo prison of the Vicaria had swallowed up a good part of that youth.

To save me from my poisonous reading, my father — perhaps with the Baron's help — found me a job in the service of the Wodehouse family, which had a wine business in Marsala and even had stores and an office in Castro. But work didn't

keep me far from reading, instead it served to create relation-
ships for me with the men of liberal ideas in the towns of Marsala and Castelvetrano and neighbouring areas, for which, from
then on, I was nearer to gaol than my father thought.

The times were imperceptibly changing, although I wasn't
aware of it then, because time I saw before me like a huge boul-
der, and I wanted to push it ahead of me with a heave of my
shoulders, flinging myself behind it. But now, looking at the
past, I can see how in the ten years between 1850 and 1860 time
worked to change men's feelings and even the very face of
things. Soon after the arrests of 1850, a Sub-Intendant came to
Castro who only occupied himself with his family, which was
large, and the public administration. He paid no attention to
spies and anonymous letters, and he associated with citizens
known to be liberals, protecting them and warning them of anything which might be harmful to them. Then a King's Judge
arrived with the same feelings, so that the police found themselves in a vacuum, cogs which no longer meshed with other
cogs. And the fact that all the efforts of the Bishop and the
Baron to remove both the King's Judge and the Sub-Intendant
were unfruitful was another sign of the changed nature of
things. On the contrary, in 1854 the Bishop was transferred to
a diocese in Calabria, right up in the mountains; and, a thing
which he grieved over so much that, as far as one heard he died
from it, was that it was a very poor diocese, infested with
brigands who had no equal for ferocity. The new Bishop didn't
concern himself so much with police matters, dedicating himself
totally to renovating the seminary and to restoring the finances
which, inexplicably, Monsignor Calabrò had left in a state of
bankruptcy.

Then Castro, which up to that time had been a seaside town
without fishing, always importing its fish from Trapani or Marsala, began to try the sea. The boats went out for fish in the
evening now, no more than ten of them, but they were enough
to provide fish for the town and at a good price. There were
also one or two cargo boats which put out, equipped by dealers
of the town, carrying dried figs and wine as far as Malta. In
agriculture, precisely because of the English demand, the vine-
yards began to make the surrounding countryside more human

and inhabited. There were bad years caused by the phylloxera which attacked the vines, but, on the whole, the life of the town revived and got better.

The Baron thought things were going from bad to worse, what with a King's Judge and a Sub-Intendant who behaved in a manner of mutual understanding with the enemies of order and the King, and a Bishop who saw to the affairs of church and the seminary. From the visit of Lieutenant Desimone to the arrival of Garibaldi, the only satisfaction he had was the annihilation of the Pisacane expedition. 'A fine end that came to! Under the peasants' pitchforks! That's the way to deal with those enemies of God, with pitchforks! And that leader of theirs: what a name, Pisacane! Well, he came to a dog's* end.'

It was in that year of Pisacane's expedition that Cristina, in the spring, married Don Saverio Valenti from Castelvetrano, whom Baron Garziano held to be of faithful Bourbon sentiments, as the Valenti family had given a Minister to King Ferdinand who was still in office, and a Lieutenant General who had been dead for some years. But his son-in-law later showed himself to be leaning towards subversive ideas, and subsequently, in the risings of 4th April 1860, which took place more tumultuously in Castelvetrano than in Castro, he compromised himself to the point of being arrested and taken to prison in Trapani, along with many others.

On 4th April 1860, in Castro, nothing happened apart from some insults to the police and some lilies chiselled off, and as usual, the Sub-Intendant and the King's Judge pretended not to hear the inflamed speeches which took place in the club and in the piazza. When it was known that the revolution in Palermo and other centres had failed, those compromised by their speeches and acts of contempt against the Government left town for a few days. I went away too, with the excuse of having been called to Marsala for my work. When I learnt there was no move against us in Castro, I promptly returned. The Baron, who by now knew how I felt, said on meeting me on my return from Marsala, 'What did you want, another "Forty-eight"? Fucking blind, you and all the others! That wretch of a son-in-law of mine, too.' I said nothing, not wanting to create any

* Cane = dog in Italian — *Trans.*

trouble for my father or myself.

Two or three days after this meeting with the Baron, I found myself in a smithy in the highest part of the town, when, in a pause between the hammer blows, when the silence suddenly seemed to spread out like water, I heard a hollow, far-off sound, regular and rhythmic, which I thought was one of the usual firing exercises of the British ships. Then, on reflection, considering that the April risings in the cities had not been entirely smoothed down, I began to feel a little agitated and disturbed. I went back into town and informed my friends; together we went up a hill, the better to hear the shots. Then we decided that one of us should go by horse to Marsala. A young man of my age went, Vito Costa, who later fell in the Battle of Milazzo, but there was no need to reach Marsala, as halfway there he met Giuseppe Calà who, on the part of our friends in Marsala, was bringing to us in Castro the news of Garibaldi's landing. Night had already fallen when the news reached us; we shouted 'Long live Garibaldi! Long live liberty!' in the piazza. We gathered people together and made speeches. I felt I loved the whole world, joy filled me until I was moved to tears.

It was late in the night by the time I reached home, and while I was knocking softly at the door, the Baron's voice reached me from a high window. I looked up and saw his face like a white spot in the dark, 'So he's landed, eh? You're all happy, now, but you'll realize a thing to two, tomorrow, when the King's army makes mincemeat of him and all the delinquents following him. . . He'll end up worse than that. . . what's his name?. . . the one with 'dog' in his name. . . We'll talk about this tomorrow, tomorrow. . .' and he closed the window with a bang.

But the next day the Baron was twisting himself into knots, 'Bastards, bastards, the lot of them!. . . Admirals, generals. . . traitorous bastards! How can they let a handful of brigands set foot on land? Four well-aimed cannonades would have been enough to sink them. And instead they let them advance, it won't be anything before we see them here in Castro!'

Garibaldi remained in Salemi until the 15th, and the Baron received the news that the King's army was prepared to meet those bandits in battle. Many young men from Castro had already gone to join Garibaldi, and on the morning of the 16th, I left myself. But I took no part in the Battle of Calatafimi: from a high ridge I saw the feverish assault of the *Garibaldini*, like waves against a strong wall. Then the wall started to break up, as the wave of men rose up from their ramparts, as if held up by the lacerating cry of the trumpet. The tricolour disappeared in a tangle of blue jackets and red shirts, there was a moment of confusion among the men rising and dashing forward, but, with the advance they made, it was as if they had only paused a moment for breath. Beyond the line of resistance held by the riflemen who were shooting steadily and accurately, the Neapolitans — although they could see *Garibaldini* rolling over, hit, — were already grouping together in retreat, the wall was becoming weaker, then suddenly it appeared to be submerged, the riflemen too retreating at a run, and the *Garibaldini* were on the height, where it seemed they dropped down as if exhausted.

I can't calculate how long the battle lasted, everything is so confused in my memory. A confusion of colours and shots, the flag disappearing, and the agony of the trumpet sound. Then there were the dead, which even from a distance you could distinguish as *Garibaldini* and Neapolitan: instead of the clamour of battle, there followed a silence that belonged to dead men stretched out in the sun, a silence that seemed to rise up like putrefaction. But we had won, that was what counted. During the battle, I had shed tears; I had been tense all over, trying to get a sight of Garibaldi in the assault, but I couldn't succeed in picking him out, even though everyone around me was saying, 'Look, there's Garibaldi, that's him, near the flag, over to the left, the one with the sabre held high', because I only knew vaguely what Garibaldi looked like and I had thought that battles were fought just as if the soldiers were marching along the street with their commanding officer at their head. Instead, a battle was nothing but a deadly confusion, men in disorder launched against other men in equal disorder who fight back and later give way.

A frosty night, thick with stars, fell on the dead of Calatafimi.

A few days later we marched towards Castro. Colonel Türr, passing along the line of men in reverse direction, had shouted that he wanted a man from the town we were approaching who was numerate. I followed after him, even though I couldn't imagine why he wanted someone from Castro who could add up. He told me it was necessary to find some sheep, and asked me if it was possible to find some in the countryside around Castro, and how many would be needed. I immediately thought of the flock at Fontana Grande, and that it would be a wonderful joke to have the *Garibaldini* eat Baron Garziano's sheep. I asked the Colonel how many were needed, because I knew exactly where to find them. 'That's why I wanted someone who could add up,' said the Colonel, 'I think we have to prepare about 1,500 rations of 400 grams each. Now you hurry up with the pounds and half-pounds, put them into kilograms for me and then into sheep. That's all I want to know: how many sheep?' Greatly fearing making a mistake, I did the sum and said, 'That's thirty-seven sheep.' Türr clapped me on the shoulder, smiling, 'Well done, don't go away, you can tell me later where to find them.' And so I found myself nearer to Garibaldi than I had ever imagined, and at the same time the thought of what the Baron would say on learning of the loss of thirty-seven sheep made me smile.

We marched in the sun, the dust sticking to our sweat, our eyebrows were white with it, but songs rose from the ranks, love songs from the Venetians and Ligurians, while the Sicilians sang one that obscenely mocked Franceschiello and his queen:

> la palummedda bianca
> ci muzzica lu pedi,
> la p. . . di to' muglieri
> a Palermo 'un ci veni cchiú. . .*

It was a song from 1848, composed for Ferdinand and now adopted for Francesco. When the songs died away, you could hear the crops rustling in the dry soughing of the wind, and with it came the desire to throw yourself down in the fields and collapse in sleep among the tall ears of corn.

Then Castro appeared, so white it seemed to be incandescent in the sun's fire. I thought I'd never seen it before, and yet, among the houses, I could make out the green of the garden in which I'd grown up, the Garziano mansion, St Michael's monastery, and the Bishop's Palace, and the ogival gate into

---

* 'The white dove/bites the foot [of Italy]/That. . . of a wife of yours/Will not come to Palermo any more — *Trans.*

which the head of our column was already passing was no less than Porta Trapani, outside which, by the side of the road, were groups of people and carriages. I went on foot behind Garibaldi, Türr and Sirtori and another four or five officers whom I still didn't know. Behind came the Intendant's carriage, creaking with the exhausted pace of the two horses pulling it and Colonel Carini's company brought up the rear. The officers stopped their horses in front of the waiting people, and dismounted. Then I saw Baron Garziano dressed in sub-fusc, with a tricolour cockade as big as a pancake on his breast, his face giving the impression of uncontainable joy. By his side were his son-in-law and Don Cecé Melisenda, and with him were all those from the club; my friends were there, too, the few true liberals in Castro. As the Baron was in front of them all, Garibaldi held out his hand to him, which the Baron squeezed between his own with devotion, giving the impression that gratitude and joy were about to make him burst into tears.

I watched as if I were hallucinating, and, in truth, the sun, exhaustion, and sleepiness buzzing inside me made the vision of Baron Garziano with a cockade, trembling with emotion, with Garibaldi's hand between his own, seem as if it were a dream. I wasn't aware of my father until he touched my shoulder with the handle of his whip. He was sitting up on the driving seat, with the usual greenish cap on. He looked like a poor old man to me. 'Get up beside me, you're dead on your feet', he said. I didn't want to lose Colonel Türr, but I climbed up next to my father when I saw that Garibaldi, with Türr and the Baron, was getting into our carriage. Noticing me, Türr said, 'Well done! Don't get lost, because you've got some sheep to find for me.' 'Are you looking for sheep?' said the Baron. 'There's my flock at Fontana Grande. . . take all you want. . . I felt even more tired, and disappointed.

Later, my father told me what had happened in the Baron's house after my departure. One night, his son-in-law arrived; he had been freed from the Trapani prison and had caught up with Garibaldi at Calatafimi. After the victorious outcome, he had rushed to Castro to warn his father-in-law and convert him to the new run of things. At first, the Baron had reacted violently, calling him a traitor and a delinquent, then he had inveighed

against the King's generals, then against the King, who, like a
fool, had allowed himself to be mocked and betrayed. In the
end he had declared that, things being as they were, it was time
that everyone looked to his own, and if the King wasn't fit to
look after himself, 'There's a fork to fork you on the Marina
plain', which is to say: it'll end up as it will. 'I don't give a fuck
what happens to him, but I know what I'm going to do!'
Straightaway he began to turn the house upside down, having
portraits and prints of the King and Royal Family removed from
the walls, together with a whole series of coloured prints showing scenes of Ferdinand's visit to Sicily, a portrait of Pius IX,
and one of Donna Concettina's brother, in a cockade hat and
bristling with decorations, who had the high office in Naples.
Waking up because of the noise, Donna Concettina had come
down in dressing gown and nightcap, asking the reason for all
the movement. The Baron replied that General Garibaldi was
on his way to Castro, and that it was necessary to prepare the
house in order to receive him in a worthy manner.

Because she had just been awakened from her sleep, Donna
Concettina understood even less then usual, and asked, 'General
Garibaldi? Who's he?'

The Baron became furious. 'What? You don't know who
General Garibaldi is? The one who's overturning the whole
world, we haven't done anything but talk about the man for the
past week and you come asking who he is! Where've you come
down from, the moon?'

Donna Concettina had got hold of herself, she turned to her
son-in-law and said, 'Tell me what your father-in-law said.' The
Baron swore and her son-in-law said, 'He said that General
Garibaldi is about to arrive in Castro.'

'This is the first time', said Donna Concettina, 'that I have
heard any talk about a General Garibaldi. Just this evening,
before going to bed, your father-in-law informed me there was
a danger that a brigand by the name of Garibaldi might arrive.
You might ask him if by any chance it has happened that His
Majesty King Francesco has appointed the brigand a general —
I think something similar happened once before.'

The Baron exploded with oaths like a barrel of gunpowder,
then he begged his son-in-law to get his wife from under his
feet. 'If not,' he said, 'I'll kill her and have her from under them

once and for all!' But while his son-in-law was trying to get Donna Concettina to go back to bed, my father began to take down the portrait of Pius IX. The Baroness screamed, 'Don't touch that portrait!'

The Baron shouted, 'Take it down', and turned on his wife. 'If, God forbid, General Garibaldi sees that portrait, you and all this house will go up in smoke. Don't you know how he gets on with the Pope? They fight like cat and dog.'

'Tell your father-in-law', said Donna Concettina, in tears, 'that I am happy, as he says, to go up in smoke: that portrait of His Holiness is staying where it is. And furthermore, tell him that if that man, general or brigand or whatever he is, enters this house, I will start to rave like a lunatic: I shall be killed, and have everything burned. . . but I will not have an enemy of God enter this house.

The Baron seemed on the point of having a stroke, he begged and threatened, shocking insults were mixed with soft expressions of love. He said that, as far as he was concerned, he would willingly give Garibaldi the poisoned mincemeat one gave to dogs, but the brigand was winning, there was nothing to be done, and there were the children, Vincenzino and Cristina. 'Don't you think about the future of your children, and about their safety?' In the end, they came to an agreement: Garibaldi would be received into the house, but in expiation of such a sin, the Baron would have a church built by the side of the mansion, a church for Donna Concettina alone, dedicated to a saint to whom would be ascribed the task of mediating between the guilt of the house of Garziano and God's mercy. Placated, Donna Concettina said she would of course choose St Ignatius, to whom she was particularly bound because of her Jesuit uncle, who had died a martyr in the East.

And so in Castro, by the side of the mansion in which a plaque has been erected to commemorate Garibaldi's stay there, today there rises the church of St Ignatius.

The Baron had had the tables laid in the garden: there were carafes of wine, ring-shaped cakes and sponge cakes; ice-cream buckets were ranged under the trees, and small tricolours were hung in their branches. The Baron spoke, 'Gentlemen, I would like you to stay as guests in my house, it's a large house and you can stay here with ease. . . while you are in Castro, it will be an honour and a pleasure to have you. . . You need have no scruples in asking for anything you require. . .' Turning to Colonel Türr, he said, 'The sheep will be arriving within an hour, and the oxen as well. . . Everything I own is at your disposal, everything. . .' He went away to give orders to the servants, and, light as a butterfly, he skimmed among the groups of Garibaldi's officers and citizens of Castro that had formed, giving out compliments and words of cheer. Following him with his gaze, Garibaldi said, 'What a heart these Sicilians have, what passion they put into things. . .'

'I would say, General, that this man shows all the enthusiasm for us that fear induces', said a young man I had seen inside the Intendant's carriage on the march: a young man with a clear profile, a high forehead, and eyes which continually changed from alertness to worry, from softness to cold. 'I have, by now, formed a firm opinion of the Sicilians, and I think this man has much to hide, much to be forgiven him, and perhaps he hates us. . .'

'My dear Nievo!' said Garibaldi, with affectionate tolerance.

'Yes, General,' continued the young man, 'it is you who have a great heart, and, in your generosity and passion, it is you who don't see the cowardice, fear and hate masquerading as celebration, waving flags to greet us. . . because we've won: if we'd remained at Calatafimi, many of these gentlemen here celebrating us, opening their mansions and cellars up for us, would have launched their peasants on us. . .'

'My dear Nievo!' said Garibaldi again.

'You see,' Nievo went on, 'they're a people who only know extremes: there are Sicilians like Carini, and there are Sicilians like. . . like this Baron, for example.'

'I agree about Carini,' said Garibaldi, 'but I don't understand why you put this poor Baron at the other extreme. He throws his house and his cellars open, yes, and that's already something. . . but I don't think he has anything to be forgiven him, or that he's hiding his hate for us.'

'Because', said Nievo, 'I believe in the Sicilians who speak little, in the Sicilians who don't get excited, in the Sicilians who worry deep inside and suffer: the poor who wave to us with a weary gesture, as if from a distance of centuries, and Colonel

Carini, always silent and distant like that, full of melancholy and worry, but ready for action at any moment, a man who seems to have not many hopes, and yet he's the very heart of hope, the fragile, silent hope of the best Sicilians. . . I mean a hope that's afraid of itself, that fears words and has death instead as a neighbour and familiar. These people should be known and loved for everything they don't speak about, for the words they nurture in their hearts, but don't utter. . .'

'That's a poem', said Sirtori.

'Oh, of course,' said Nievo, 'but to say it in prose, and the General will have to forgive me, I say that I don't like this Baron, and I don't like Sicilians like Cri. . .'

Garibaldi made a gesture cutting him off, 'Let's get back to poetry', he said.

But the Baron came back, followed by a servant carrying a tray of ices. The Baron took the first cup from the tray and offered it to the General with a bow, then he served Türr, then Sirtori, then, turning to the young man, whom he did not know, he said, 'And for you, Captain.'

'I'm not a captain', said Nievo.

Laughing, Garibaldi said, 'He's a poet, a poet who goes to war, and he'll write about our victories and about the heart of the Sicilians.'

'I'm glad', said the Baron, and as if to pay homage to poetry, he declaimed:

You hear on the right hand the sound of the trumpet,
Another replies on the left. . .

They were two lines which had stuck in his mind from the ceremonies of 1848. But, to change the subject straightaway, he said, 'I've had a room prepared for you, General. If you'd like to go up and rest a little, you'll find everything ready. Look, there's your room. . .' and he raised his stick to point out a window.

I was standing somewhat apart, leaning against the trunk of an olive tree. In the stick which was raised, in the gleam of its knob, time seemed to open up like a funnel of wind to suck me back into the past. The Baron, euphoric and assured, went on, 'It's the best room, gets the sun on all sides, as you can see. I keep it for my most illustrious guests. . . And there's many of them passed through that room!. . . Do you know who's slept there? Try to guess. . .'

'Who?' asked Garibaldi, coldly.

Looking at the Baron's face I saw that for a moment his brain had stopped like a broken watch, his eyes began to roll about desperately, like those of a drowning man. 'He'll have a stroke,' I thought, 'he's going to die.' Instead, he caught hold of himself and said, 'A relation of my wife slept there, he was a little odd. . . intelligent, but a little odd. Just imagine, he wrote books, all in Latin, saying that all the goods in the world should be shared together, women as well.'

Everyone laughed, and the Baron passed a handkerchief over his brow.

(The next day I left with Garibaldi's army, and fought in all the battles, from Ponte dell'Ammiraglio to Capua; then I transferred as an officer to the regular army, only to desert and follow Garibaldi again, right up to Aspromonte. But that's another story.)

Antimony

And the Cardinal dying and Sicily over the ears —
Trouble enough without new lands to be conquered. . .
We signed on and we sailed by the first tide. . .

— Archibald MacLeish, *Conquistador*

Author's note:

In my part of Sicily, the sulphur miners call fire-damp 'antimony'. They say the name comes from 'anti-monk', because historically the monks used to mine it, and handling it carelessly, they died from it. Antimony is used in gunpowder, in printer's type, and at one time in cosmetics. These reasons combined to suggest the title of 'Antimony' for this story.

I

They were firing from the bell-tower with machine-gun bursts or careful rifle shots, according to our movements. The little town was nothing but a blind street of low, white houses, at the end of which was a church with a rough sandstone façade, two flights of steps and a three-storey bell-tower. They were firing from the bell-tower. We had gone into the town thinking they had completely abandoned it, but the machine-gun bursts and rifle shots stopped us at the first houses. Our company was ordered to go round to the other side of the town, behind the church. But behind the church was a precipice of flat rock so sharp and smooth it seemed to have been cut by a saw. The captain decided to have us lie in wait in the cemetery on a neighbouring height, which was level with the church roof and the bell-tower. When they were aware of us, they began to direct bursts at the graves.

I had been on my knees behind the tombstone for an hour; I rubbed my face against the marble for some coolness. My head felt as if it was frying inside the burning helmet, and the air quivered from the blazing sun like the air at the mouth of an oven. To the right of me in the archway of an armorial mortuary chapel, the captain and a journalist I knew were standing, rigid, as if nailed to the door — the slightest movement would have made them targets. If I turned my eyes to the left and a little behind me, I could see half of Ventura's face (we kept close together in every action) behind a huge marble slab with a long inscription in huge words. . . *subió al cielo*. . . which, after some time, began to dance before my eyes and in my brain as if, one by one, the letters were coming incandescent from a blacksmith's forge. As for me, I was sure my time for ascending to heaven had not come, and if it ever did, it would be far better to go down into the earth, where it sticks moistly to the rooth-airs of plants. Certainly, the soldier from the grave in front of me, facing the shade of the chapel, had not ascended to heaven: his head had been blown apart and his lean body was now swollen like a wineskin; it was forty degrees in the shade, the captain said — in the shade of the chapel where he was.

'The Moors are coming', Ventura told me.

They seemed to be curled up as they came towards us, bent at the run. From the bell-tower, they switched their fire on to them. The captain and the journalist stretched their heads out like giraffes, keeping their bodies glued to the chapel door. A bullet whistled sharply past their heads and the journalist's monocle fell out on to the step, breaking with a silvery sound. 'Bastard Reds!' he said. But he had another monocle in his pocket, which he took out of its tissue paper and fixed in his eye. I knew him, since he was from my town. He could not live without his monocle. I remembered him as he was, as a young man in 1922, in his black shirt, with a hard straw hat, a hide whip hanging from his wrist, and the inevitable monocle. His friends teasingly called him 'Count', but he was the son of an old moneylender. In the summer of 1922 he set fire to the door of the Trade Union building, barely missing setting the whole town ablaze, and then he left. I did not know he had become a journalist, as the last time I had seen him had been ten years previously, when he gave a lecture on D'Annunzio in the town's theatre. I like anything to do with books, but, from his lecture, I did not like D'Annunzio. I had come across the fellow again in Spain, and made myself acquainted with him because it is a pleasure to meet a fellow townsman abroad, even if you never went near him at home because you disliked him. He said he was pleased to see a fellow citizen serving the fatherland on Spanish soil. 'Well done,' he said, 'let's gain some honour.' He had not understood a thing.

The Moors had not been unscathed, from my position I could see two men fallen, with their arms open and their faces in the sun. The faces of dead men eaten by the sun; *cara al sol*, as the Falangist hymn began, referring to the living marching with the sun in their faces, but for me the sun was that image of death. Our machine-guns ripped out furiously; the Moroccans' arrival was always encouraging, not least because they undertook risky actions just for fun.

There could not have been more than four men and two

machine-guns in the bell-tower. A moment later and the sound
of the machine-gun there ceased, and only the regular *ba-bum* of
the rifles continued. That sound reminded me of a far-off summer's day, with bandits firing from the rocks at the peasants on
the road to make them leave their mules. My father had said the
sound came from Austrian rifles. It was in the days after the
War, when the countryside was swarming with bandits. The
Moroccans behind the graves were getting excited and began to
show themselves: again bursts came from the bell-tower, but
the Moroccans took no notice. The last burst died away, and
we knew it was the last, just as the peasant on the threshing
floor says, 'The wind's going to change, this direction's
finished.' To those in the bell-tower, their machine-guns were
no longer going to be any use.

We left an Italian patrol in the cemetery, and the rest of us ran
back to the first houses in the town. Firing from both sides of
the street, hugging the walls of the houses, the Moors advanced
towards the church; rifle shots came from the bell-tower, a
Moor fell heavily on to the cobbles.

'What a bunch', said the journalist.

'They're tarred with the pitch of hell', said Ventura.

The Moors reached the flight of steps, and only then was I
aware that the church was exactly the same as that of Santa
Maria in my own town. Shots no longer came from the bell-
tower, then we heard a rending voice, like that of a frightened
boy about to burst into tears.

'They're surrendering', said the journalist.

The Moors squatted on the steps, rifles pointing at the door.
I heard the silence growing around me. When men were surrendering, I felt a fever rise in me, blades of cold ran down the
length of my spine, there was a knot of pain in the pit of my
stomach, and dreamlike things entered my head, a cabala of
things.

The church door opened with a creaking noise and two
figures in overalls appeared, one of them wounded, with a
deathlike pallor. They were FAI* — I had known they were
from the moment I realized there was no possibility of escape,
and that they had known it, too. We all moved in. The

---

* Federazione Anarchica Italiana, Italian Anarchist Federation — *Trans.*

wounded man sank down on a step, the other took off his helmet: straw-coloured hair rained over the face and a hand's gesture to arrange it turned her into a woman with large grey eyes.
The Spanish colonel began questioning her, she replied rapidly
and we gathered that, between one reply and another, she was
pleading with the colonel for her wounded companion. The
journalist explained for us. 'There were four of them, two are
dead in the bell-tower. She's German. . .'

Smiling, the colonel spoke to the Moors, the woman
screamed, and the Moors dragged her away with howls of
delight. The journalist said, 'He's made them a present of her,
they'll give her a good time. She'll get more than she bargained
for', and his eye gleamed maliciously behind its monocle.

They took away the wounded man, who was one howl of
pain. Ventura and I sat down on the church steps and took out
our papers and tobacco, but I spilled mine through the trembling in my hands. Some doors began to open, two or three
windows sprouted with flags, red-yellow-red ones.

'If he gets into my sight at the right moment,' said Ventura,
'I'll send a bullet into the glass eye of that journalist from your
town.'

'And into that colonel', I said.

'The colonel, too,' he said, 'I'll put him with those right at
the top of the list. I've been making one for six months now,
it's getting too long, I'll have to make a start. . .'

Ventura had *mafia*-like tendencies, he said that during the
Great War, his father, his uncle, a friend of his uncle and a
cousin of his mother — in short, all those from his town who
found themselves at the front together — would not think twice
during an attack about getting rid of the officers and sergeants
who were 'stinkers'. Going by what he said, the Italian army
must have lost more officers and N.C.O.'s from the bullets of
its own men than from the Austrians. I joined in his game,
because I found it a release, it served to loosen that knot of fear
I felt inside me. Ventura was a good comrade; perhaps he said it
all to cheer me up. We had been together since Malaga, always
together in the moments of danger. We had become friends the
day he had taken his fists to a Calabrian who liked to 'Watch the
firing squads'. As soon as he had a spare moment, he said, 'I'm
off to watch the firing squads', as happily as if he were going to

see the fireworks for Santa Rosalia. Ventura told him he should not mention them any more, and that if he had a liking for them, which only a right bastard would, he should go off without bothering people whose stomachs turned at the thought. The Calabrian's reaction was to try and jab him with his bayonet, but Ventura punched him in the face until it swelled up. After the scuffle, I invited him for a glass of wine, and we passed an hour munching soft-shell crabs and drinking wine, which was perfumed like the wine of Pantelleria. It was only then that I began to understand what the war in Spain was, because I had thought the 'Reds' were the rebels who wanted to overthrow a government of law and order. Ventura explained that the rebellion had been started by the Spanish Fascists, who had not been able to bring the government down by themselves, so they had asked Mussolini for some help. Mussolini had said, 'What am I going to do with all these unemployed? I'll send them to Spain, then I'll be straight.' And so it was not true there was a Communist government in Spain.

'And then,' said Ventura, 'what can the Communists do to you? What can they do to you and me? I don't care a thing about Communism or Fascism, I could spit on them both. America's where I want to go.'

'And how will you get there?'

'That's why I've come to Spain', he said, 'to cross the front. The Americans are helping the Republic, Americans are fighting in the Brigades — there's one that's all Americans — I'll cross the lines and join the Brigade. If they kill me, if you kill me. . .', the thought that I or one of us might kill him surprised him, 'But I won't be left dead in this mix-up, I'll get to America, even if I leave some piece of me behind, I'll get there. . . My mother's in America, my brother, two married sisters, nephews and nieces. . . I went there when I was two, with my mother and father, then my father died, and I got in with all the villains in the Bronx. One night they killed a policeman, and I got involved in it without knowing how — because it wasn't me who fired — and within fifteen days I found myself on a ship taking me to Italy. . . I was still a boy, my mother wanted to come with me, but they persuaded her to stay, saying a good lawyer would occupy himself with the case, a Senator, too, to enable me to come back. . . My mother's been chasing after the lawyer and the Senator for ten years, with me in Italy in despair, not doing a thing, because they never let me go short of dollars, just waiting. . . I've tried to cross into France more than once, but they've always caught me. . . As soon as I heard about the war in Spain, and they wanted volunteers, I became the most fanatical Fascist in town, they had me leaving with the first to be sent: but I'd as soon spit on Fascism, and Communism, too.'

I think the wine might have made him want to talk so much, to confide in someone as a release, because he should not have spoken like that to someone whom he had only just met. So many confidences and so many dangerous things made me afraid. Some days later, however, he told me that he had not told me the confidences because of the wine, he had known he could trust me, because he understood men. I continued to think it was the wine, and constantly advised him not to let himself go above half a bottle.

'You,' he told me that day, when the wine had already mellowed him towards me, 'you're one of the ones that Mussolini's got from underneath his feet; you're one of the unemployed, let's have the poor unemployed man fight the war. He goes hungry in Italy, becomes a hero in Spain. He'll do incredible things for the grandeur of the Duce. . .'

Now, sitting on the steps of the church, which was the same in every detail as the one in my home town, rolling misshapen cigarettes between my fingers, I felt a great desire to talk and talk, like a drunk: I wanted to talk about myself, about my town, my wife, the sulphur mine I had worked in, and about my escape from it to the bullets of Spain.

Rifle shots were heard. 'They've shot the wounded man', Ventura said.

'I'd come with you to the other side for that,' I said, 'so as not to hear the firing squads any more, so as not to see the wounded being butchered, so as not to see what I saw now with the German girl, so as not to see the Moors any more, or the colonels of the *tercio**, the Crucifixes and the Sacred Hearts. . .'

'You wouldn't see the jackets of the *tercio*, the Moors, the Crucifixes and the Sacred Hearts, but no one can wipe out the firing squads and the rest from your mind.'

---

* The Spanish Infantry, known as the 'third' in the Civil War — *Trans.*

I knew it was true. But to me it seemed a lot not even seeing
the Crucifixes any more, which, in their devotion, the Falangists attached to everything that sowed death, to their cannons
and their armoured cars, and not hearing the great Mother of
God invoked by those Navarrese who relaxed during attacks by
shooting prisoners, and not seeing the chaplains giving their
blessings, and that monk who passed ardently through the lines,
with his hand raised exhorting us in the name of God and the
Virgin. . .

'Right now in my town,' I said, 'there's the Feast of the
Assumption — the Madonna of Mid-August, the peasants call
her — here they shoot the peasants for the glory of the Madonna
of Mid-August. . . The peasants form a procession with their
mules wearing bell-collars, and each mule has a brand new
pack-saddle full of wheat, they reach the church and unload the
wheat, hundredweights and hundredweights of wheat in
thanksgiving for the rain, which came at the right time, for the
baby's recovery from the attack of worms, for the kick from
the mule which only grazed the peasant's head. . . Of course,
many babies die, there's been good rain for the wheat, but the
almonds had a bad frost, and it's not going to be a good year for
oil, and some peasant's had a mule kick right in the head or
belly. . . But in our faith, it's only the good things that count.
God doesn't come into the sufferings , it's destiny which brings
them. We have a good Sunday, there's soup and meat, and my
mother says we must thank God. They bring my father home,
burned by antimony, and my mother says it's vile destiny that's
burned him. . . I'd like to have my mother here, and show her
that, here in Spain, God and destiny have one and the same
face.'

'I don't want to hear anything about it,' said Ventura, 'either
about God or destiny; only stupid people think about destiny —
it's like standing next to an anthill and thinking 'Shall I kick it
with my heel or not? Is it destiny I should give it a kick or
destiny I should leave it alone? If you start thinking about
destiny you can go out of your mind, standing there looking at
an anthill. As far as God's concerned, it's a little more complicated. In ten years of doing nothing, I've had time to think
about God as well, and I'm convinced that God is death, every
man carries the God of his own death inside him, like a worm.

But it's not something simple, there are moments when you wish death was like sleep, and that something of you remained suspended in a dream, a mirror that continues to hold your image, while you're already far away. . . That's the reason men create a god. But I don't want to know about it, perhaps in this moment I feel abandoned, like a baby that starts to walk, and after a while it becomes aware that its mother's hand isn't there ready to hold it up, and down it tumbles: I've got to walk alone here, without God; might as well have never had him. But if I'd had to create a God for myself, it would've been a benevolent God, and he would certainly have left me alone in Spain. . . The God of the *tercio* and the Navarrese isn't a benevolent God.'

'That's what I'd tell my mother,' I said, 'that her God's on the side of the *tercio*.'

'She'd say it was right. Perhaps she's saying a novena right now for the *tercio* and the Navarrese, the priest will have given his sermon from the pulpit "and say your novena to the Madonna of Mid-August with the intention of invoking God's strength and protection for the armies that are fighting in his name and for his glory".'

'I hate the Spaniards', I said.

'Because they've pulled God on to their side, as if he were a blanket, and left you out in the open: your God is your mother's God. But there's no God in the Republic; there are those who've always known it, like me, and others who're shivering with cold because the Falangists have pulled the blanket of God all on to their side.'

'It's not only that,' I said, 'it's because they're so cruel.'

'Listen,' said Ventura, 'I've come to risk my life in Spain, because of this great desire I've got to get back to America. America's rich, it's civilized, full of good things; there's freedom; from being a nobody, a man can become as rich as Ford, or become President, become anything he likes. But two innocent men were sent to the electric chair, and the whole of America knew they were innocent; the judges knew, the President knew, those who make the newspapers and those who sell them. To me, that's a more terrible fact than the firing squads here. And those two were condemned in a free, ordered and rich country, with all the protection of the law, for the very reasons that the Falangists butcher the FAI here. Never heard of

Sacco and Vanzetti?'

'No,' I said, 'never heard of them.'

He told me the story of Sacco and Vanzetti, and really, there was nothing to be surprised about in Spain.

'And think about Sicily,' said Ventura, 'think about the Sicily of the sulphur miners and the peasants who work on a day-to-day basis: think about the peasants' winter, when there's no work and the house is full of hungry children, and the women moving about the house, their legs swollen with dropsy, the donkey and the goat by the bed. I'd go mad, I would. And if one fine day the peasants and sulphur miners killed the Mayor, the Fascist Party secretary, Don Giuseppe Catalanotto, the sulphur-mine owner, and the Prince of Castro, who owns the lands in fief — if this happened in my town, and your town began to rise as well, and if the same wind began to blow in all the towns of Sicily, you know what would happen? All the country gentlemen, who're Fascists, would join up with the priests, the Carabinieri, and the police chiefs, and start to shoot the peasants and the sulphur miners, and the peasants and the sulphur miners would kill the priests, the Carabinieri and the gentlemen, there'd be no end to the killing, then the Germans would come and arrange a couple of bombardments that would make the Sicilians lose their longing for rebellion for ever, and the gentlemen would win.'

'It'll end up like that in Spain', I said.

'Thanks to us,' said Ventura, 'because without the Italians and the Germans, the gentlemen would be dying like flies here. We're worse than the Moors, we are.'

I wish I could remember the name of that town; I remember the church was dedicated to St Isidore, who was a peasant saint, but in that church the peasants had used him for target practice. The journalist took photographs of St Isidore with his head blown off, looking like a flower pot, and no arms, like the soldier who lost them at Guadalajara. I began to understand many things, sitting on the steps of that church: about Spain and Italy, about the world at large, and the world of men.

At Malaga, the Calabrian who went to watch the firing squads had said, 'It's like the theatre, even the ladies come: they stand a little way off and watch — there's one old lady who

watches through a pair of mother-of-pearl binoculars.' The picture of that old lady caught my imagination; she seemed to sym-
bolize Spain's fanaticism and its cruelty. At the same time, she
reminded me of Donna Maria Grazia, who let us live in ground-
floor rooms in her mansion, where my mother reduced the rent
by washing the floors and steps, twice a week. Donna Maria
Grazia used to watch her through a lorgnette, saying, 'You've
left all the suds over the staircase, wipe the cloth over this
corner, go over the salon again.' Twice a week my mother came
down from the house worn out, so tired she didn't even want
to eat. Donna Maria Grazia had a very poor opinion of me; to
my mother she said, 'Your son's growing up badly, he's not
obliging, he barely greets me, and he's dressed as as if he were
a gentleman. I wonder what wicked ideas are in his
head. . . You'd better teach him that people must stay where
Providence has put them — the poor man who plays the proud
always comes to a bad end.' My mother said, 'Greet her, for my
sake, greet her.' But I had never gone without greeting her, I
used to take off my beret and say, 'Good afternoon', but she
wanted me to say 'Your servant, Madame', so she would look
at me through her lorgnette and not reply. She would have to
come with a pair of binoculars to see me being shot by firing
squad.

I understood nothing about Fascism until I came to Spain.
For me, it was as if it did not exist. My father had worked in the
sulphur mine, my grandfather too, and like them, I worked
there as well. I read the newspapers: Italy was a great country,
it was respected; it had conquered an Empire, and Mussolini
made speeches that were a pleasure to hear. But I had no sympathy for the priests, both because of what I had read about
them in books and the way they used confession. I was not
happy that my mother or my wife went to tell the priest everything that happened at home: their sins, my sins and those of
the neighbours. That is how the womenfolk confess in Sicilian
towns, they say more about the sins of other people than their
own. The country gentlemen annoyed me, too — those who
lived off income from the land or mines. When I saw them in
uniform on Sundays, I thought Fascism was rendering a kind of
justice by making them dress up in a ridiculous manner and having them parade about in the piazza. But I believed in God, went

to mass and I respected Fascism. I loved my wife, whom I had married for love, without a penny of dowry. I worked in the sulphur mine, one week on the night shift, the next on the day shift, without a word of complaint. The only thing was my great fear of antimony, because it had burned my father in the same mine. It was a mine which, according to the memories of the oldest, the owners had always exploited without caring about the workers' safety; 'accidents' were frequent — a roof caving in or an explosion of antimony. And the families of those who had been crushed or burned took it as destiny. There was one time, in 1919 or 1920, when instead of taking it as destiny, the miners who had escaped took against the owner, organized a strike and made threats. But the time for strikes was past. To tell the truth, I did not think strikes were a good thing in a nation of order such as Italy had become.

On 8th September, 1936, the day of the Infant Mary, when bonfires are lit in her honour in the countryside around town (my mother later said it was a 'notable' day, you didn't work on 'notable' days), I was on the day shift. I got up at three in the morning, left the house at half-past, an hour's walk, then I was 'dropped' into the shaft at five. For some days, my uncle, Pietro Griffeo, my mother's brother, who was an old hand in the mine, had been advising us, 'Keep your lamps low, lads. There's something I don't like.' He gave us the same advice on that day, too. Our sector was the least ventilated, there were no supports, and the 'fillings' had to be done. We stripped off, and felt the air on our naked bodies like a wet sheet. Our lamps were acetylene ones, as the management kept the safety lamps like one of us kept his Sunday best — they only 'appeared' when the engineers came on an inspection. Besides, the old miners did not want them. 'When destiny calls,' they said, 'you can die with a safety lamp, too.' I have no idea why they looked down on them, but they loved the old acetylene lights.

After a meal break — we almost all ate bread, salted sardines and raw onion — we set to work again. Again my uncle advised us, 'Keep your acetylenes low!' then a minute later, there came a roar of flame from the end of the gallery; the flames came roaring toward us, just like I had seen at the cinema, when water shoots out from an open lock. But I'm thinking this now, I'm not sure it was actually like that. I saw the flames above me, and couldn't understand a thing. My uncle was shouting 'Anti-mony!' and dragged me off, but I was already running as if in a dream. I ran even after I came out of the mouth of the mine, and, naked and shoeless, I ran through the countryside until I could feel my heart bursting inside me, then I threw myself down on the ground, trembling, crying heavily like a child.

That night, my head swam, I wasn't feverish, but I couldn't sleep. Every single word said to me, every single noise I heard, every single thought that rose, seemed to explode in me like a photographer's flash: then the flash died and there was a violet light, the light I imagined the blind had inside them. I had always been afraid of antimony, because I knew that it burned the internal organs — that was how my father had died — or the eyes: I knew many men who had been blinded by antimony.

The next day I felt a hundred years old. I decided I would never go back to the sulphur mine. I knew about the war in Spain, and that many men had gone to the one in Africa and made some money, and only one man from town had died there. And then, dying in the light of the sun did not frighten me (and in all the war in Spain I was never frightened of death, only the thought of the flamethrowers made me break out into a fearful sweat). I dressed up in my Sunday best and went down to the Fascist Party building. The political secretary there had been a schoolmate of mine, later going on to become the prim-ary school teacher himself. He did not dislike me, even if he was worried I might treat him with an old schoolmate's familiarity, and use the informal *tu* with him. But I spoke to him with great respect.

'I'd like to go and fight in Spain', I said.

'Ah, yes,' he said, 'actually, there's something, an appeal for volunteers has just arrived, but that doesn't mean to say you'll go to Spain. . .'

'I'll go to hell and back', I said.

'Yes, all right, but they want Militia, militiamen have prece-dence. You're not a member of the Militia.'

'Then enrol me', I said.

'That's not so simple.'

'Look, I'm in the Fascist Trade Union,' I said, 'I was a Young Fascist, I was a member of a Junior Training Corps and I've done my military service. I don't know why you didn't enrol me as a militiaman when I came back.'

'You had to ask', he said.

'Well, I'm asking now, I didn't fight in the war in Africa, but I want to fight in this one. I was a Bersagliere, I'm in good health, and I think someone like me has a right to fight in a war — or I could write to the Duce personally and offer myself as a volunteer directly.'

This was a good argument, because a worker had once written to the Duce for an award that they had not wanted to give him, and he had sown a seed that the political secretary still remembered. Naturally, they had made the worker pay for it, later on.

'We'll see what we can do,' said the political secretary. 'I'll speak to the Consul and we'll see. Come back on Monday.'

They enlisted me. My mother and my wife cried. I left with my heart at ease: the sulphur mine really frightened me; in comparison, the war in Spain seemed like a trip out to the country.

Cadiz was beautiful; it was like Trapani, but the whiteness of its houses was more luminous; Malaga, too, was beautiful in those February days, with their lively sun, the sun's good wine and its brandy. From November to February the war was also fine, it was fine being in the *tercio* with its officers who went into the attack without drawing their pistols, simply holding a riding-whip in their gloved hands. I thought the essence of our war there was the man with the pointed beard, whom the Spaniards applauded. He was not an officer, but he was certainly a Fascist bigwig: he wore the symbols of the *fascio*, the Cross and the bow and arrows of the Falange on his black shirt. He was a handsome man, and looked extremely well on horseback. The Spaniards said he might accomplish great deeds, and later I got to know that a Frenchman had written a book about him, telling of the tremendous things that the man had done. I would like to read it.

At Malaga, I began to hear about the firing squads, and then my meeting with Ventura began to open my eyes. But the Spaniards in Malaga cheered us, they all wanted to offer us something, or talk to us, and the women smiled at us. The men said, 'I'm on the Right', and invited us to drink something. I didn't know what they meant, and thought that declaring yourself to be 'on the Right' was a compliment or a greeting the Spaniards used. Ventura explained that the Fascists were a political party of the Right, and that the Communists and Socialists were on the Left. All the Spaniards in Malaga were on the Right. Six years later, and I have seen all the Fascists in my own town declare themselves to be on the Left! The city was intact, the streets bright with women, but there was no end to the firing squads.

Up to Malaga, you could not say I had risked my life. I had only taken part in small engagements around villages and towns, and in Malaga I was only a walk-on part in the march past. I began to feel the real war a month later, in the battle for Madrid, which later took its name from the town of Guadalajara. That is a memory of hell: more for the wind, which cut sharp as a razor, for the snow, the mud and the loudspeakers, than for the shelling and the scything machine-gun fire which came at us from all sides. The loudspeakers made your head swim, the voices seemed to come out of the woods, from the very branches above our heads; they were on the wind, as if they shared its nature, and in the snow. Trees, wind and snow said, 'Comrades, workers and peasants of Italy, why are you fighting against us? Do you want to die trying to stop the Spanish workers and peasants living in freedom? They've fooled you: go back to your homes and families. Or rather, come over to us! Your comrades who are now our prisoners will tell you we have opened our arms to them. . .'. Then you heard another voice, 'Listen, mates, we've been fooled and betrayed. It's not true the Reds shoot their prisoners, that they're better armed, and eat better. . . It's not true they don't have generals, I've seen them myself, they've questioned me. . . This is Pinto speaking, Calogero Pinto. . .' and with every name coming out of the loudspeaker, the officers said, 'It's not true, I saw Pinto (or whoever it was) fall myself, he's dead. They've found his identity tags.' Perhaps it was true, they did use identity tags, but it was suspicious so many officers seeing the same man fall.

Ventura told me, 'I'm off, I'm going to find out where the American Brigade is, I want to get over to the Americans, right away.' But he did not go, I think he felt obliged not to while things were going badly. On 15th March, we were on patrol, when at one point we stopped, suspended and intent on the silence, as if each one of us had heard a mysterious warning, but I really think we must have heard something, because I do not believe in mysterious warnings. We moved, and a voice said, 'Throw your weapons down!' Like puppets, we turned our heads in search of the voice's direction; a volley was fired high over our heads, and again the voice said, 'Throw your weapons down and surrender!' The accent and the words were Italian, spoken as calmly as if they were offering friendship. The lieutenant was fooled, and said, 'Stop joking, will you, it's us!' The voice was amused, and replied, 'Of course it's you, we recognise you very well: throw your weapons down!' Ventura made a rapid movement, a grenade exploded in the trees, a hail of fire came, and we threw ourselves down onto the ground, behind the tree trunks; the lieutenant and a soldier were killed. When we reached our lines, and were drying ourselves by a small fire, Ventura said to me, 'I'll go when I want to go, the men capable of taking Luigi Ventura for a sucker have yet to be born.'

We were in a hovel, which had been blown in half; the corner which was still standing would have served well as a stage for the Nativity. There was a mantle of snow on the remaining piece of roof, and snow all around to soften the destruction. We had placed a little wine to mull on the fire.

'They were Italians,' I said, 'perhaps your grenade killed some of them.'

'I'm sorry,' said Ventura, 'but even if they'd been the Americans I'm looking for, I'd still have thrown it. In some circumstances, there's neither Italy nor America, neither Communism nor Fascism. Today was one of those circumstances: there was Luigi Ventura and a guy who wanted to take him prisoner. There was a rumpus, once, in a bar in New York, the police arrived and they put us against the wall, with our hands up. I was stuck against the wall for ten minutes. It's not very nice for a man to have to stay with his face to the wall and his hands in the air. And I thought, right, from today, the first man to tell me to put my hands up, it's either his skin or mine. You've no dignity, standing there with your hands up, while someone points a rifle at you. The firing squads make me want to throw up: there's no dignity putting a man against a wall and shooting at him with a dozen rifles. Those who order the firing squads and those who perform them are dishonourable, that's what they are: dishonourable. They've no honour in them at all.'

'There's no honour in killing', I said.

'No,' said Ventura, 'there can be honour in killing, when it's done in the heat of the moment, when it's either his skin or yours, or when you kill the ones who are rotten, those who play the spy through cowardice or by profession, or those stinkers in command: you can even kill them in cold blood and it's an honourable thing.'

For him, killing a policeman in the Bronx or a carabiniere in the Naro countryside, or shooting an officer in the back, were honourable things. It was a way of thinking that was not new to me: the contractors in the sulphur mine, who took money from us and from the owners, thought the same way, too. They ensured a job for us and an efficient output for the owners, and those who did not pay offended their honour. They were people I detested, and Ventura was a little like them. Perhaps, in the sulphur mine, I would have hated him, but in that war, his motives of honour turned out to be better, nearer to man's dignity, than the motives Fascism had behind its own flag and that of Italy. For myself, for Ventura and for many of us, in a war we had accepted without understanding, and which was slowly drawing us over towards the motives and feelings of the enemy, there were no flags. Each one of us had an obligation of honour to himself not to show fear, not to surrender and not to leave his post. It is possible that all wars are fought like that, without flags, with men who are simply men; and that for the men who fight the wars there is no Italy, Spain, or Russia, or even Fascism, Communism or the Church: only the dignity of each man gambling with his own life, and accepting the risk of death. It is possible, as I say, because as far as I am concerned, I would have been pleased to have a real, human flag under which to fight. When the voices inviting us to desert were over, they played the workers' hymn over the loudspeakers. The invitations and declarations of brotherhood gave me a strong feeling of repugnance: even real things shouted and broadcast from loudspeakers take on the appearance of a deception, but the workers' hymn gave me a different feeling.

My father had died in 1926, when I was sixteen. The thought of his life and the way he had died had never left me, even though I had forgotten he had been a Socialist. At that sound of the workers' hymn I saw my father holding me by the hand, the band that was playing and then a man in a bow tie, who came out on to a balcony and spoke. My father said, 'Well said!' and clapped his hands. And who remembers anything more about the hymn? It was good music, at certain moments you thought it might even tear the dark clouds apart, as the words said, 'The sun of the future shines on the flag of freedom ' — they really seemed to hold out hope.

But what was Socialism? Certainly, it was a good flag. My father said it was 'Justice and Equality', but there can be no equality if there is no God, you can't create a kingdom of equality before a solicitor for oaths, you can only do that before God. Or before Death, if, in each moment, we could all see ourselves reflected in Death. But that would not be right, if we could only live in a world of equality by living in the name of God, or by seeing ourselves reflected in Death. However you can have justice without God. I've thought that God was justice. God is a long way from our hope for justice. My father was not happy with justice alone, he wanted equality. He thought those big lawyers with their big hats and bow ties were in the place of God: Ferri, the lawyer, and Cigna, the lawyer, in the place of God.

But Socialism too must be a little like religion, a pot in which lots of things can boil, where everyone adds a bone to make a broth according to their own tastes. For me, it was the memory of my father, his faith, the way he had died, and myself, who had risked having the same death. Then there was Donna Maria Grazia, who said of me, 'He's got the same twisted ideas as his father.' But I had neither straight nor twisted ideas, only a gentle memory of my father and the pain of how he died, a great fear of antimony, and a little hope in justice.

After Guadalajara it was said we had been beaten because, on the Madrid front, Communism was beginning to circulate among us like a disease; perhaps they believed that the great blather from the loudspeakers and the pamphlets they rained down on us from their aeroplanes (they rained bombs as well, and you can't accept truth and bombs together) had, as they said, eaten away at the morale of the troops. Afterwards, there were investigations and some of us were repatriated. One day,

I remember, they had us all line up and Teruzzi, who commanded the whole of the Militia, came and reviewed us. After a while, he stopped in front of a legionary and asked, 'You, why have you come to Spain?' The legionary began to stammer, 'It was a friend who told me, "There's a war in Spain, put in a request". . . I'd only been married a while, I had some land for share-cropping with my father and brother, I married and they pushed me out, my father said, "Find some share-cropping land of your own" and I told him, "You think it's that easy to find share-cropping land? Where can I find any?". . . I was lucky my friend came along and told me about the war in Spain.' Teruzzi looked at him as if the soldier were letting him in on a secret, becoming attentive and full of thought. Before Fascism, they said he had been a sergeant, and in that moment, he understood the soldier as a sergeant, as a poor man, as he had once been himself, not as the Commanding Officer of the Militia. But the colonel accompanying him said, 'Idiot!' to the legionary and, without saying a word, Teruzzi passed on, looking distractedly at the legionaries' faces. Then he stopped again and asked, 'You, let's hear why you've come to Spain.' But, in order not to be called an idiot by the colonel — by now we had all understood how to reply — the legionary said in a firm voice, 'For the glory of Italy and the salvation of Spain.' Teruzzi heaved a sigh of relief and said, 'Well done!' and to the colonel, 'We'll give this legionary an award', and later on they really did give him twenty-five pesetas. On the other hand, the one who had replied with the story about his friend and the share-cropping land was repatriated. Performed in this way, the investigation was stupid, but the colonel came back on his own to question us and Ventura, who was a glib talker, cut a great figure, talking about the Duce, Fascist Italy and religion as if he were a Federation secretary and priest in the pulpit rolled into one — and he was someone who hated Fascism and priests. As always, the Fascists wanted lies. Every one of us, except for a few ardent Fascists, had come to Spain for the pay they gave us, constrained to do so either because of unemployment or the conditions of work: but we fought with dedication, and men died. Without a doubt, it disturbed us that Spanish peasants and miners found themselves on the other side, and that the Falangists would shoot them. Not even knowing anything about Socialism, that music and that flag were enough to give rise to dangerous memories, like my own memory of my father.

The battle for Madrid at Guadalajara was hell: from the gentle Malaga spring I would never have believed you could have met such a violent winter. My lips and hands were cracked by the snow blizzards, and we wallowed in mud. We rarely saw our aeroplanes: those of the Republic passed over us as if they wanted to decapitate us, you felt as if they were taking your head off, and they had tanks like houses, while ours were really like sardine tins by comparison. On all the walls they had written *Madrid es el baluarte del antifascismo*, and they fought with great courage and discipline to keep it. Up to Malaga, we had been fighting against bands of peasants and workers who had no order nor due care and were wiped out by our machine-guns, or else they hid behind the walls enclosing fields, on roofs and in bell-towers to make a desperate last stand, and often they were only armed with a double-barrelled shotgun. There was a good number of Republican soldiers taken prisoner at Malaga, ten thousand of them; they could have made a better stand, and perhaps beaten us, but they knew nothing about order. I knew nothing of the art of war, but the way they milled around in attack and retreat gave me the sense that they had no proper chain of command. Perhaps they had thrown themselves into the war with the same dream of equality that my father used to have, thinking they could give birth to the world of equality right there in the war: no officers and everyone an officer — my father would have liked to have thrown himself into that kind of a war. But in war you need someone who is going to take command, even if they happen to have a watermelon for a head. They had finally begun to understand this, and for the defence of Madrid they had disciplined soldiers and good officers; our officers said that Russian officers had arrived who continually used the firing squad to impose discipline. I don't believe it was true, however, because I never saw a Russian prisoner. I saw German ones, American and French, and I even saw an Italian fall prisoner, but never a Russian. The fact is that they had begun to understand; having started badly, they were now tackling the war on the right footing.

I would be recounting things which I only learned ten years later if I said that I had understood the battle and had felt the sense of a defeat. In those days I felt a great admiration for the generals because, from all that confusion of tanks and men in the mud, among the trees, under snow, wind and fire, they managed to disentangle some semblance of lines, and see where we were, and where the Republicans were. But seeing that we were beaten, possibly they didn't see things that clearly. Or else, as we said among ourselves, it was General Franco who had cheated us. On the front held by his troops he left the Republicans in peace, as if there was a pact that the battle for Madrid had to be won by Mussolini's troops. It's certain that, underneath, the Spaniards secretly gloated over our defeat. Whenever a quarrel broke out between Spanish and Italian soldiers, they mentioned 'Guadalajara' to offend us, and the name even annoyed me, who never quarrelled.

We had our revenge when, at Santander, the Republican army wanted to negotiate its surrender with the Italians, because they trusted the word of our generals and not that of Franco, and to tell the truth I would not have trusted his word either. Portraits circulated of a youthful Franco, looking like S. Luigi Gonzaga with a little moustache; I had seen him close to, much older, but still with that air of a man who had just finished praying. He was like Don Carmelo Ferraro in my home town, who held the golden umbrella over the Holy Sacrament in the Corpus Domini Day processions, went to church every afternoon to lead the saying of the rosary, with the old men and women murmuring behind his beautiful deep voice, and who always walked along looking up to heaven, as if his eyes were drawn there by magnetic force, yet who lent money out at huge rates of interest, and took an olive grove off Baron Fiandaca for fifty thousand lira when it was worth more than a million, crippling him with interest payments, and flaying the poor with them as well. Like Don Carmelo, Franco had a full, smooth face, whose eyes appealed to heaven. I became convinced he was one of those men, of whom I know so many in my home town and in the rest of Sicily, who look as if they have come down from an altar, and yet do all the evil a man can do, robbing and having people killed, and then making bequests to churches and hospitals in their wills. Better the general who spoke every evening on the radio, whom the Spaniards enjoyed as much as a farce, called Queipo de Llano, who did what he did at Malaga, but that was to be expected, going from his brutish face and the obscene things he said on the radio. Franco, calm and elegant, was a man who had just risen from his velvet hassock, and you cannot expect anything good to come from a man who prays on a velvet hassock. So, the army at Santander wanted to surrender to the Italians, who guaranteed the prisoners' lives, and it was satisfying to have the Republicans know us as humane. But it was soured, because Franco got up off his velvet hassock and said that General Bastico was beginning to get on his. . . Of course, he did not put it that way, his anger would certainly have found a clean expression. He informed Mussolini that it was crazy that an Italian general should not give a hoot about hs orders and should hinder him in bringing *limpieza* to Santander, cleanliness to the Red city, and so Mussolini whistled for Bastico to come back home. Mussolini understood — you can just imagine him not understanding — the need for bringing *limpieza*, as he too held by cleanliness: Bastico left, and the Falange began to have a great time in Santander as well.

But while I was sitting on the steps of St Isidore's church, in that town whose name I have forgotten, the battle for Santander had barely begun. It was 15th August 1937. We were circling around Madrid like moths at night around a candle which come near enough to feel burnt and then widen their flight, coming near again, then, because of a swirl of wind, the flame catches them. Madrid was like that. The gust of wind was at Brunete, when the Republicans came at us unexpectedly, and my admiration for the generals suddenly fell, because the Republicans could have taken us, as they say, in our sleep, and that they did not make an overwhelming advance was because they were surprised, perhaps, by that gap, fearing a prearranged trap, where instead there was nothing. They passed the crossroads at Brunete, then the rush fizzled out. Lister, their general, gave too much credit to our generals on that occasion; like the farm-hand he had been, and like me, he thought generals could see everything, and that leaving a gap like that on the Madrid front was a secret calculation. By the time he realized he could have pushed further, it was already too late; his forces were pressing around Brunete, which had many of our soldiers inside it, but we had already moved into a counter-attack to block further advances and to break the pincer movement which had closed around our troops. We could not manage to break it, but we compelled Lister's forces to move to the defensive, and in the course of ten days, the initial success he had not exploited to the full was completely wiped out. And then we began to clean up the villages again. The one we took on the day of the Madonna of Mid-August was in the area of Brunete; I seem to remember there was a small stream, and a town we passed through called Maqueda. It was said that a Duke of this area had been a Viceroy of Sicily in the past, for which reason the most beautiful street in Palermo is named Maqueda after him. But perhaps I don't remember too well, and we passed through Maqueda some days before or after. I don't know why, but I have no clear memory of the towns and cities in Spain, not even of Seville, which is the most beautiful city I have ever seen. I don't have a good memory for places, and even less for those in Spain. Perhaps it was because the towns were very similar to the ones I had known since childhood, my own town and the neighbouring ones, and I dismissed them saying, 'This town's like Grotte. . . It's like being in Milocca here. . . this piazza's like the one in my town. . .' and even in Seville there were moments when I seemed to be walking through the streets of Palermo around Piazza Marina.

The countryside, too, was like that of Sicily: lonely and desolate around Castile, like it is between Caltanissetta and Enna, but greater in its desolation and solitude, as if after having flung Sicily down the Almighty had enjoyed himself playing a game of enlargement with one of those instruments they sell at fairs, called pantographs, which engineers use as well. And what an idea to go and plant a capital city right in the middle of Castile! It seemed incredible that there could be a large beautiful city in the middle of that desert, it was like a hallucination, like a vision of spring water rising up in a parched man's thoughts. But there it was, Madrid, glaring red at night in the fires which our aeroplanes went in to attack; only in odd moments did I think there were children and old people in the city, women screaming in pain, and houses in which thousands of people were living. 'Antimony, fire. . .' I thought. But the glare was so far off and that city of hallucination had caused us so much blood and sorrow, that I usually watched that red halo of death like a child in the country who watches the far-off Catherine-wheels of the Festival of S. Calogero, a faraway game in the night.

Evening fell on that small town in Castile or Estramadura, with its countryside of clay, brambles and burnt stubble, in which you could feel the feudal system, with its violent overseers, thieving Excise men, and the Duke, who lived in Palermo or Madrid, burning up the income on women and cars, and its peasants slaving in the clay soils under the hostile eye of the overseer. For me, the countryside gave off a sadness: it was like that when I had come out of the mine and met the smell of earth and sun, and a desire to become a peasant welled up inside me. We pushed on past the last houses. A man dressed in dark clothes greeted us with his hand stretched up high. 'Long live Italy!' he said, and Ventura replied, '*Arriba España*'. Usually I liked that exchange of greetings, in which the names of Italy and Spain crossed.

The man stopped, and said, '*Es magnífico.*'

'*Sì*', said Ventura.

'*Mussolini*', said the man, '*nos ha prestado un gran servicio. . . Es magnífico.*'

'*Cómo no!*' said Ventura.

'*Una pandilla de asesinos, los rojos*', said the man.

'This guy's beginning to get on my . . .' said Ventura, and asked, '*Por qué?*'

'*Qué opinión tiene usted?*' asked the man, suddenly anxious.

'Arriba España', said Ventura.

The man breathed again. '*Falange ama España sobre todas las cosas,*' and then, '*Es terrible estar entre cuatro paredes cuando fuera. . . Los dias son largos entre cuatro paredes. . . Pues, ahora empieza nuestro triunfo. . .*'

'*Cómo no!*' said Ventura, '*Ahora limpieza: y hombre profético partido único sindicato vertical. . .*', he read the Spanish newspapers and knew a lot.

'*Claro,*' said the man, '*España no se aparta de Dios.*'

'Spain will not swerve from God', translated Ventura, and said to the man, '*Naturalmente: así es. . . Manos a la obra, ahora: limpieza.*'

'*Es magnífico*', said the man again, as if enchanted for a moment with his own private vision, then, moving his hands as if they held a machine-gun in a scything motion, '*Falange fusil-ará a todos, a todos. . . Es terrible estar entre cuatro paredes. . .*'

'*Arriba Falange*', said Ventura, turning his back on him.

'Long live Mussolini', said the man.

'The bastard,' said Ventura, 'wants to shoot half of Spain to get his own back for the days he's spent shut up in his house. He'll be the chemist, or the Municipal doctor or the brother of the rural dean. These folk are the power behind Fascism in our towns back home, in other words: middle-class gents.'

They had placed a radio in the square in front of the church, it was coughing and spluttering and giving off sounds like guitar strings breaking, then, as every evening, a voice announced, '*El excelentísimo señor general don Gonzalo Queipo de Llano, gobernador de la Andalucía y jefe del glorioso ejército del sur. . .*' The *charla* began. 'Degenerate!' said Ventura, 'He's the man who's taught me all the nasty Spanish words I know.'

II

Zaragoza was full of prostitutes. I had never seen a city with so many; they buzzed about the bars like flies; every soldier found one for himself, and there were thousands of soldiers in Zaragoza. When the Republicans shelled, bars and restaurants suddenly turned into convent refectories with all those women invoking the Virgin of Pilar, reeling out their prayers, one or two taking out their rosaries and going down on their knees. The change over of a group of half-drunk, happy women into a mournful bunch of dutiful Christians had a special flavour to it, a pleasure made up of many things, like a dish made up of many different ingredients which you would never eat on their own, but whose individual taste you no longer recognize when combined.

Zaragoza was protected by the Virgin of Pilar, who had performed a famous miracle before, in the days of Napoleon. She continued giving her protection with the rank of Captain-General of the troops of Aragón (the Falangist ones), with a concomitant salary. My mother crossed herself when I told her about the Madonna of Pilar having a rank and salary in the army: she thought I had made up such a piece of out-and-out devilry to annoy her, as the Madonna takes no part nor rank in wars in which young men are killed, and then a salary. . .! She was only convinced after I had sworn on the souls of the family departed that such a thing could be. But as the Madonna could not draw a salary, so some priest would draw it, thus she did not really look after the Aragón troops, or rather, she thought about the troops of Aragón and about a Sicilian like me and about all those fighting the war in Spain, praying to God to have him end the slaughter.

Zaragoza was not many kilometres from the front lines, but the war seemed a thousand miles away. Only the odd shelling, which caused no great damage, served to remind us of the war close by. The fixed lines made a change for us, it had become a war of positions, with trenches and outposts that were taken, left, then retaken. We had a difficult time at Belchite, but by the middle of September the front had, as they say, returned to normal: that is, we lost few men, and we killed few. The weather was good, there were some heavy downpours followed by bright, cloudless skies, the countryside could be clearly seen and the Ebro was like a living vein in the earth.

Facing us was Lister, whom we nearly took one day in a lightning attack; his things had been left behind and a monkey they said was his, which he took around with him for good luck, or perhaps it amused him. I have a photograph of Lister's monkey held by a legionary who looked just like it — the lieutenant had picked him on purpose — with us arranged in a semi-circle with smiling faces. Lister was the very devil, always escaping us, but he was a good commander. I have never seen a portrait of him, and don't know what he really had been, a farmworker or a philosopher. I would like to know what happened to him, and if he is still alive. There are so many things, not only about Lister, that I would like to know about that war.

Coming back to Zaragoza from the front, I always went in search of the same woman: she was called Maria Dolores; her husband had gone off with the Republicans, but her sentiments were otherwise, her father had supported the Catholic side and the Reds had shot him. She hoped her husband was already dead, and was certain he would never come back.

Maria Dolores was full of hate, she wanted all those who fought for the Republic killed, in revenge for her father and to make sure her husband did not get away. Mussolini was a man who had pitched into the Spanish war for her, to free her from a husband who had gone to the dogs through drink and politics and to avenge the death of her father; she went to bed with Italians as if to do Mussolini a favour in return. I would never have managed to make friends with a Spanish man who was as full of hate as she was, but with a woman it was different; her hate became, for me, an act of love, and not because a love for me grew in her from a hate for others, but because I actually liked her hate, because she made a magic out of it, and because it made her something of an enchantress. The pleasure of love is very complicated: greater when there is a dark sense of damnation in the woman, a mysterious, evil centre to her being: and I mean the pleasure of love, because love itself is something simpler and clearer. That woman attracted me more than any other, not only because with her body, her eyes, her hair, her voice, she 'got my blood up', as they say in my home town when a woman is irresistibly attractive, but also because she loved violently all that my conscience rejected.

In those days, the thought that my wife might be unfaithful, and was perhaps being unfaithful, did not sear me any more as it had in the early days of my being away: between the raw pleasure of love, complicated and turbid, and the painful clarity which the war was beginning to acquire in my eyes, I found a strange equilibrium. I felt indifferent to, and far away from, the life I had lived before, as if it no longer belonged to me, except for those facts which had brought me to Spain: poverty, the sulphur mine and Fascism. Memories of my father, his death, and the vision of my mother at sixty, with her arthritic pains, going as a charwoman to the houses of the rich, never left me: but only because I had had the brutal revelation of having come to Spain to fight against their hope, against the hope of people like them and like myself. My wife, however, was becoming an image of love which, with every passing day, with every letter I received, was moving farther away, becoming insignificant and out of focus. Her letters were wandering and stupid; she told me about her domestic troubles as if I had gone on holiday, not to war: how it weighed on her having to queue up to draw the money I earned for her with that war, how she passed some days in a solitude enough to drive you mad, how my mother scolded her for certain expenditures she thought useless or excessive; and she told me about the dresses she sewed and about the people she met. She wrote an entire letter telling me about Mussolini who had passed through the local station, and how she had gone to see him, how he was a really good-looking man, better than in the photographs, with a likeable, bronzed face. So many people had gone down to the station, that, after a while, Mussolini had become worried about the youth squads and the little girls of Italy who might have ended up under the wheels of the train, if pushed by the crowd.

On the other hand, my mother wrote that she prayed for me, and for all the young men like me, she prayed the war would soon be over, and she always said, 'I don't know what your wife says about me, but don't think I act the mother-in-law with her, I only advise her to save up and think how bitterly earned the money is they give her.' My mother could not imagine the bitterness in carrying a war, remorse and shame in your heart. She was thinking about war's bitter work, the firing squads and the bombs, and about the death which could have plucked me away from one minute to the next. As my mother did not know how to write, she dictated her letters to a neighbour, who, after a while, amused herself on her own account by telling me about what was happening in town. I knew my mother well, and she would never have written to her son fighting in a war about how the Feast of S. Calogero had gone or about the Bishop who had come to the parish to give Confirmation.

I had married for love, which, in Sicilian towns, is a business of furtive glances and wordless meetings. You take your usual way down a street and after a time you notice a beautiful girl on a balcony. The day before, perhaps, she had been just a child, but from that day on, passing by, you look up at that balcony, and every day she looks back at you; and then, every Sunday, you go to midday mass just to see her; and in your eyes she becomes still more beautiful. You are in love, and, looking back at you, so is she. And, except that she wants you, you know nothing of her thoughts, her life and the things she likes and the things she fears; you know nothing of her heart, of her way of feeling happiness or pity for the world. But love should be born from the quiet discovery that a man and a woman are well-matched for facing up to the suffering — above all, the suffering — of life; for being together in life, knowing about pain, and helping one another in this knowledge; for being together in pleasure, which is only a moment, but which leaves us with our hearts naked, understanding ourselves better at heart. In this way, the meaning of love became clear to me, and I found that I did not love my wife. So I satisfied myself in pleasure, a soldier's woman was enough for me, a woman who had the evil of that war inside her. I went in search of her like a man dying of thirst, but after several days, returning to the front, I left her with a sense of relief. It gave me a sour pleasure thinking that other soldiers might take my place in her *cuarto*, and feel the hate in her, the dark pleasure of her hate.

Ventura passed from one woman to another. Once he went with Maria Dolores, too. They had left me at the bar and they went off together. I suffered a bit over it, but because Ventura was my friend, not because she went with others. Thinking about it, it was stupid: Ventura wanted to enjoy himself at Zaragoza, and wanted to forget about the war. Every time we returned to the front he became more sullen and angry, he quarrelled and became still more incautious in the way he spoke. His desire to be off seemed to have passed.

That autumn, on the front lines of Aragón, the war was not as hard as it had been at Guadalajara and Brunete; the black days would come with winter. We took part in small actions, sometimes I had the impression they were making us run about like a dog trying to catch its tail, whirling us around like a top. There must have been some confusion in our orders, and perhaps Lister knew it. One night, we were about to go to sleep in a farmhouse near Zaragoza, when they woke us with an alarm: the news spread that enemy cavalry had infiltrated our lines and had occupied a village in our sector. We did an hour's march, in darkness you could have cut with a knife, it was so thick and seemed almost solid around each one of us, and we felt the damp night soaking right into our bones. We reached a village so full of dogs we seemed to be moving in the middle of a flock of sheep. Everyone petted them, saying '*Perro, perrito*', and, in the darkness, threw down the pieces of bread he had in his pocket, for fear of being bitten. You could hear the clack of their jaws in the dark as they bit into the pieces of bread, and the violent gnawing, because the bread must have been as hard as bone. They told us to halt. The next village, four or five kilometres up the road, was the one the enemy cavalry had occupied. It was three o'clock, so the officers said we could settle down for some rest until dawn. In my memory (and then, too) the movement of men and dogs in the darkness, the calling to the dogs, the swearing and the dogs' gnawing seemed like something from out of a dream.

A livid dawn rose, the dogs yawning like we did. A couple of motorcyclists left. Half an hour, an hour. . . They did not return. The officers had a consultation; a lieutenant came towards us, a young Sicilian who was always next to the major, whom I found likeable, and said, 'Twenty or so men come with me, let's have a little look what's happening.' Ventura was the first to step forward, I was the next. The sun was already beating down by the time we came in sight of the village; in Spain and Sicily, the autumn sun is sometimes worse than that of summer. There was a deathly silence. It would not have been the first time that Republican soldiers had taken a village and then gone to sleep without leaving sentries, heavy with fatigue and wine, and had themselves captured by us in their sleep.

But there was the fact of our two motorcyclists, who had not returned. Taking all precautions, we moved into the first houses. Nothing. We came out into a little square as if on tiptoe, and there was a priest with three or four old women: the priest and old women of the first mass, just like a Sicilian village. Seeing us appear at the street corner, rifles at the ready, they nearly died with fright. For my part, I have never felt so much joy in seeing a priest as I did on that occasion, because it meant there were no Reds in the village — or there would have been no priest there. He had become like a slab of salt cod with the shock, and it took a little while before he could manage to return the lieutenant's greeting. The lieutenant asked about the Reds, because, he said, the village had been put down as being in their hands. The priest gave a start, instinctively gathering up his skirts, as priests and women do when they are about to run. It needed all the lieutenant's patience to get him to calm down and tell him that there was not even talk of Reds in the village, nor in the neighbouring ones. And the motorcyclists? The priest could give us no news of them, either. Again, we set off down the road, where there was another, larger village a few kilometres further on. There were two motorbikes in front of a large house, and a sentry: over the front door was a wooden board saying 'Command Post'. Furious, the lieutenant rushed through the door, coming out five minutes later with a major, who was saying, in a complaining voice, 'Look, son, I can't understand a thing around here, they all do just as they like, officers and men. Yesterday, a lieutenant says, "Major, Sir, I'm off", and I say, "Off? Where to?", "I don't feel well", he says, "I'm off to hospital", so I say, "Hospital my. . . You're in better health than I am, it's me they should be taking away on a stretcher", but he says, "I'm off, I'm ill." Now what should I do? Ruin him, that's what I should do. And that business with the lieutenant was just one of many: I won't tell you how many troubles I go through. Here, they're the biggest layabouts, it seems they pick them on purpose for me, one after another, "We'll give them to Major D'Assunta, he's patient, his nerves are all right", but it's the opposite, my nerves are stretched like guitar strings. I'm going to get one of them and fix him for good, I'll ruin him.'

'And the enemy cavalry?' asked the lieutenant.

'That, son, is another matter. Or rather, no, it's the same thing. I've got to do everything myself here. I have to go on the ramparts every day and have a look around with the binoculars, and that's nothing, I do plenty of other things I shouldn't have to. Anyway, yesterday, I have a look over on that side' (he gestured toward the village where we had met the priest) 'and see men on horseback and others on foot, carrying planks in the valley bottom where there's a stream, they were bringing them from the foothills, up there, down to its banks. So I think, "Oh, they want to fool me, do they?" I call everyone in to make their reports, and one says, "What's this tale about the planks? I knew about that a couple of days ago." You follow me, son? A couple of days! And he keeps it to himself, like he's seen a nice young bit of stuff in Via Toledo. They do just as they like, I tell you. A war? They think they're on their holidays in Capri. Anyway, I send a coded message, "Infiltrations of enemy cavalry". Now you're here, we'll neutralize 'em in no time. . .'

He passed a hand over his face, which had a few days' growth on it, and said, 'Have you got a barber among your men? Mine hasn't been seen for two days, son of a gun.'

We sent the two motorcyclists back, and the rest came up to join us. Our major made a survey with his binoculars, and sent out patrols. They came back in a cheerful mood, because in the valley bottom they had met up with a detachment of mounted *requetés* and labourers who were working on building a bridge. Major D'Assunta , clean shaven and happy, said, 'Well, that's not so bad, I was really worried they wanted to fool me.' He then began to relate to our major the troubles he had been through with his men, but more to be cheerful than to complain about them; he was like a father telling about the naughty escapades his children got up to, who would have disliked it if they no longer did them. 'Poor lads, they've been in this village

over a month, they've got used to it, they've got a *novia*, a nice
warm bed, fresh eggs, and get themselves well thought of by
the whole village here, and they think well of me, too, you
know, they get me angry at times, but they think well of
me. . . "Major, Sir, milked with my own hands": a nice beaker
of milk. . . "Major, Sir, it's still warm": an egg. . . "Major, Sir,
some of the *chorizo* you like": a sausage long as your arm. . .'
Major B. (I remember his name, but prefer not to write it,
because there are other things I want to say about him), who
commanded our battalion, looked at him like a mastiff, as if he
would tear him apart from one minute to the next. Major D'Assunta interrupted his account of the affectionate attentions of his
men to ask, 'Do you like *chorizo?*'

That was the last straw, Major B.'s anger erupted, 'I haven't
come to Spain to eat *chorizo*, I've come to fight a war, and fight
well.'

'Of course,' said Major D'Assunta, 'we're fighting a war,
who says we're not? We're fighting a war, what else have we
come to Spain to do, have the Festival of Piedigrotta? Perhaps I
don't fight it as well as you do, if here that means. . . Oh, forget
it. Well, anyway, I like *chorizo*.'

Major B. gave him the Roman salute and turned his back on
him.

'Tomorrow,' said Ventura, 'Major D'Assunta won't have
either his fresh eggs or his milk straight from the cow. I wonder
which front they'll send him to. . .'

Lorries came to collect us, and we returned to Zaragoza.

The first time I went from my home town to Palermo I was ten
years old. I was with my father and we were going to see off a
brother of his who was leaving for America. It was my first
train journey, and the train, the railwaymen, the stations and
the countryside were all a wonderful novelty for me; there and
back, I did the journey standing up, looking out of the window.
It was then I had the idea that I would be a railwayman when I
grew up: getting off the train a moment before it stopped, blowing the whistle, shouting out the name of the station, then
remounting with a sure-footed leap as the train was pulling out.
At a certain point in the journey, the railwayman shouted,
'Change for Aragona!' Those who were not going to Girgenti

got out, loaded with suitcases and bundles, to get onto another train that was waiting. In the game I later played with the other boys in the district, I kept that cry for myself; it was like the voice of destiny itself, which had some men born to live to the east of Aragona, and others to the west, although I could not say exactly what fascination the cry had for me then. I remember the town of Aragona as it appears from the train, a few minutes before it arrives at the station. It seems to rotate on a pivot, doing a half turn around the large mansion which dominates the town, with the bare countryside below. It is only a few kilometres from my town, but I have never been to Aragona — I only have an image of it from the train.

In the Aragon of Spain, a region which has many towns like the Aragona in the province of Girgenti, I remembered that far-off journey and the game I played afterwards with the other boys, and that cry always came floating across my mind, 'Change for Aragona', just like a tune or the words of a song spring to mind, and develop and come in variations for days. I thought, 'Change, my life is changing trains. . . or, I'm about to get on the train of death. . . Change for Aragona. . . change here. . . change here. . .' and the thought became a musical obsession. I believe in the mystery of words, I believe that words can become life, or destiny, in the same way that they can become beauty.

So many people study, go to university and become good doctors, engineers and lawyers, or become civil servants, M.P.s and government ministers: and I would like to ask these people, 'Do you know what the war in Spain was? Do you know what it really was? Because if you don't, you won't ever understand what's happening under your own noses, you won't understand Fascism, Communism, religion or mankind, you won't ever understand anything about anything, because all the world's mistakes and its hopes were concentrated in that war, like a lens concentrates the sun's rays, causing fire, and Spain was lit by all the world's hopes and its mistakes, and the same fire's splitting the world today.'

When I went to Spain, I was barely literate, I could just about read the newspaper, the *History of the Royal Families of France* and write a letter home. When I came back, it seemed as if I could read the most difficult things a man could think and write about. And I know why Fascism is not dying, and I am sure I have met all the things which should die with its death, and I know what will have to die in me and in all other men so that Fascism will die out for ever.

'*Hoy España, mañana el mundo*', said Hitler from the propaganda postcards the Republicans dropped: they pictured him with an arm outstretched over Spain, with squadrons of aircraft appearing to drop from his gesture, and a wreath of weeping children's faces over the Spanish earth. 'Today Spain, tomorrow the world', said Hitler, and I felt they were not words invented by the propaganda machine, the whole world *would* become Spain; breaking the bank there would not mean that the game was all over. No one, except for Mussolini, wanted to play all his cards there. The Germans were testing their new, accurate instruments of war, while Italy was throwing in everything: new fighter planes and old Austrian cannon, tanks good enough for the regimental review and machine-guns from 1914, and the poor soldiers with their footcloths, puttees, and the grey-green uniforms that became as hard as a crust in the rain: the wretched unemployed of the Two Sicilies. And the best of it was that not even the Francoist Spanish were grateful for all our efforts, they had even made a joke of our initials, *Corpo Truppe Volontarie* [Volunteer Corps] with the phrase *Cuando Te vas?* which means 'When are you leaving?', as if we were in Spain simply to annoy them. I would like to have seen them get by alone, all those priests, country gentlemen, pious women, young men of the parish club, career officers and the few thousand *carabineros* and Civil Guard — I would like to have seen them against the peasants and miners, against the Red hate of the Spanish poor. Or perhaps it was humiliating and shameful for them to have us see that misery and that blood, like being forced to have your friends see how poor you are at home and how mad your family is: there was all of Spain's irrational pride in that wish to have us leave. There were even those with Franco who secretly felt unhappy and anxious about what they saw happening on their side, it was not merely a few who said, 'If only José were here, everything would be different,' Without José Antonio they were not convinced by the general's revolt: '*no es justo que el conde Romanones poséa todas las tierras de Guadalajara*', and they were sadly certain that Franco would not take a hectare of land off

Romanones. They felt shame at tearing Spain apart with foreign weapons and soldiers, with the Germans crushing whole cities with bombs just like someone out on a walk might squash an anthill, and with the Moors — led by the Spanish — coming to avenge themselves, after centuries, on the sons of that Christian Spain that had expelled them. When the prostitutes and bourgeois gentlemen of a captured city watched the Moors march past and applauded, '*Moros, moritos*', I could read the mortification and hate in the faces of some of the Spanish soldiers. As far as we Italians were concerned, the fact that we accused them of putting too many people up against the wall — and it seems our commanding officers were continually protesting about it — provoked antagonism in those who wanted the firing squads, and shame in those who did not, and so there was not a single Spaniard who was not upset by our presence.

All these feelings and reactions became intensified at Zaragoza, perhaps because of the prostitutes and next to a woman, prostitute or not, a man wants to be himself, and then there was the wine, that moment of truth that wine gives before the glass that makes you drunk. And in Zaragoza there were Moors and Germans, *requetés* and Falangists, Aragonese and Andalucians, and among the Italians too there was the dyed-in-the-wool Fascist from the north, who had enrolled to come and give the anti-Fascists in Spain a good hiding, who regarded the Sicilian unemployed in the same way that the Castilian soldier regarded the Moors. So with wine inside him and a woman by his side, everyone was either at his best or his worst.

I would say that the least peasant in my home district, the most 'benighted', as we say, that is, the most ignorant, the one most cut off from a knowledge of the world, if he had been brought to the Aragon front and had been told to find out which side people like himself were on and go to them, he would have made for the Republican trenches without hesitation, because for the most part, on our side, the countryside remained uncultivated, while on the Republican side the peasants worked away even under shell fire. As far as I can gather, the Republicans had divided the land up among the peasants and, seeing that the young ones were fighting the war, the old had attached themselves to their piece of land with so much fury that not even the shelling and the thought that the cultivated land might become disfigured with trenches from one moment to the next, could keep them away from it. Looking from a hill with binoculars on clear mornings, you could see the peasants beyond the Republican lines, with their black trousers, bluish shirts and straw hats, guiding the plough which a pair of mules, or a single mule, was pulling behind it. The ploughs were made in the shape of a cross, with a ploughshare no bigger than an axehead — the same that the peasants in my area still use — which makes a furrow like a mere scratch, barely turning over the dry crust of the earth. Ventura had a pair of binoculars, and I loved to watch the ploughing, when I could forget the war and feel as if I were in the countryside around my home town. It is a beautiful countryside in autumn: the whirr of partridges suddenly rising up, the slight mist from which the earth emerges, brown and blue. Aragon is a land of hills, the mist gets trapped between them and they become more beautiful in the mist and sunshine; not that it is a really beautiful landscape, which seems beautiful straightaway to everybody, it is beautiful in a special way, you would need to be born there to realize its beauty and love it.

The front was a zig-zag line, like the braid on a general's peaked cap. There had been no great movements from the start of the war, even the business of Belchite had not brought about anything new. There were actions which were like a fracas in hell, which seemed as if they would drag the front so much further forward, or even backwards, up to the houses of Zaragoza, but it all ended in nothing. We went to take possession of trenches that had belonged to the Reds the day before, or else the Reds would come and occupy ours, and then, again, we would go back to the trenches of the day before. Ventura liked this kind of exchange because he found American books and newspapers in the Republican trenches and he was in love with anything that came from America.

This situation lasted until the first days of December. Except for having a city nearby, with the rest and women that Zaragoza offered, it was no great advantage being on the Aragon front. When a war stagnates for months in the same place, even though the risk to life is reduced to stray bullets and clashes between patrols, in your throat you feel the nausea of war, of what is really nauseating in war, just like when the doctor sticks an instrument down your throat and makes you feel sick. The earth seems to be decomposing, there is a smell of rotten eggs and urine, as if men had carved trenches and approaches into the diseased body of the earth, or into a putrescent growth. In fact, that smell of death comes not from the earth, but from man making his foxhole there, from man reverting to being a wild animal, digging his hole there, and like every other animal, tainting it with his smell. In this sense, I think there is nothing more degrading for man than trench warfare: he is forced to live in his own savage smell, and swallow his food while the earth exhales the breath of vomit and faeces, and drink greedily the water that seems to have collected, drop by drop, in the slobbery drain of a water trough.

Snow, when it falls and covers roofs and countryside, brings cheer, because it gives everything a smooth profile and a luminous aspect — when it falls on my town at home it warms the heart, and you rediscover your own home as if there were an unusual grace to living inside it — but on a battlefield of trenches, snow brings despair, because a man looks out from the trenches with the same eyes as a fox on the edge of its hole.

I think that the offensive the Republicans launched against Teruel, with all that it cost me, saved me from a hideous winter in the trenches. I would have gone mad there in those two months of December and January; it was nothing but a howling wind above a world of white death.

The town of Teruel is high up, like Enna, and no larger than Enna. Right from the beginning of the war it had been in the hands of the Falangists. It seems the Civil Guard had butchered the Reds there, not only those in the town, but also the Republican soldiers who rushed to occupy it, tricked by the Civil Guard pretending to be still faithful to the Government, who then mowed them down like flies. It was a good position for keeping Valencia under the threat of attack, and so the Republicans decided to take it off Franco.

It was a strange war, on the Republican side (but I would like to have been on it), it was as if it were words which determined actions, a little like in religion or poetry, where words make things sacred or beautiful: like the bread that becomes the body, blood and soul of Jesus Christ, or a countryside or town that you looked at vacantly at first, and then, because poetry has passed over it, you find beautiful. I am not sure if I can manage to be clear: what I mean is that, from certain phrases they wrote on walls, or in manifestos and flysheets, I had the feeling of an event already determined, even before the action which was to determine it had begun, and I imagined those words assuming an inevitable truth and beauty in every soldier of the Republic, that they would become determination and strength. *Madrid es el baluarte del antifascismo. . . Teruel sera hoy nuestro. . .* slogans like these had a sense of destiny for me. Great streams of words issued forth, but after a while a few words or a slogan would come up as if on a high wave and engrave themselves with the power of truth or faith. *El comisario del XIX Cuerpo de Ejercito* said some wonderful things in a proclamation — the attack on Teruel had already been launched — and the Commissar said, '*Que en estas tierras ásperas de Aragón, sea donde florezcan las primicias de nuestra vittoria definitiva.*' But, flowing along like that, they were only words; it was the more naked necessary ones which had certainty: *Teruel sera hoy nuestro.*

So on 15th December 1937, the Republicans launched their attack against Teruel. Not that it was a surprise for us, because it was a war in which there were no surprises, for either side. There must have been as many spies in Spain as there were worms in a rotten cheese. In actual fact, the Republicans had made a move before the 15th. In the preceding days, we had had Anarchist soldiers opposite us in the trenches, who used to amuse themselves by letting off a thousand or more shots, always over our heads, first throwing out brotherly invitations with their megaphones, and then furious insults. On the whole, they were men who would have come over for a round of cards, if we had invited them, and although they persisted in making their bullets whistle a good few inches over our heads, it was more from the irresistible temptation to squeeze a trigger, which a Spaniard feels as soon as a rifle is put into his hands, than for trying to kill any of us. In actual fact the Anarchists had a decided preference for hand grenades: it was only distance which persuaded them to use rifles. As they yielded to the temptation to shoot or launch a grenade, even at the most inopportune moments, we lost count of the times their sorties ended in bloody defeat, especially those at night, when a rifle shot or grenade explosion warned us just in time for us to welcome

them with a hellish fire. But it is not to be discounted that there
was someone among them who specifically wanted to warn us.
All Franco's 'Fifth Columnists' went to infiltrate the Anarchist
battalions, to profit from the fact that the real Anarchists were
so mad and showed such absurd courage that they would not
notice if, when one of their number put us on our guard, it was
either through impatience or betrayal.

I liked the Anarchists, the real ones, of course. It is not that
you can win a war with people like that; on the contrary you are
bound to lose. From the way things turned out, I am of the
opinion that if the Republic had had more Communists and
fewer Anarchists, Franco would not have won. Just as you cannot live with other people if you say everything you think about
them, so you cannot fight a war like the one in Spain, exploding
bombs under everything you hate. And the Anarchists hated
too many things: bishops and Stalinists, statues of saints and
kings, monasteries and brothels. They died more for things they
hated than for those they loved. The reason why they had insane
courage and a thirst for self-sacrifice was because each one of
them felt a little like Jesus Christ and saw the world redeemed
by his own blood. And you can understand how, if someone
wants to have himself crucified, and be simply a picture of sacrifice, he has no need of officers telling him when it is time to
move and when it is time to halt. I could be wrong, because my
judgement comes from their actions, as I know nothing of their
doctrines, but the Anarchist thinks of himself as a bomb, made
to be thrown and exploded; and just as in action he is impatient
to launch the grenade in his hand against the first sign or movement of the enemy, so he is impatient to launch and explode
himself against the things he hates. Opposite him in the
trenches, you could have asked him for his rations, in the name
of your hunger, and he would have brought them for you
gladly, you could even have asked him for his rifle, if yours was
jammed, but a minute later, even without his rifle, he would
have come over to attack your trenches with all his hate.

Even in a war like that there had to be hypocrisy, and the
Communists had it. If they had been holding the reins from the
very beginning, there would have been *Te Deums* in the Republic's churches, not target practices, and there would have been
wagonloads of priests to sing mass for the Republic's victories

with no hesitation, instead of ending up in front of a platoon of Republican soldiers. The Spanish bourgeoisie, the good ones who go to mass, killed the peasants in their thousands simply because they were peasants, nothing more, and the world closed its eyes in order not to see; but the first priest to fall under the Anarchists' bullets, or the first church put to flames, made the world leap with horror and sealed the Republic's fate. At bottom, killing a priest because he is a priest is more just than killing a peasant because he is a peasant, because a priest is a soldier for his faith, whereas a peasant is only a peasant. But the world prefers not to know this.

Teruel was an episcopal seat, and the Bishop was in the town when the Republicans began to tighten their pincer of fire around it. There were women and children there, too, and soldiers and Civil Guards who could not have escaped, but the whole of Franco's Spain protested only for the Bishop. At one point they said the Reds had shot him, but I read of the Bishop of Teruel's death about a year later, when the Anarchists killed him before they crossed over into France. Seeing that even a Bishop cannot die twice, it is clear that the Republicans did not kill him when they took Teruel.

When we occupied a town, and the middle-class gentlemen came out, limp and pale, from their hideouts, and the priests, with their soutanes hanging about them as if they were hung on a clotheshorse, their anxiety having made them so thin, and the rich ladies, with their eyes huge in faces sharp with fear, and the gentlemen and ladies all came out as if to watch a gala bullfight, with the priests ready to give the last rites to those Republicans who wished to avail themselves of it; when, as one day in Zaragoza, I saw the people swarming out of doors from the Grand Hotel, and thought it was for some smart celebration, and instead they were going to see the prisoners about to be shot filing past: a hundred men tied together in threes, and the Moors around them with their rifles at the ready, and an officer at the head of the parade with a long-barrelled pistol in his hand, and a priest wearing his stole (and there were even young boys among the prisoners, walking and stumbling along like sleep-walkers, from the steady pace of the other condemned men, pulling them along in jerks on that terrible march); when I saw all those things, the thought that the Republicans might return, even for a few hours, gave me bitter consolation. Of course, if I had been on the Republican side, and had seen priests and gentlemen tied together going to the firing squad, I would have been shocked by it: but it was different seeing people like myself, men who had left the pickaxe and the plough to fight their war, going to their death. So I found a certain justice in the fact that the Republicans should take Teruel, that they should surprise men who thought they were safe and victorious, the bourgeoisie and Civil Guards who had vented themselves ferociously on working-class people. A civil war is not a stupid thing, like a war between nations, the Italians fighting the English, or the Germans against the Russians, where I, a Sicilian sulphur miner, kill an English miner, and the Russian peasant shoots at the German peasant; a civil war is something more logical, a man starts shooting for the people and the things he loves, for the things he wants and against the people he hates; and no one makes a mistake about choosing which side to be on — only those who start shouting 'Peace!' are wrong. And I think that, of all Mussolini's faults, that of having sent over thousands of Italian poor to fight the Spanish poor can never be forgiven him. Despite its atrocities, a civil war is a kind of *hora de la verdad*, a moment of truth, as the Spanish call the bullfight's climax. Working-class people, for example, say 'Cops', despising the men who are the arm of the law, the men whose job it is to ensure that people keep the peace: so their scorn appears to be unjust and uncivil, the more so if you remember that the cop comes from the working-class. But a civil war makes you realize immediately what a cop is, and why the working-class despise him. I have often asked myself what reasons the Civil Guard had for being on Franco's side: they were betraying their oath of loyalty to the Republic and betraying the people whose sons they were; nor can you think they were on Franco's side through force of circumstance, fear of their officers, or simply through obedience, because they deserted the Republic at risk to their lives, a few at a time or in groups. The only reason can be this: they were cops, with all the arrogance and nastiness that the working-class attibute to them, and they knew that in Franco's Spain they could carry on being cops, striking fear into people, and from the dregs of humanity that they were, they could rise up before the working-class in quivering authority.

The Spanish say 'With respect', when they happen to mention the Civil Guard, like Sicilian peasants do when they mention certain part of the body or unclean things; but not all the Spanish, you understand.

The death knell sounded for many of the Civil Guard (with respect) at Teruel. But, to their credit, I should say that in war they were no cowards, they knew how to fight and die, too — moreover, during the whole war, I never saw a Spaniard show any fear of death. From the moment they were taken prisoner, they accepted their fate with indifference, some even looked at us with ironic sympathy. The youngest — and there were many boys in that war — you could see would have cried if they had been on their own, but they were able to model their behaviour on the self-control of their elders. Ventura said that, in the face of death, the Spanish were the most dignified people in the world.

When an army launches a huge offensive, as the Republicans did against Teruel, the enemy army on either side can do very little to stop it, unless there is a prolonged resistance by the forces against whom the offensive is directed. I know nothing about the art of war, and make this observation from my single experience of Teruel, but we were at the side of Lister's division, so to say, like a dog that runs by the side of a car: the car accelerates and the dog sees it can do no more and comes to a stop by the edge of the road, panting, In little less than a week, the Republicans had taken Teruel, and it required another week before we could then seriously begin to attack Lister ourselves.

For snow and wind, I thought that Spain could not have produced more than it had done at Guadalajara, but around Teruel it was worse. I felt I was made of glass, and the wind was cutting into me with diamond tips, even the images the pupils gathered seemed fractured into a spider's web, as if they were on a pane of glass that had been hit by an invisible bullet. I felt these sensations, perhaps, because of the sound the wind continually made, similar to the noise glaziers make when cutting glass, and from the brittle crunch of the snow beneath our feet, and from the stinging tears in my eyes.

I passed the most atrocious winter of my life below Concud, which Lister was holding like a guard dog. All the images of peace and home, of midnight mass, the game of cards around the brazier, the smell of capon boiling in the kitchen, the colour of oranges on the white table cloth, rose up in me, making a contrast with the reality of the war. Our celebration, in a stable half destroyed through shelling, was some acid wine, which still tasted of must, and a couple of packets of American cigarettes. Each man saw himself reflected in the others, with his long beard, glazed eyes and blanket over his shoulders. We were figures to make you think more of prisoners than combat troops, and we felt a little like prisoners, not so much because the Reds were winning and we could have fallen into their hands from one moment to the next, but because of the war they were making us fight, both those of us who intuitively understood and those of us who would never understand: it was not our war, either for those who thought it a good idea to fight against Franco, or for those who thought it a problem that the Spanish should settle among themselves. That night I became aware that, in each soldier, the war gave rise to thoughts which, for one reason or another, revealed the true face of Fascism: for most it was a face of madness, the madness of a man who, with the help of cowards and clowns, was directing the destinies of millions of Italians, and who could say to what precipice he was leading them.

In Ventura, Christmas and the wine produced a rigorous logic. There was, he said, a thread linking the madness of Mussolini and that of the millions of people going to church at that moment for the birth of the Infant Jesus, and this thread was in the hands of the crafty: they gave a tug in the thread, and the war in Spain exploded. 'Jesus Christ', he said, 'was born in a stable like this. Along come the crafty and put up columns of gold around the stable, and a roof of gold over it, and make a church. Then they build their mansions by the side of it, and make a city, the city of the crafty. Along comes the peasant from the country and sees how beautiful the city is. "I'd like to live here", he says, and the crafty take him to church and let him see the stable, and say, "You've got a stable like this and you want to come and live in a mansion? Look where Jesus wished to be born, to be the same as you, now don't you go and offend him by leaving your stable." The peasant goes back to his stable and thinks again, "And if Jesus Christ wished to be born in a stable," he says, "perhaps it means that it's not right to keep men in stables", and he goes to the mansions and says, "Let's organize things, because to me they don't seem to be going according to the word of God." The crafty get angry, and say, "If you really want to reason this matter, we can satisfy you right away", and they call for Mussolini. . .'

'And Mussolini begins to reason with a cudgel', interrupted a man from Palermo. 'It's just like that. I remember one day, I wasn't yet ten years old, my father came home with his face all strained and was sick for the whole day, he was dying, they'd given him so much castor oil, " I wanted to talk reason with someone who said they should string up the railwaymen on strike," he said, "and the man called his mates over and they beat me up." It's like that as soon as you begin to reason, the fists start flying.'

'Let's forget all this sort of talk,' said the sergeant , a Neapolitan with a tribe of children, a wife and in-laws to support, and whose troubles the whole battalion had come to know about by then, 'Let's forget it, it's Christmas, it's a family festival, Christmas and Easter with your own folk, let's think about our families.'

'And what do you want to think about them?' someone joked. 'Right now your in-laws are celebrating, perhaps they're saying, "Here's to the idiot who goes to war to support us!".'

'You don't know my in-laws,' said the sergeant, 'you think you're joking, you say it just to get me annoyed, but they really do think like that. If I die tomorrow, they'll think they've hit the jackpot. . . for pity's sake don't make me think about it.'

'Then don't think about it,' said Ventura, 'think about Mussolini instead. What would you say to him if you saw him appear right now in this stable?'

'I'd say, Duce, we're one with you!'

'And Mussolini would say, "Bravo, carry on working in this little war, and in the meantime I'll prepare another one for you, perhaps even a bigger one."'

'Mussolini's always thinking about wars', said a soldier from Catania.

'Long live our Duce!' said the Neapolitan. 'Let's salute the Duce, the founder of the Empire!'

On 28th December we attacked Lister in great strength, and the offensive broke against his positions like a demijohn against a wall, but we had news that on the opposite side the Republicans were giving way. The journalists who roamed among us, looking at Teruel through their binoculars began to write for their papers that Franco had retaken it. The war in Spain has taught me not to believe journalists: it is an occupation similar to that of a dealer, who would have you think a stone pit is a garden, and a horse ready for the knacker's yard is fit for a Galahad. Teruel was retaken at the end of January 1938, I am not sure of the exact day, but I am sure that the Republicans fought back until 18th January because after that date I left the Teruel front and the Spanish war for good.

In the early days of January, Ventura learned that the American Brigade had entered the Front. He did not tell me he intended to go away, only the news that the Americans were there; nor did I ask him any questions. The last time I saw him was the 15th. We were crawling up a slope, it was getting dark and in the air above our heads bullets from a machine-gun were exploding like sparks flying from a grindstone. They were special bullets, Ventura told me, 'They don't kill, but watch out for your eyes.' He was by the side of me, then, a moment later, he was no longer there, and I would never see him again.

The day before, something had happened which had disturbed me, and my admiration for him had grown. We had performed a small action of what is known as forming a bridgehead, and while we were among the trees, from which the shelling had stripped every branch, and the sky was riddled with thick snow, a Republican soldier came out of nowhere like a phantom; he had his rifle over his shoulders and his hands up, and he was saying, 'Fascist, Fascist', his face open in an anxious smile. Major B. opened fire, the smile on the soldier's face closed up like a zip fastener, his eyes those of someone who gets to the top of a ladder, then slips, and he fell down on his knees. Major B. was a great shot, firing two rounds, chopping his left hand flat over the pistol, like Matt Dillon: it was just as well he was only a couple of strides away. The scene happened as if in the flash of a photograph, for ten seconds we saw without understanding, just like a camera which is simply an eye, taking in images. When we took our eyes away from that body stretched out, face down, on the snow, and looked each other in the eye, the Sicilian lieutenant, the one I found likeable, was sagging at the knees, just like the Red soldier had a moment before under the Major's shots. You could read the horror and disgust in his face. Major B. was aware of this and glowered at him witheringly, the lieutenant pulled himself together again, and looked up into the sky to let the snow fall on his face. 'We can't afford the luxury of taking prisoners', said the Major, but the lieutenant's attitude had got on his nerves, you could see.

A couple of hours later, a patrol came back with two prisoners. I thought, 'The Major'll shoot them now', but he asked if they had been taken with their weapons in their hands, because Franco, ever since the days of Guadalajara, had promised to spare the life of any Reds who were captured unarmed. These two had been taken with their rifles in their hands. With his eyes, the Major fished for the Lieutenant, and fixed them on him as if to tell him he was doing this for his own good, and that he had to get used to certain things, and he ordered him to take the prisoners away and liquidate them, and have them buried as best he could. For a moment, the lieutenant was suspended on the threshold of fury, then he said, 'Yessir!' He called four of us, the nearest ones, and we went off with the prisoners in front. Ventura was not among those called, but he came with us. We, the six Italians who set out, were as much in fear as the two prisoners. They were two boys, who had understood they were going to die, and who had those silent tears, like children tired of crying out aloud who begin to sob silently. With his pistol in his hand, the lieutenant was trembling all over, the beads of sweat rolling down his face like tears. He looked at us fearfully, and then at the prisoners. After a hundred or so metres, he halted and said, 'Here.' We halted, and so did the prisoners. One of them asked, '*qué hora es?*' Ventura looked at his watch and said, '*las once y cinco*', and then he said, '*más adelante*', then, to the lieutenant, 'Farther on,' The lieutenant obeyed him, and we set off again.

Ventura said to the prisoners, '*Clama: nada que temer.*' The prisoners looked at him with the eyes of animals who are suffering unutterably, without understanding.

'*Alto!*' said Ventura, after a while. We were behind a hillock, where brambles were wound into skeins with snow. The lieutenant and Ventura looked each other in the eyes, then Ventura turned to the prisoners and said, '*con cuidado: a la izquierda*', pointing with his left hand, to the left, indicating that they could go.

The prisoners looked both hopeful and incredulous, but they did not move.

'*A vuestras casas*,' said Ventura, '*adios.*'

The boys looked at each other, understood, and made their way off towards the left, continually turning round to look at us. We stood as stiff as statues, and they disappeared behind a hedge. Ventura took the pistol from the lieutenant's hand, fired four shots into the snow, and handed the pistol back to him. Mechanically, the lieutenant replaced it in its holster.

'Let's have a cigarette', said Ventura.

The following afternoon, he disappeared, and they gave him up for dead, as they always find someone who says, 'I saw him fall.' But I searched for him looking at all the dead, one by one, and I never found him. Perhaps he really is dead, or he ended up as a prisoner, or he succeeded in finding the 15th Brigade, the American one. But I have asked all the Sicilians from America I have later met, and none has been able to tell me anything of Ventura. I hope he is alive with his relatives in the Bronx, and that he is a gangster, or sells beer and ice creams, as he used to promise himself and me. I hope he is alive and happy.

On 18th January, another huge offensive was launched. After the first rush forwards, our detachment was halted by a machine-gun shooting accurately at us among the trees, using those exploding bullets. I was behind the trunk of a tree, and as they say that the ostrich hides its head in the sand and thinks it has found shelter, so I, with my head under cover, thought the machine-gun could not get me. I was stretched out, face down, with my left hand, which had grown numb, also stretched out, but not under cover. It was as if the air around my hand suddenly became boiling water. What you feel, unexpectedly seeing your hand bloody, a hand that is no longer a hand, is like being sprung out of your body, just like it happens in the special effects in the cinema, when a person looks at himself in the mirror and his image there starts to move, while he remains still.

I dragged myself behind the lines. The fingers that were no

longer there pained me with a burning feeling, there was a curious sensation they were still there and that they were burning. In the field-hospital, the doctor began working on it and I no longer felt a thing. Perhaps I fainted for a moment.

Four days later, I was in hospital in Valladolid: the war in Spain was over for me.

III

The war in Spain was over for me: the snow, wind and sun of Spain, the days in the trenches, the attacks on them, on the farms, on the cottages, the battles of the French *carretera* and the Ebro, the anguishing spectacle of the prisoners, and the women of the executed men, in their black garb, with their sunken eyes, and the women of the Grand Hotels and the prostitutes: all these things were over for me. I would no longer see Major B., the *tercio* officers, the Civil Guards, the Navarrese and their Sacred Hearts and all the flags of the war; its hope, its hate and its death, which created flags and raised them up in the Spanish sky like a ship glowing with flags for a festival. But inside me, in my thoughts and in my blood, the war in Spain was still alive: each moment of my life would be imbued with the experience, in which by now my life-roots had taken hold, moving silently in that dark nutriment; my left arm was like a dead branch, but my life-roots were growing.

The idea of a tree came to me in a dream I had in hospital in Valladolid: I seemed to be as naked as in the inspection for recruits, a man with no face was touching me with ice-cold hands and talking as if to himself; from his words I learned that he thought of me as a tree; I wanted to tell him I was a man, but I had no voice, I felt the words bursting silently in my throat like soap bubbles. The man was touching my left hand, which, in the dream, was whole again, and saying, 'We'll have to cut it off, it's a dry twig. The tree'll put out new branches, new roots. . .' Without any voice, I shouted that my hand was good, that it was a hand, not a branch; but everything was growing dark and in the darkness I heard the click of pruning shears. I had many dreams in hospital in which I saw my hand whole, and they all ended with something falling on it and crushing it, or someone taking it off with a slash or cut and I would wake up with the pain.

I did not suffer greatly because of the missing hand, although I did a little when they took the dressing off, because with the bandages on I felt as if the hand was still there in some way. When they exposed the stump, whose colour and shape made you think of a fresh sausage where it is tied for hanging up, I was in despair for the first few days; I sweated in despair when dressing and undressing, with the buttons, shoelaces and puttees, and when lighting a cigarette. But after a few months, I was no longer aware of it, it was as if I had been born with just one hand — except when lighting a cigarette, even today I feel despair over that.

The war had condemned my body. But when a man has understood that he is an image of dignity, you can even reduce him to a stump, lacerate him all over, and he will still be the greatest thing God has created. When fresh troops arrive on a front and have been thrown into battle, the generals and journalists say, 'They've had their baptism of fire' — one of the many solemn and stupid phrases usually thrown out about the bestiality of war: but from the war in Spain, and the fire of the war there, I really do feel I have had a baptism: a sign of liberation in my heart; a sign of consciousness and of justice.

In the hours I spent outside the hospital in Valladolid, I went for walks alone along narrow Calle Santiago, letting my thoughts unwind, sitting down in Café Cantábrico, letting the hours fly by in thought. Sometimes my thoughts became jumbled up, like skeins of yarn, with God and religion confusing everything, and I could no longer find the beginning of a thread and unravel them all.

I used to go to the College of St Gregory and enter the courtyard; my thoughts rose away from me, above words, above the stone and light made into harmony by the hand of man. The stone was no longer that of the *sierre*, and the light no longer that raw light which beats down on the countryside of Castile. I had come from a world in which man's heart was like mountain stone and the light ate up the faces of the dead. I discovered that, with his heart alive, with peace in his heart, a man could bind stone and light together in harmony, that he could uplift and order everything above himself.

Even the façade of St Gregory's captivated me. It was clustered with all the symbols of Spanish history, though I knew little of Spanish history; but that history and all the beauties of Spain were reflected there in that façade. Valladolid is a beautiful and ancient city, I could have stayed there for ever. I like small, ancient cities, and hope to end my days in a city like Valladolid, such as Siena: a city in which man's past is in every stone. But for me the war was over: on the 'loyalty and honour' with which I had served, on my lost left hand, the stamps of various command posts and embarkation points fell, and Spain became a last nocturnal sign of land and houses, as if it had become a land of peace again in the freezing February night. While the ship was moving off, a soldier sang ironically, 'When Spain sleeps in her clear, still night', which was a song of a few years before, one of those songs which brings the evil eye (in a manner of speaking, because I do not believe in it: but it is strange that in those years troubles came to those countries which had songs written affectionately about them: perhaps they put strange ideas into Mussolini's head). In the dark, a voice shouted out in fury, 'Oh, dry up!'

IV

Friends and relatives came to visit me. They showed a little concern over the hand I had lost, but they thought about my future
as a man with a pension, and found that, at bottom, you could
thank God that nothing worse had happened. Then they asked,
'What's Spain like?' almost as if I had gone on a pleasure trip
and that it was only because of an accident that I had one hand
less.

'Terrible', I replied.

They were surprised. The bullfights, the guitars, the women
behind the arabesques of the gratings, the jasmine and the processions: wasn't that Spain?

I had not heard a single guitar string quiver, I had left a
bullfight after the first bull, and I had seen the women drunk in
bars, not mysterious behind the gratings, and I had seen other
women turned sour, a black mass of tears behind command-
post doors, and I had not smelt the nocturnal smell of jasmine,
nor seen the processions of gold and incense.

'But it is beautiful, isn't it?' they insisted.

'It's like Sicily,' I said, 'beautiful towards the sea, full of trees
and vines, but in the interior, it's dry, 'baked-crust earth' as we
say, but with little bread.'

'Are the Spanish poor?'

'The poor are worse than we are, and the rich are frighten-
ingly rich. It takes a whole night by train to cross the lands of
one duke: it's a feudal estate that goes on forever.'

'Here's to his ruin', said my friends. 'Here Mussolini's turned
against the feudal system, says he'll divide the estates up among
the peasants. They've put posters up in the square, it's written
there, *The attack against the large estates*, in huge letters, so high.'

'While in Spain, we're fighting against those who want to
share the estates out among the peasants.'

'We're fighting for the rich in Spain?'

'For the rich, the priests and the coppers', I said.

'How can that be? For the priests and the cops, you can understand, but Mussolini treats the rich like pigs.'

'He can say all he likes in his speeches', I explained, 'but neither you nor I will see anything taken off the rich as long as Mussolini is around.'

My mother heard me making these comments, and gestured with her eyes and lips for me to shut up. When we were alone, she advised me to be cautious, and said that her heart stopped whenever people came round and I started to speak out. My Uncle Pietro said he no longer recognized me. I had left barely being able to string three words together in a row, and now there I was holding forth like a lawyer defending a lost cause: he said it was insane, after having lost a hand in war, to set about getting interned. My wife said nothing. The bank book and the ten thousand lire she had managed to save seemed to compensate for everything: the war, the missing hand, the repulsion she felt whenever she saw the stump or was touched by it. I used to feel her quiver, as if shuddering, whenever I touched her. There never had been any love between us; in the few months we had been together, we had had pleasure; now the maimed wrist, which was always cold, like a dog's nose, was enough to quench her desire. In the same way, certain flowers take on a burnt colour as soon as they are touched. She was beautiful, my desire for her took me like a flame; but as soon as it was satisfied, my life was empty of her, just as marks disappear from a blackboard when a cloth rubs over them. She had become more beautiful, her body was more perfect, and she pretended to have her moment of love with dedication; the more distant she was from me, the more she pretended to feel desire. She was a good wife. Or perhaps I was wronging her; I felt different towards her in my body and my mind, and imagined the trickery and deception in her. I condemned the excitement she showed over the bank book, and what could be done with the money, as greed, the grasping joy of a woman who only loves money, whereas perhaps it was the poverty from which we came that made the money gleam in her eyes, and my mother saw an untroubled future in that money, as well, and in the pension I was to be paid. But I suffered over that money; I saw myself as a hired assassin who had done his terrible deed and had been paid, a

Judas with his thirty pieces of silver. I could remember the moment, the one moment in the war, when the cold pleasure of killing took hold of me. The Republicans were retreating, and I fired, calculating my aim a little ahead of the running man I wanted to hit, and I remember the fierce joy in seeing a man fall heavily to the ground, hit. I cannot understand why the pleasure of killing should have come to me in that moment, both with such violence and such clarity. Above all, war is terrible for that, because in a moment it reveals us to be assassins, reveals the pleasure of killing in us, as violent as the desire to possess a woman. And I felt I had earned that money in the red bank book for that moment in which I had been an assassin. My mother would have understood me, perhaps, if I had told her that, in my eyes and to my mind, that money represented shame: for a war that was not mine, against people who were like me, and for the moment in which I had been an assassin. She would have understood, but according to her, with regard to my peace both present and eternal, if I went down on my knees and spoke my thoughts to a priest, taking a small part of the money as an offering for Our Lady, everything would be resolved. It is this that really annoys me about religion: that people can take their consciences to it as they would a dirty sheet to the wash, and once it is clean again, they put it over themselves and go to sleep. My wife did not even understand this washing of the conscience; she had an appetite for life and joy, and went to church like some people touch wood when they see an evil omen. The most that her effort to understand and her sense of beauty could bring her to was to copy a design in crochetwork. To have a child with her was a thought that filled me with horror.

In that period I was like a child with a new toy, a complicated toy, and I would not leave it alone, even for a moment. I had found that thinking about myself, and others, and about all the things in the world, was an inexhaustible game, like making an endless chain of numbers. Not that I was conscious of the discovery, or that I willingly pushed myself into this terrible game; it was a fact of nature, like a plant stunted in its pot that bursts out with roots and leaves when transplanted to the country. As children in primary school we had played a game with numbers: a nought after one and we read out 'Ten', another nought 'One hundred', and then more noughts, one after the other , until we reached numbers that not even the schoolmaster could read, and still we added more noughts — and thinking is like that. I felt like an acrobat who soars on the trapeze, he looks at the world in a thrill of flying, and then he turns, hands upside down, and sees death below him, the trapeze suspends him above a vortex of lights, human heads and the drum which beats the death roll. In a word, the fury of wanting to see everything from the inside came to me, as if each person, each object, each fact, was a book to be opened and read: a book is also an object, you can simply put it on a table and look at it, you can balance an uneven table with it, or even use it to hit someone over the head, but if you open it up and start to read, it becomes a world. Why then should not everything be opened and read and be a world?

What hurt me most and made me feel more alone was everyone's indifference to the dreadful things I had experienced, which Spain was still living through. I felt like someone who finds himself at a funeral on a festival day like S. Calogero or the Assumption; people are stupid with joy, the square is flowing with bright colours, and you walk behind the black-and-yellow carriage that holds a corpse, your heart gloomy with suffering, and you have to walk through a whole gallery of joy, and you feel bitter because of the festival and because of the people enjoying themselves. Perhaps all war veterans are stung by the indifference of others and shut themselves up within themselves until everyday life, work, the family, friends, reabsorb and assimilate them. But when someone comes back from a war like the one in Spain, with the certainty that his own house will burn with the same fire, he cannot manage to turn his experience into a memory and take up the sleep of daily habits: indeed, he wants everyone else to wake up, he wants them all to know.

But the others want to sleep. My town was like that, so poor, and mean in its poverty, that they all said to me, enviously, 'You've made some money, you can take things easy now.' Even the rich said the same. If I had not lost a hand, I would have gone back to the sulphur mine, which was also a Spain: men exploited like animals, and the fire of death lying in wait to spread out from a gash, and man with his cursing and hate, with his fragile hope, like white shoots of wheat on Good Friday, inside that cursing and hate. With my lost hand, however,

I was condemned to while away the time talking to the old men in the miners' club, or in long, solitary walks. I could talk endlessly to the old men, who listened to me as if I were telling them stories of French knights in the Middle Ages, of far-off things, with blood only a bright colour as on the paintings of the donkey-carts.

The local Party secretary looked upon me as if I had gone to fight in Spain on his behalf, in his name: he was proud of my lost hand which weighed our town's merit in the victory balance. 'We have written a page of valour', he said. It was the phrase which ended the citation for the medal they had given me; he had had the citation written out by a teacher, in a hand full of excessive flourishes, surrounded by watercolours of the fasces and flags. It was hung in a frame between the Diploma of S. Sepolcro* of a fellow townsman and the portrait of another who had fallen in Abyssinia. Photographs of the fallen, diplomas and citations for medals covered the walls of the Fascist Party offices. Behind the secretary's 'work' table was framed a commandment from the Fascist Decalogue: 'One serves the Fatherland even by standing sentry over a can of petrol.' It was not without reason that the secretary had put this commandment on show; Mussolini could count on him to stand sentry over a can of petrol, because he would then sell the petrol. The secretary sent for me nearly every day, saying that the fatherland would never forget its debt of gratitude to the best of its sons; the secretary was working to remind the fatherland of its debt to me: he wanted it to give me a suitable job, but the fatherland had many heroic sons to reward and perhaps it was a little forgetful. He wanted me to tell him about episodes from the war; he was a fan of General Bergonzoli, who was called 'Electric Beard', just as if General Bergonzoli had been a football player or bullfighter. I told him things about Bergonzoli I had read in the newspapers, because I had never actually seen that beard. Then I told him the most dreadful scenes I had witnessed, things that would make you want to spit on Fascism; I recounted them to him absolutely baldly, without putting a single tremor of indignation in my voice. He listened and grew

* Given to members of the Fascist combat troops, formed in Piazza S. Sepolcro, Milan, on March 23rd, 1919 — *Trans.*

enthusiastic, 'Well, yes,' he said, 'the country people [he meant the peasants] are an ugly lot, if you treat them well, they'll only bite you. . . And the sulphur miners, too. There are chaps like you, but the majority are people to be given the big stick. . . Spain wanted them in hand, eh?. . . But the Duce's waking up, Communism had better not show up in our waters. . .

'Actually,' I said, 'there were few real Communists in Spain; most are Anarchists, Republicans or Socialists.'

'They're all Reds,' said the secretary, 'all slaves of Moscow, and the Anarchists are the most dangerous of the lot, they're like wild animals.'

One day he sent for me, because the fatherland had replied to his solicitation: it had remembered me and was offering me a position as caretaker of a school, but the fatherland's school-caretakers, that is, the positions as caretaker dispensed by the State, were in towns where there were secondary schools; caretakers in primary schools were not State employees. It was necessary, therefore, and the secretary was sorry about it, for me to take up my position in another town, but perhaps it could be one close by. . .

'No,' I said, 'it's better in a town a long way off, outside Sicily, a large city.'

'Why?' asked the secretary, surprised.

'I want to see something new,' I said.

EQUAL DANGER

Leonardo Sciascia

'One of the major writers of the age' *Times Literary Supplement*

'Only very rarely can we say of such works [crime novels] that they look at questions of social justice with the informed eye of the intelligent artist. We can, however, make that claim for the stories of Leonardo Sciascia' Frank Kermode

District Attorney Varga is shot dead. Then Judge Sanza is killed. Then Judge Azar. Are these random murders, or part of a conspiracy? Inspector Rogas thinks he might know, but as soon as he makes progress he is transferred and encouraged to pin the crimes on the Left. But how committed are the cynical, fashionable, comfortable revolutionaries to revolution – or anything? Who is doing what to whom?

This is one of Sciascia's best political thrillers and was made into a movie – 'Illustrious Corpses' – by Francesco Rosi.

THE DAY OF THE OWL

Leonardo Sciascia

'Sciascia made out of his curious Sicilian experience a literature that is not quite like anything else ever done by a European' Gore Vidal

This short novel about the mafia is also a mesmerising demonstration of how that organisation sustains itself. It is both a beautifully written story and a brave act of denunciation. A dark-suited man is shot as he runs for a bus in the piazza of a small town. The investigating officer is a man who believes in the values of a democratic and modern society, and soon finds himself up against a wall of silence and vested interests. The narrative moves on two levels: that of the investigator, who reveals a chain of nasty crimes; and that of the bystanders and watchers, of those complicit with secret power, whose gossipy furtive conversations have only one end: to stop the truth coming out.